A FINE LAYER OF DUST

a novel

USA TODAY BESTSELLING AUTHOR
BARBARA CONREY

A Fine Layer of Dust
Red Adept Publishing, LLC
104 Bugenfield Court
Garner, NC 27529
https://RedAdeptPublishing.com/

Cover Art by Streetlight Graphics[1]

This is a work of fiction. Names, characters, places, and incidents either are the product of the author's imagination or are used fictitiously, and any resemblance to locales, events, business establishments, or actual persons—living or dead—is entirely coincidental.

To my brother, Tim. Your life was too short.

Chapter 1

As a junior partner, Jake was seated at Cranston, Clark, and Cunningham's teak conference-room table to get a feel for how the big boys played—so that when his time came, he would achieve his goal of becoming a senior partner at one of the most prestigious law firms in Vermont. But as a husband, he owed it to his wife to be on time for a meeting that was important to her. As he checked his watch, he hoped Stephen would soon wrap this up.

Stephen Cranston, *the* senior partner, the only one with his name on the wall who mattered since Clark and Cunningham had long since retired and spent their free time—all their time—at the Old Mount Calvary and Greenmount cemeteries, respectively, sat at the head of the table, looking somewhat bored.

Brian, the firm's newest junior partner, tried desperately to engage Stephen by expounding on the latest in a multitude of snags with the class action suit against the emergency air transportation company AIR FAST. The case was long overdue for settlement, but so far, Stephen had done nothing more than yawn.

Just as Brian reached the meat of the matter, Stephen looked up as if someone had tapped him on the shoulder.

"What time is it?"

Six lawyers cocked their wrists simultaneously.

But the winner was Brian, who nearly squealed, "One fifteen!"

Stephen stood and looked around the table. "That's all for today, folks. I've got another meeting."

Jake was the first one out the door. When he reached his office, he grabbed his briefcase, dug his hand into his pocket for his car keys, then decided it would be faster to catch a cab.

On the way out, he stopped at his secretary's desk. "I'm meeting Sophia shortly. Not sure when I'll be back."

Amy nodded and returned to the files covering her desk.

Once he reached the sidewalk, Jake flagged a cab and threw himself into the back. "South Willard. I'm in a rush." He slammed the door shut, anticipating that the cabbie understood his need for speed and would act accordingly.

"Gonna give me the rest of the address, Mr. In a Big Hurry?" The cabbie was not impressed.

"Sorry." Drawing a blank, he plugged the name into his phone. "2544."

The cabbie pulled away from the curb. If We Make Families accepted them, their lives would quickly change. Rechecking his watch, he saw he was cutting it close. His life would take a dive bomb if he were late. Sophia had had her fill of his inability to pull himself away from the office.

Jake had been confused when Sophia first brought up the idea of surrogacy. Her career at the Shelburne Museum was on solid ground. At fifteen, their daughter Emily was practically grown. Why take chances with Sophia's health? Their lives.

"There are risks to crossing the street," she'd countered.

The memory made him smile. She'd make a damn fine lawyer.

"I'm not getting any younger. If I want to do this, the time is now. There are so many families who cannot have children. Surrogacy is a way for me to give back for this privileged life I've led."

They'd been hiking Mount Abe at the time, close to the summit, when she'd added, "If I get pregnant, I'm thinking of taking a sabbatical. I didn't work when I was pregnant with Emily. No reason why I should when I'm sixteen years older."

That alone told him how serious she was about becoming a surrogate. Sophia loved her job.

Minutes later, the cabbie pulled up in front of the address. Jake flung a few bills into the front seat and jumped out.

"Buddy, you really need to take it easy. You know what I mean?" The cabbie breathed in deeply and let it out slowly. "Be in your moment." Then he laughed and pulled away from the curb.

Straightening his tie, Jake strode into the building.

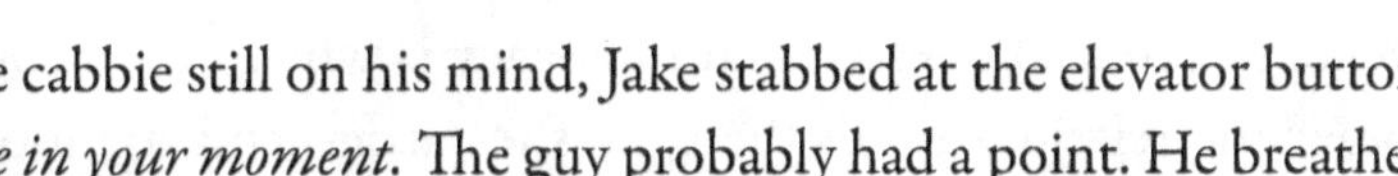

The cabbie still on his mind, Jake stabbed at the elevator button. *Be in your moment.* The guy probably had a point. He breathed in deeply and let it out slowly. He did it again and felt the kink in his neck give way. He should have given him a bigger tip.

The receptionist at We Make Families directed him into an office similar to his own except for the great view of a small park and Mount Mansfield in the distance.

He imagined the woman sitting behind the desk, swiveling her chair toward the window whenever she wanted to stare into that lush landscape. He'd kill for this office. When he'd first been named junior partner, he had practically swaggered into his new digs. He'd accomplished his first goal—an office with a window. His excitement had been palpable until he looked out the window and stared at a brick wall. Not exactly an image that brought to mind wide-open spaces and fresh air.

After swooping in for a quick kiss, Jake slid into the chair beside Sophia right on time. Ms. Boden, according to the nameplate on the desk, stood and reached out to shake his hand.

"Nice to meet you, Mr. Trenton. I just started giving Sophia some background information. Our staff includes lawyers, accountants, social workers, program managers, and coordinators. At least half of us have been surrogates and found the experience so rewarding that we are committed to helping others on their journey to becoming parents. As you might imagine, surrogacy is very personal to us."

Ms. Boden moved to the front of her desk, perched on a corner, and continued. "If you and Sophia meet the qualifications and decide to pursue surrogacy, a simple online application will get you started. I'm here to answer any of your questions. And speaking of questions, is there anything I can clear up for you before I continue?"

Jake shifted slightly in his chair. "No, so far, I'm good."

"Great. Let me define some terms you'll hear frequently if you decide to proceed. Gestational surrogacy is when the surrogate has no genetic relationship to the baby she carries, and traditional surrogacy—which is not all that common anymore—is when the surrogate *does* have a genetic relationship. It's important to understand these terms so there's no misunderstanding during discussions or when there are questions."

Jake almost laughed. He'd briefly looked at their website once he saw how serious Sophia was about becoming a surrogate, and those were the terms that required the most thought.

Ms. Boden handed Sophia several brochures then continued, "From our original phone call, Sophia is interested in gestational surrogacy for a couple or a single person, the intended parents or parent, who cannot have their own child."

Sophia leaned forward as if she were afraid she would miss something, even though Jake would bet she already knew everything Ms. Boden was saying. He reached over and squeezed her hand.

"There are several types of intended parents to consider. Once you've completed the background checks, physicals, and psychological examinations, we can discuss your thoughts about a match."

He'd read briefly about the matching process but hadn't given it much thought. "What do you mean by 'types of intended parents'?"

"Heterosexual couples who struggle with infertility or are concerned about a genetic defect or health issue that they don't want to pass on to their children enroll in our program, as well as single women who want to become mothers without a husband or partner but cannot carry a baby to term and same-gender couples who want to have a family."

"Really?"

Sophia leaned toward Jake. "Why don't we let Ms. Boden finish, honey?"

"Please, call me Becky." Becky looked from Sophia to Jake and gave him a let-me-explain-this-in-the-simplest-terms-possible smile. "If two men are a family and want to have children, they use an egg donor and, generally, the sperm of one of them. Sometimes, their sperm is mixed. When that happens, they both consider themselves the father. We also assist female couples if neither can conceive or maintain a pregnancy."

They had a lot to think about.

"If you have additional questions, please go to our website, and complete the online application once you're comfortable." Handing him a business card, Becky added, "And if there's anything you don't understand, call me. But please remember, you both must agree before we move forward."

As they walked from the surrogacy center to the underground parking garage, Jake wrapped his arm around Sophia's waist, exhaling a much-needed deep laugh. "*That* was a lot."

"It was."

"I wasn't expecting her to talk about intended families including same-gender couples."

"Look at you, all into the right lingo."

"I'm trying, babe. Can you picture the look on my dad's face if we tell him you are going to be a surrogate for people other than what he considers 'traditional'?"

"I totally can. If that's the case, we'll flip to see who has the honor of telling him."

"Everyone thinks you are all sweet and nice, but you can get down and dirty with the best of them." He stopped and pulled her to him. "Maybe you tell him, and I'll snap a photo of the look on his face."

She grinned. "Now who's bad?" Sophia looked around the small parking garage. "I don't see your car."

"I took a cab." Sheepishly, he added, "It was quicker. Care to give me a ride back to work?"

"Quicker because you were cutting it close? Again?"

"Maybe."

Shaking her head, Sophia slipped behind the wheel and released the lock on the passenger side so Jake could slide in. Within minutes, she entered the office parking lot. Jake leaned across the seat to kiss her, unable to hide his smirk.

"What?" She flashed a smile when she caught his grin. "What's so funny?"

"You know the new junior partner? Brian? At this morning's partner meeting, he was like a little kid trying to get Stephen's attention. When Stephen asked the time, I thought Brian would choke if he didn't get the answer out first."

"You shouldn't make fun."

"But he makes it so easy." He kissed her quickly. He'd lost a good hour and a half out of his day. "Don't count on me for dinner."

"Again?"

The car door was open, and with one foot on the ground, he turned back to commiserate. "I know. And I'm sorry. I promise to make it up to you."

"Oh?" As quickly as it had surfaced, her exasperation evaporated. "And how do you propose to do that?" The gleam in Sophia's eye told him they both had the same idea on exactly how he could make it up to her.

"Don't you worry. I'll think of something."

He *had* been crazy busy for months—years—and didn't see an end in sight. Not if he wanted that promotion. *Don't forget about family, bud.* As tired as he was when he finally headed home that night, he grinned. Sophia would never let him forget about family.

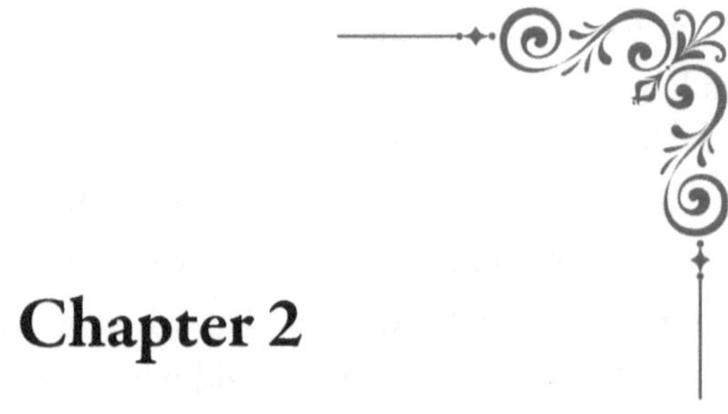

Chapter 2

When Jake walked in the door that night, photographs and shiny brochures covered every kitchen surface. Emily, eating a sandwich—peanut butter, by the smell of it—was rifling through the mess.

He grabbed one of the brochures. "What's up with all this? Or do I even want to know?"

"Of course you want to know!" She giggled. "Look at these puppies!" She practically danced around the table, shoving her sandwich into her mouth and grabbing photos of beagle puppies that looked a couple of days old. "Can we adopt one?"

Before he could respond, she plucked a photo from the pile and held it out—two adult beagles caught mid-run, one with a red ball in its mouth and the other seemingly determined to capture it. "Aren't these older dogs cute too? This organization rescues beagles, and I want to adopt one. Maybe a puppy. Maybe an older one." She laughed. "Whatever they have."

The grandfather clock in the entryway struck midnight.

"Why are you still up?"

She held up the remains of her sandwich. "Hungry. So, what do you think about a puppy? Or an older dog?"

There was no way he would answer that question without first talking to Sophia. "I just came home, Em. Let's see what Mom has to say."

Emily's eyes lit up like lanterns, and her grin was bigger than the one she'd carved on last year's jack-o'-lantern. She looked just like Sophia when she had pulled one over on him. With her dark curly hair and hazel eyes, they could be twins. They even had the same sprinkling of freckles. Whenever he looked at Emily, he found it hard to believe she was healthy and whole. And his.

"What's that big grin about?"

"Mom loves puppies."

As if I don't know that. "We'll still talk. Tomorrow."

Sophia stirred when Jake crawled into bed. Yawning, she wrapped her arms around him.

"You're home."

"Sorry. Didn't mean to wake you." He kissed the top of her head and pulled her closer.

"Wasn't totally asleep. Emily's puppy enthusiasm is hard to sleep through. She's something, isn't she?"

"Em? She is. Just like you. She's got the biggest heart, and when she sees something that needs fixing, she doesn't come up for air until she's done her best."

Propping herself up on one elbow, she laid joyful eyes on him. "Does that mean we're getting a puppy?"

"Don't look so hopeful. I told her we'd talk about it."

"Spoilsport." She ran her hand through his thick blond hair. "How was work tonight?"

"Long. And it won't be the last late night. Not if I want to be the next senior partner."

That was his goal. He wanted to walk into his father's law office and casually place his new business card on his desk, and he wanted that card engraved with his name, Jake Trenton, and title, senior partner.

When Sophia didn't respond, he thought she'd fallen asleep, but her body stiffened, and he feared their long-standing argument about how much time he devoted to his career would resurface with a vengeance.

"You are so obsessed with becoming a senior partner," she sputtered in exasperation. "Nothing else matters to you." She pulled herself up then crossed her arms over her chest and stared at him.

"That's not true." Swallowing his frustration, he leaned against the headboard, pretty sure sleep was out of the question. He pushed the image of slapping a new business card on the old man's desk from his mind and concentrated on Sophia.

"It *is* true. None of this is important to me. This house. The way we live." She waved her hand around their bedroom filled with antiques and Williamsburg reproductions as if he wasn't aware of what was in the room and how much it had cost.

As if she'd read his mind, she added, "You don't have to prove anything to your family."

She didn't care about any of it. Jake's ambition was all about him. She was right. Expecting her to sacrifice their family life for his dream was unfair. In his defense, he tried to be a good parent and husband and still prove to his father that he was as good as the son he'd lost. But Sophia obviously didn't see it that way.

"This won't be forever."

"You've said that before." The look on her face said there wasn't a chance in hell that she believed him.

"I mean it."

"You'll slow down? Spend more time at home?"

The doubt in her voice hurt, but he would prove it. "Yes. I promise."

Sophia relaxed slowly, eventually snuggling into him, and their tension melted slightly. "Can we set aside some time tomorrow to talk more about the surrogacy program?"

"You bet."

They had a lot to talk about. Sophia's job, the added stress to their family life, Emily. Surrogacy was important to her, but it couldn't have come at a worse time, if he were honest. But he couldn't tell her he didn't have time for her to be pregnant.

"How about a date night? Then we won't be interrupted."

"Seriously?" She poked him in the shoulder. "You know as well as I do how our date nights end. I'm not sure we'll have enough energy left to make important decisions."

"Well, how about we give it a try? I'll see if I can make a dinner reservation for tomorrow night."

He had just enough energy to lean in and kiss her full on the mouth before his body drifted toward sleep. Tomorrow was Saturday, and he could forget about his father *and* Cranston, Clark, and Cunningham for a few hours.

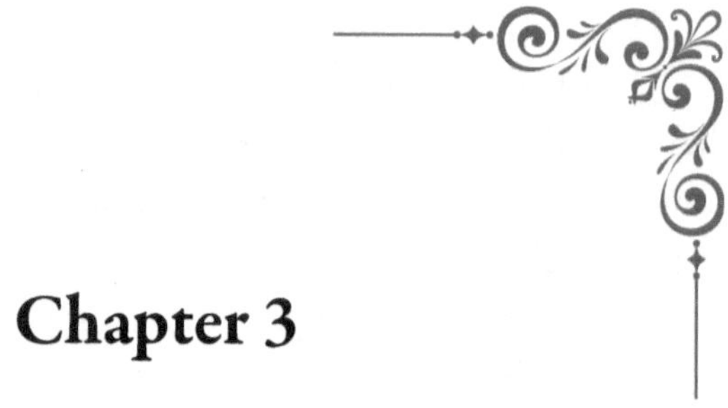

Chapter 3

Jake aimed high. No matter how the evening went, he wanted the conversation to start in a place they both loved. Bistro de Margot was what they needed.

Snagging a reservation in less than twenty-four hours would be akin to holding a royal flush in a poker game, but he explained that the night was a special occasion, and he hoped they could accommodate him. He considered throwing a prayer into the universe when the reservationist put him on hold but settled for crossing his fingers.

Luckily, a last-minute cancellation provided them with an intimate table for two housed in a small room where they could watch the other diners if they chose but were virtually invisible to anyone else. It sounded like what Jake was looking for. They could enjoy a delicious dinner and have a private conversation without worrying that the people at the next table would chime in with their opinion on whether they should pursue surrogacy.

He had just disconnected the call when Sophia came in from the garden.

"Any luck?"

He smirked and twirled her around the kitchen.

"Prepare to be wined and dined this evening at your favorite restaurant. Wear something saucy."

Sophia's eyebrow jutted upward. "Saucy? Define saucy."

He leered. "Something that comes off easily once we get home."

Emily breezed through the kitchen and caught his last words. "Guys. Get a room."

His eyes lit up. "That's what we should do. A night at the Lang House is what we need."

Sophia, pushing herself out of his arms, vetoed an all-nighter before he could pick up his phone to check on a vacancy.

They started with cocktails—French gimlets, steak tartare for an appetizer, and red snapper with citrus and fennel salad for their entrée. Raspberry and chocolate macarons for dessert would be the finishing touch. Unlike anyone they knew, they always selected the same meal from any menu they perused. Their friends found it endearing. They thought they were boring as hell but still couldn't stop themselves.

They clinked their glasses.

"Here's to making a decision that will bring us both joy," she said.

"I'll drink to that. But remember, if you do this, it'll be Shirley Temples for you."

"True. Is it too early to order a second?"

Jake nearly choked on his drink. "Who are you, and what did you do with my wife? I've never seen you have more than one drink in an evening."

"I guess we put no drinking for the next nine months or so in the con column. If I get pregnant."

He could see that Sophia had already made up her mind, but he was determined to take it slow.

"What are the chances of a successful pregnancy for a thirty-five-year-old surrogate?"

"Wow. Talk about starting at the top." She took another sip of her drink. "Nothing in life is guaranteed one hundred percent. You know that. And when have I ever failed at anything?"

"Never. But you've never been a surrogate before."

They kept their voices low, but he was still glad they were separated from the main dining room.

"That's fair. But I'm healthy, and that's one of the most critical factors."

"But you could conceivably spend nine months pregnant with nothing to show for it."

She swallowed. "That's an awful way to look at it."

He agreed. His words were harsh, but they were still valid. This wasn't the time to tiptoe around the facts. "Look, I admit I haven't spent much time thinking about this, but my gut feeling is that this is not a good idea. You're at an age when there's a risk to your health."

"Jesus, Jake. People take a risk every day just climbing out of bed."

"Let me finish, okay?"

Before he could say another word, the waiter appeared with the appetizer and asked if they wanted another drink. Sophia demurred, but he nodded. Wanting had nothing to do with how much he needed a second drink.

Jake took a large swallow when his fresh drink arrived and continued, "I know that becoming a surrogate means a lot to you. It's a wonderful way to give a baby to someone who desperately wants one, but other women are doing the same thing. And those women might desperately need the compensation that comes with giving up a year of their lives. You don't need that money."

Sophia pushed her steak tartare aside as if it were the very last thing she wanted to put in her mouth. "How long did it take you to think that one up?"

Ignoring her, he continued, "I know you've looked at the We Make Families website. So have I. I've looked at every surrogacy center in Vermont. They all lead with the compensation package. Why do you think that is?"

He dug into his appetizer, and Sophia pushed hers toward him when he finished.

"Is that what you think? Women do this for the money?" Every bit of joy drained from her face.

He reached for her hand, and, surprisingly, she let him cover her fingers with his.

"No. I don't think money is the primary reason. I think most women want to do something wonderful for someone else. But I think money can be a factor for women who want to do something amazing but also need the money."

She looked crestfallen, and he felt like a shit. He waited for her to say something. If he were a betting man, he'd bet he wouldn't be unwrapping Sophia from her dress when they got home.

"I understand what you're saying. The thing is, the demand for surrogates is high, so I don't think anyone who needs the money will be affected by my becoming one. I agree with you about the compensation—we don't need it. We can forgo the money. So..." She grinned, once again in control of the situation. "Are we in agreement?"

Sophia was so earnest about this last shot at pregnancy, and when Jake thought about what an ass he'd been when she was pregnant with Emily, he understood that she was looking for a joyful experience. But still, he gave it one more shot.

"What about our vacation?" He was grasping at straws.

"*What* vacation? You know as well as I do that we intentionally didn't plan a trip this year because you've been so busy. But *if* you can see your way clear to spend some time with your family, I say we wait to see if I get pregnant. If I do, let's plan a beach vacation, so I can soak up the sun. If I don't, let's go somewhere wild and crazy."

He couldn't help but laugh. "Is this what Becky meant when she said we both had to agree?"

Sophia grinned again, and when the waiter served the entrée, she dug in with gusto.

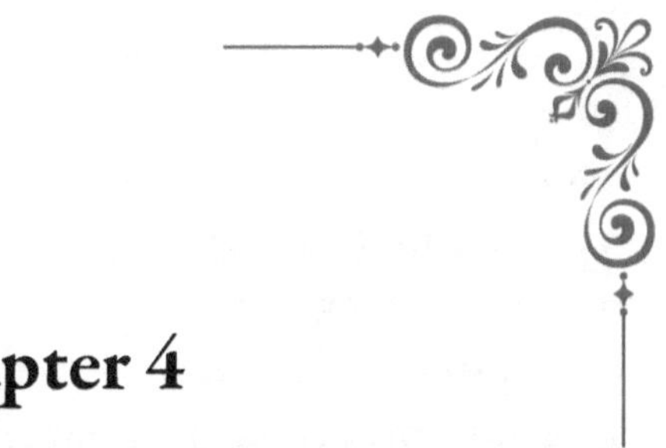

Chapter 4

Like most Sunday mornings, Jake played racquetball with Matt before heading to the office for a few hours. He needed the fast pace of the game to blow off steam—the thrum of his feet hitting the floor to keep pace with his heartbeat and his good friend and next-door neighbor never disappointed.

Matt grabbed a towel to wipe the sweat off his forehead. "How'd the meeting go with the surrogacy center?"

"It was good." Jake smiled. Last night's date night was even better. He wasn't against Sophia becoming a surrogate. He had some reservations, but ultimately, he felt the decision was hers. In Sophia's mind, that meant they agreed.

"There's a lot to this. You don't just drop by and offer to carry a baby for someone, and they welcome you with open arms."

"I suppose not. But if you and Sophia decide to do this, Christine said you have our full support. We'll even supply references."

Jake almost choked on a mouthful of water. "References? It's not like we're adopting a dog."

"Guess not. Remember my cousin Charlie and his wife? You met them last summer at our Memorial Day barbecue. They went through IVF for their first baby, and now, they're thinking about having another one with the same surrogate."

"I'd forgotten. Really? With the same surrogate?" Jake wiped off his racquet and zipped it into its cover.

"Yep. Little Chuck is almost two, and now, they'd like a girl." Matt tossed his damp towel into his gym bag. "Maybe after this baby, Sophia will get a second request."

Hefting his gym bag over his shoulder, Jake snorted. "I'm pretty sure she's thinking of this as a one-time thing. Besides, if we're approved, I still need to explain this to my old man, and one surrogacy will be more than enough for him. If I tell him Sophia's starting a baby-making business, I may have to move out of town."

Matt's laughter filled the court. "A little drastic, don't you think?"

"You've met my dad."

"So, what are you thinking? The Northeast Kingdom or all the way across the country?"

"I'm thinking it's time for lunch."

In the family room after dinner that night, Emily reached for the television remote, but Jake grabbed it before she could hit the power button.

"Hey! It's time for *Law and Order: SVU* or *Criminal Intent*—I forget which one is on, but it's time to watch."

Jake frowned. "Why do you watch that stuff? You know that's not how the law works."

"I know, but a girl can dream. So until I sit in a big, fancy office like you, I'll watch all the legal shows. At least until I go to law school."

"My office is hardly fancy. How about tonight, we forget the law and talk about this rescue organization you're so keen on?"

"Really?" Without missing a beat, Emily moved to the old pine table that displayed her carved initials from when she was too young to know better and fired up her laptop. Soon, the bold colors of the rescue website filled the screen, highlighting the exhaustion of the dogs pictured there.

Jake couldn't turn away from the anguish in their eyes. He wanted to shield Emily from experiencing the sorrow these pictures triggered, but instead of disgust or dismay, he saw hope written all over her heart-shaped, freckled face.

"The organization started years ago when a laboratory contacted an animal rescue and advocacy group and asked them to take two beagles no longer used for experiments. They found forever homes for the dogs then contacted other labs to see if they could have the dogs they no longer needed."

"Are forever homes what I think they are?"

"Yep. Depending on the health of the rescued dogs, they might stay with foster families until they're well enough to be placed for adoption—to their forever home." The light in Emily's eyes dimmed as she mindlessly traced her initials carved into the pine table. "It used to be legal for the facilities to kill the dogs they no longer wanted, but now, some are released. In some states, anyway."

Emily drew in a deep breath. "Homeward Bound is a worldwide organization. Even though most rescues occur in California—their main headquarters—they've saved dogs as far away as China." With the biggest smile, she added, "Isn't that great?"

Her words tugged at his heart, but he wasn't sure this was reason enough to adopt a dog.

"Can we get one?" Emily looked at him with big watery eyes, and he nearly caved. "They're practically free."

"Nothing's 'practically free.'" Jake regretted his words the moment they shot out of his mouth. He sounded like his old man. Viewing one listing after another, he ignored the pictures and concentrated on the details. "We know nothing about these dogs or where they come from. Just that they're rescues from product testing facilities." Jake didn't want to destroy Emily's enthusiasm, but she needed to learn not to lead with her heart. "I'm not sure this is a good idea."

Emily didn't even blink. "It's a great idea! I don't want to *marry* them. They deserve to have a home and someone to love them. And if we take good care of it and it gets all its shots and stuff, it'll be healthy." She never took her eyes off him.

Jake rarely denied her anything, and she might have been counting on him not starting that night.

"Plus, this is a nonprofit organization, so we should donate *and* adopt a puppy." Batting her eyes at him, she added, "Can we at least go look at them?"

Ignoring Emily's question, he asked one of his own. "How'd you find this place?"

"I'd been looking at a website for someone who breeds registered beagles, and I fell in love with the gorgeous beagle puppies—I knew I was meant to have one," she said. "But the kennel is in Kentucky, and since you're so busy at work, I figured I'd have a better chance if I found a place closer to home. That's when I found the rescue organization, and once I started looking at this site, I knew I wanted one of these dogs."

He clicked through the pages, looked at more pictures, and watched a few short videos of released dogs experiencing freedom for the first time. He fought against closing his eyes when he saw how frightened the dogs were, how the volunteers moved slowly and spoke softly to not terrify them further. Jake wasn't sure how Emily could look at all of this. The articles about the laboratory conditions made him wish he hadn't eaten dinner.

He wanted to help, but he also never wanted to think about this place again. "But I thought you wanted a puppy?"

"That's the thing. Sometimes, there are puppies. Sometimes, they rescue pregnant moms, and the puppies are born into freedom.

Sometimes, the labs give them up because they don't want to care for them until they're old enough to be used for testing."

Sophia had been quiet all this time, but her eyes were hopeful. Jake could easily see that even if he were dead set against Emily's idea, he'd be facing a losing battle.

"Dad, are you paying attention? We need to help these dogs. Even if they don't have puppies, I'll take one of the older dogs. And I almost forgot the most important thing! The products made in these laboratories? They could be products we use. We can't buy their stuff anymore. We can't support companies that use animals for testing."

Emily sucked in a mouthful of air before adding the last of her information. "There's a place on this website that lists companies that don't condone animal product testing so that people can make better choices. That's what we're going to do."

❧

Days later, Jake handed Emily two plane tickets.

"What are these for?"

"That beagle breeder you were looking at in Kentucky. I thought we'd visit. Go see some puppies." Strutting around the kitchen like a peacock, he was confident his daughter would be thrilled.

Emily gave him a why-don't-you-ever-listen-to-me look. "I already told you I want to go through Homeward Bound. I want a rescue. Besides, aren't you too busy to fly to Kentucky?"

Even Emily was busting on him for his time in the office.

"I'm *making* time. I know what you said, but it won't hurt to look." He hoped that if he presented Emily with this option, it would be easier to sway her toward puppies nurtured from conception.

He was still willing to donate to the rescue organization and steer clear of products that supported animal testing. He just didn't want her exposed to the ravages of mistreated dogs. "You should check all your options before committing to something as important as a puppy."

"You just don't want me to see what those dogs look like. I've seen the pictures. I know what they look like."

He couldn't get what he'd seen on the rescue site out of his head. "Pictures are different than looking into a dog's eyes and seeing the pain he's suffered."

"I *know*, Dad! I'm not a kid."

Laughing at the indignity on Emily's face, he pulled her in for a hug. "You'll always be my kid, no matter how old you are."

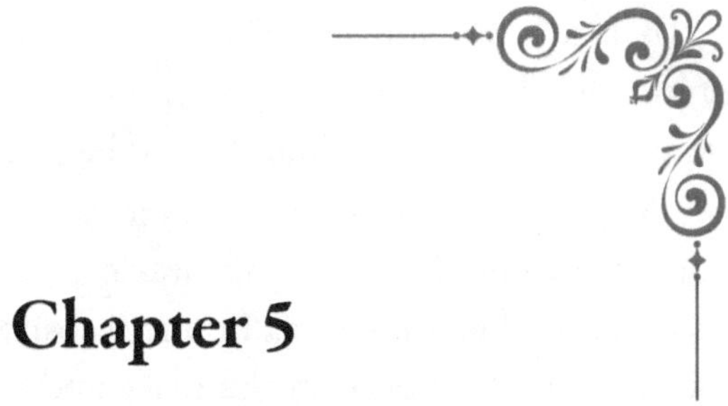

Chapter 5

Emily ripped off her sweatshirt as soon as they landed at the Louisville airport. "Why do airplanes have to be so cold?"

"To keep us annoyed?" Jake lost no time pulling off his sweater.

Sophia was lucky to be bogged down at the Shelburne. She hated the sound of her own teeth chattering. Other than the temperature, the flight had been great, and by the time they'd caught a shuttle to the car rental agency, he was wearing his sunglasses to avoid the glare of the midday sun.

The one thing he regretted about this trip was that it was in the middle of summer. No one in their right mind flew south in the summer. Once he completed the car rental paperwork, they climbed into the Lexus and drove to Bagdad, stopping at a Bojangles for a burger. "So, what do you think, kid? We're on our own adventure."

"I think you're trying to bribe me—I hope you realize I am not bribed easily."

He almost snorted. "And why is that?"

"Because I'm your daughter."

And she was. From the moment she'd grasped his finger as an infant and refused to let go, Jake had noticed she wanted to be with him, be like him, *be* him.

Not thirty minutes later, they pulled into the Mill Road Breeding Farm driveway and followed it to a big white farmhouse at the end, where the owners, Ted and Martha Winters, waited for them on their front porch.

Before Jake could unbuckle his seat belt, Emily was out of the car, practically skipping to the porch. He shook his head. Keeping her from wanting *all* the puppies would be damn near impossible.

After introductions, the Winterses led them into a building that housed the puppies. The space was the exact opposite of what they had seen on the Homeward Bound website, where although scrupulously clean, dogs overran the place and everything looked slightly frayed around the edges.

This building was air-conditioned, with lots of sunlight streaming through the windows. The toys on the floor looked like they'd recently come out of the packaging. The puppies were all cuddled together, even though there were enough beds for everyone.

"They like to be together," Ted explained, "but every once in a while, one of them will get in a huff and go off by himself, so the beds are there in case they need them."

Now only eight weeks old, the puppies would grow into thirteen-inch tricolor beagles. Emily sank to the floor, and the puppies moved closer one by one to sniff her extended hand. Two were brave enough to lick her fingers, making her giggle.

Jake knelt beside Emily. "They're pretty cute, aren't they?"

"They're adorable."

He and the Winterses waited outside in the sunshine while Emily played with each pup. Unbeknownst to her—and Sophia, for that matter—the Winterses had verified his references, and he had paid a deposit for whichever puppy Emily wanted most. Jake was so confident that she would fall in love with one that he'd paid an extra charge to have first pick of this litter. He'd even arranged to fly a puppy home with them, so he was more than a little surprised when she thanked the Winterses and headed toward the car.

"Hey." He had to pick up his pace to catch up with her. "Did you pick your favorite?"

"That would be impossible. They are all fabulous."

He waved to the Winterses, indicating he'd call them later. Emily probably needed time to decide. Jake put the car in gear and headed down the driveway so they could check into their hotel and talk about puppies. Maybe go for a swim. Neither of them liked this heat. Reaching over, he gently touched her cheek.

"Well, I can't buy them all. Your mother would surely object, but you can have whichever one you want."

"Dad!" Emily shot him a look as if he were just a typical parent who never listened. "I don't want any of them. I told you that. These dogs are beautiful, and you are the best to bring me here, but I want a rescue. And I know you'll think I'm joking, but instead of a birthday party this year, I want you to donate whatever you would spend on a party as a gift to Homeward Bound."

Jake would never understand how he deserved this child. But he had Sophia to thank for her.

Chapter 6

Sophia's eyes bounced between Jake and Emily, an I-told-you-so look plastered on her face as soon as they walked in the door from the airport.

"Where's the puppy?"

"I never said I was bringing home a puppy," Jake huffed. He dropped his overnight bag on the kitchen floor then leaned over and nuzzled her neck, whispering, "I missed you," before grabbing a beer from the fridge.

Sophia smirked. "Oh, but you were planning to."

His ears grew warm, and he faced her with a sheepish grin. That had been the plan.

"The puppies were awesome, but Dad is such a dork. He thought he could sway me with gorgeous puppies raised in pristine conditions. Those dogs don't need me. They'll have people fighting over them."

Laughing, Sophia kissed Emily then glanced at Jake.

"Your dad means well."

He considered sticking out his tongue.

"Mom and I figured you'd pull out all the stops to convince me that a purebred was the way to go. She warned me to hold my ground if I wanted a rescue."

"And that you did. I'm proud of you." After opening his beer and taking a long pull, he conceded, "Maybe I was planning on a puppy, but our girl here is not changing her mind. Like she said, she wants a puppy who needs her, not the other way around."

"So, when are you going to take me to Homeward Bound?" Emily made her eyes big and round. "It's all I'll ever want."

"I know, sweetheart. Everything you want is always the only thing you'll ever want. Let me look at my schedule."

"Awesome! Mom, you heard him. You're my witness!"

Taking in the harried look on Sophia's face, he pulled out the chair next to hers. Her laptop was open to the surrogacy website.

"How's it going?"

"I just started filling out the application."

Emily's focus moved from the open fridge to her mother. "Are you getting a new job?"

"No, of course not. It's a surrogacy application."

"What do you mean?"

Sophia drew in a deep breath. "It's—"

"*Stop*." Holding up her hand as if she were a crossing guard, Emily added, "I know what surrogacy means. When I was little, I begged you for a baby sister, and you said you didn't need to have more kids because I was enough. And somehow, that swayed me into believing you didn't like being pregnant." Emily's voice edged toward indignation. "And now you're having a baby for someone else?"

They hadn't talked about telling Emily yet. What to say. Most everything they found on discussing surrogacy with children referred to much younger children. Children more inclined to take what they were told at face value. Not children who questioned everything that came out of their parents' mouths.

Eyes on Jake, Sophia answered, "Yes, I'm hoping to have a baby for someone unable to have their own, but it won't be my baby. I am thrilled to be your mother, and I loved being pregnant with you, but the decisions your dad and I made were based on our lives then. Things change. Situations change."

Emily pulled out a chair across from her mother. "So, are you sorry *now* that you didn't have more kids?"

The question stilled his heart. He had been bewildered the day Sophia told him she was pregnant with Emily.

"We agreed on no children," he choked out, refusing to accept the reality.

Uncharacteristically, she sniped, "I didn't exactly get pregnant by myself, Jake. It just happened. Accidents happen."

They walked on eggshells around each other for the next several weeks. He moved into the guest room, and they limited their conversations to when he would and would not be home for dinner.

After they reached a nonverbal détente, he went through the motions of becoming a soon-to-be-parent, but it wasn't until Emily was born, and he could see she was fine, that he embraced fatherhood with every breath in his body. Even then, he watched for her to exhibit his brother's behavior patterns, but she never did. And finally, he stopped looking for problems, even going so far as to say she was perfect. Which, of course, she was.

He pushed aside the memory when Sophia asked Emily if she still wished she had a sibling.

"God, no. Maddie's little brother is a pain. He thinks he should do the same things we do even though he's five years younger. He wants to be in Maddie's room with us whenever I'm there." She rolled her eyes so hard he was surprised they didn't fall out. "He's so annoying."

"So we're good then? With my becoming a surrogate?"

"Will you be able to give it up?"

"The baby?"

Nodding, Emily added, "Won't it be hard?"

Sophia took her hand off the mouse. "I don't know if it'll be hard. I don't think so. Women enter into this knowing that the baby isn't theirs. There's no genetic connection in the type of surrogacy I want to do, so I think this differs from having your own baby." She seemed to think about that for a minute. "I'm hoping so, anyway."

"This is really cool, Mom." Heading out of the kitchen, Emily added, "Got to call Maddie."

"Em?" Maddie's name had caught his attention. "Best friend or not, nothing about surrogacy. A lot has to happen before Mom knows if she'll be a surrogate."

"Got it."

"Well, one hurdle down. I didn't think we'd be telling her so soon, but it seems safe to say she thinks you're Wonder Woman."

"I was a little worried that she's too young, but we can't exactly wait until the baby comes and *then* tell her it's not ours."

"Good point." He leaned even closer and inhaled the scent of her hair. He had no idea why it always smelled like peaches. "You loved being pregnant?" Again, his thoughts returned to when she was expecting Emily. "We weren't in a good place for most of your pregnancy."

"True." Sophia stared out the kitchen window then added, "A big part of being pregnant is between the mother and baby. I knew you weren't happy. I wasn't happy either, but I refused to let our problems diminish my joy in carrying our baby."

"But this will be different. It won't be your baby. Do you really think you can disassociate yourself from this baby?"

"I do. One of the women in my book club knows someone who has been a surrogate several times. During each pregnancy, she enjoyed all the good parts, suffered through the morning sickness, yet never felt like she did when she carried her own baby. She did admit that, when she delivered, she felt the same joy as when her son was born, the same rush, but she attributed that momentary euphoria to hormones."

"Several times? You're not considering doing this more than once, are you?"

"I can't say I'd want to do it again since I haven't done it once, but realistically, my age is against me. So no, I'm thinking of this as a one-time experience." She glanced at him and added, "Don't look so relieved."

"Sorry. It's a lot, you know?"

"I do know. And I appreciate your support."

He tightened his arms around her. "So now that Emily knows, we need to tell our families. We can pretty much bet on my old man's reaction. I doubt he has much experience with women who have babies for other people."

His father would want to know why. *Why* would Sophia want to do this? Jake doubted he would understand the need to give something to someone simply because they needed it. He rarely saw anyone's needs other than his own.

Worse, he would look for the reason that made it *his* fault his wife wanted to become a surrogate. "My dad will say that you must be unhappy and I must be the cause of your unhappiness." He kissed her ear. "Are you not happy?"

She grinned. "Do I *look* unhappy?"

"No. But you do look delectable." He kissed her repeatedly until she laughed so hard tears ran down her face.

"Stop! You are going to make me pee myself."

Finally, they returned to discussing their families, and both agreed that his mother would be thrilled.

"How do you think your family will react?"

Sophia cackled. "I picture my mother pounding her chest in the vicinity of her heart, gasping that her beloved daughter has fallen from God's good graces and will spend eternity in hell if she so much as considers becoming a surrogate."

Sophia painted an accurate description of Rose Marie.

"What about your dad?"

"You know my dad. He salutes to Mom. But even though Emily knows, we're not telling either family until *after* I'm pregnant. That gives them less time to complain."

"What? You're not expecting them to congratulate you?"

"Not on your life."

Sophia turned back to her laptop, and he leaned in closer. "So, what's all on here?"

"Information about the contracts, background checks. The medical and psychological evaluations. The match between the intended parents and me. We need to agree on specific things."

"Like what? Names?" He was kidding, but Sophia's humor seemed to desert her.

"No, of course not. Like different laws if the intended parents live in a different state or even a different country. How often each expects or wants to talk or meet." She hesitated before adding, "Selective reduction or termination, things like that."

"What the hell?"

"If something's wrong with the baby before it's born, both the intended parents and the surrogate need to agree if the pregnancy should be terminated."

"You'd agree to that?"

Again, the memory of her pregnancy with Emily came unbidden. He'd suggested she have an abortion when she announced her pregnancy. No way was he bringing a child into the world who might have psychological problems like his brother Robbie—that was what he'd thought at the time—but Sophia had looked at him like he'd asked her to fillet a puppy.

"Yes. I'd agree to it. It wouldn't be my baby. It wouldn't be my choice to make."

"But it's your body, and I thought you were against abortion."

"I'm *for* the right to choose. It's more complicated when surrogacy is involved. I couldn't bring a child into this world knowing that it wouldn't survive, and the parents couldn't possibly deal with the agony of waiting for their child to be born only to bury it. Abortion is their choice, not mine.

He wasn't sure he believed her but was willing to let it go, especially after she moved from her chair to his, whispering, "Tell me again how much our daughter thinks I'm Wonder Woman."

Chapter 7

They rocked the physical and psychological exams, and the background checks proved they were upright citizens with one traffic violation between them. It was a momentous first step that called for a celebration. Besides, if Sophia became pregnant, her champagne-drinking days were over, so they agreed to celebrate while they still could.

All that was left was the match. Jake assumed the center entered all their data into a program, ran it through their database, and spit out a selection of intended parents. How hard could it be?

Sophia had apparently hidden her anxiety about the match until the day he found her on the patio, perched on a bench, staring into space. He doubted she knew he was there or even noticed the warbling of the goldfinches flocking around the feeder Emily had made in sixth grade. He wouldn't bet that she saw the butterfly hovering nearby either.

Jake kept his voice low so as not to startle her. "Everything okay?"

She stared at him then shook herself and laughed. "Everything's fine."

"Work's good?"

"Yep."

"You seem lost in thought out here."

"I guess I am. I was thinking about the surrogacy center. Wondering when they'll come up with a match for us."

He checked the date on his watch. "It's barely been a couple of weeks. How long does it normally take?"

Sophia laughed. "You know, I have no idea. But you know me. I want what I want, and I want it now. I'm a little impatient."

His eyebrow twitched at the massive understatement. "Maybe a lot impatient."

When the call finally came, Sophia put the phone on speaker so they could both listen. They absorbed the information as the We Make Families representative described the couple's profile. A traditionally married couple—Jake wouldn't have to explain to his father two men or two women wanting to have a baby. At least not if this couple turned out to be the match. He was almost disappointed. The look on the old man's face would have been classic.

The couple, Marianne and Adam Barclay, lived in the Northeast Kingdom in St. Johnsbury. He and Sophia enjoyed that part of Vermont, especially in the fall, with the leaves changing colors and the air crisp and cool. As newlyweds, they'd stopped in Lyndon for a late lunch at the Miss Lyndonville Diner after a morning hike. St. Johnsbury was a stone's throw from there. They liked the area so much that they'd looked for a house there, but the advantages of living in a city won them over.

He hadn't considered that the intended parents might live so close. *But who knows how many couples we might interview?*

Everyone agreed on the twenty-fourth for the first meeting.

Sophia's voice betrayed her excitement when she trooped behind him to his office. "Can you double-check your calendar?"

She was still smiling at dinner when she made the big announcement to Emily.

"How cool is this? If you like these people, and they like you, this might be your family."

Sophia grinned, but he played the spoilsport.

"Let's not get ahead of ourselves, Em. There might be several families to talk to before making that decision."

Later that night, he overheard Emily on the phone talking about the potential surrogacy, and he didn't have the heart to remind her that it was too soon to be bragging to her friends. So much was still up in the air. Even if the Barclays were a good match, the embryo transfer had to be successful before Sophia would become a surrogate. But he let it slide, happy she was so enthusiastic.

Jake rarely came home from work early, but he didn't think walking into his kitchen in the middle of the day a week later warranted the third degree.

"What are you doing here?" Sophia asked.

"I live here?"

"Not at three in the afternoon on a Wednesday, you don't," Emily countered, taking a cookie tray from Sophia, sliding it into the oven, and setting the timer.

Jake slipped off his shoes and placed his briefcase near the door so he wouldn't forget it on his way out the following day. "I need to pack. I have an early flight in the morning to present the final agreement to my client in Colorado."

All thoughts of him standing in the kitchen on a weekday were forgotten when Emily yelled, "You closed the SNIPES deal? When will they start building?"

"The deal's not closed yet. I'm bringing them the final papers and answering any additional questions. Then, we wait." His grin was wide. "But yes, we're close to one of the biggest retailers in the country opening a store in Vermont."

Sophia jumped in before Emily could ask more questions. "How long will you be gone? We have the videoconference with the intended parents next week. You didn't forget, did you?"

"No, I didn't forget. I'll be back by the weekend."

"But what if you're not? Every trip you take for this client seems to last longer than scheduled."

"I know, and I'm sorry." Jake loosened his tie. "You've been a sport through this whole deal. I can't tell you how much I appreciate your support."

Ducking her head, Sophia was suddenly interested in giving the cookie dough another stir when he leaned in for a kiss. But that only made him try harder.

"Hey, I promise. I'll be back in time. You know how important this client is." After kissing the top of her head, he moved toward the stairs then returned. "But if I *don't* get back—and I will, I'm just saying if there's some random emergency I can't talk my way out of—make sure Emily's home." He grinned. "That way, they can see you've already birthed a perfect child. They'll be impressed." He winked before heading upstairs to pack.

Chapter 8

By the time Jake returned from Colorado late Thursday evening, more than a week later than planned because Stephen insisted he stay and schmooze the clients within an inch of their lives, he only wanted to rip off his tie and climb into bed. He needed sleep more than he needed air.

But as soon as he slid between the sheets, Sophia moved toward him, her warmth taking the chill from his body.

"How was your trip?"

The joy in her voice relieved him. She hadn't been happy when he'd told her he wouldn't be home for the meeting with the Barclays.

"It was good." No matter how tired he was, he couldn't help the grin that slipped into place. "I think I'm close to sealing the deal."

"Oh, Jake, congratulations. I'm happy for you!"

He was not a superstitious man, but there was no point in taking chances. "Don't congratulate me yet. Things could still go south."

She laid her hand on his chest. "I have complete faith in your ability to bring this deal home." Yawning, she added, "Emily and I had a great meeting with the Barclays the other night. Wait until you meet them." She chuckled. "They love each other so much. We both might have something to celebrate."

"Oh?"

"They desperately want a baby." Sophia's happiness was palpable. "I think they could be the right couple."

He owed it to Sophia to be supportive, no matter how exhausted he was, but he couldn't help the doubt that crept into his voice. "Isn't it a little early to be so optimistic?"

"I don't think so. We really clicked, and Emily liked them too."

"That's great, but our daughter is fifteen. I'm not sure her opinion matters."

Her hand trembled on his chest. He could almost feel the effort she put into her following comment. "Don't be such a killjoy."

But when he didn't respond, her words tightened.

"You weren't there, Jake. I'm not sure how much your opinion counts either."

"I'm sorry I couldn't get home." Careful to keep his voice calm, he added, "You know how nervous Stephen is about this client."

He knew her anger about his absence had been slightly below the surface of her warm welcome, and even though he'd apologized as soon as he found out he wouldn't be home on the twenty-fourth, she was definitely still pissed. He got it. This wasn't the first time he had disappointed her, and it most likely wouldn't be the last, but her meeting with the Barclays had been important, and he'd let her down.

On top of that, it seemed he had touched a nerve about this couple. As much as he wanted to soothe Sophia, he was afraid she was being premature.

"I'm just saying that these are the first people you've met." He didn't want to spoil her excitement, but it seemed like she was moving too fast. "Maybe we should talk to other couples?"

Sophia was silent, and he hoped she was considering his suggestion.

"Remember when you asked me to marry you? You told me it didn't matter that we hadn't known each other long. I was the one for you. That's how I feel about the Barclays. They *are* the right people."

Sophia wasn't usually enamored with someone so quickly. Her words settled like a fine layer of dust, and Jake feared they would occupy every future conversation about the Barclays until the mere mention of them rubbed him raw.

He winced. *Talk about being negative.* He tried to shake off his feelings when his father's voice plowed into his thoughts. '*What does she even know about these people?*'

It took a second for him to realize Sophia was still talking.

"You should have seen Adam kiss Marianne's hand while they shared how long they've wanted a baby. It took my breath away."

Whether the memory of the Barclays' love prompted her or the fact he'd been gone for over a week, sudden expectation filled her voice, and his body responded.

He pulled her closer, whispering, "Well then, I definitely defer to you." His fingers grazed her bare breast. And then... and then he felt nothing. Startled, he searched for a reason but found none. Pulling back slightly, he freed his hand from under her shirt.

"Jake?"

The surprise and hurt when she spoke his name distressed him more than he wanted to admit.

"I'm sorry." He kissed the bare skin of her shoulder where her T-shirt had slipped down. "I guess I'm more tired than I thought." As if it were normal for him to be unable to make love when he couldn't remember it ever happening before.

After Sophia's gentle snores assured him she was asleep, he unwrapped himself from her and slipped quietly down the stairs to his study, too exhausted to sleep and more than a little disturbed by his inability to make love.

His brain was still wound tight around the deal with SNIPES. That had to be the answer. He poured himself a bourbon and gulped a good half of it, hoping it would relax him so that he could put this day to rest, although Sophia's warm body hadn't been enough to allow him to give way to sleep. Maybe he needed a double.

Sophia's mention of his desire to marry quickly brought back all their early history. And she was right. He couldn't wait until she was his. The first time he'd seen her, standing next to his longtime friend, Clive, from prep school, he had wanted her. He'd been running late, and when he pulled up in front of the Commons Building at Bennington and parked his MGB, Clive stood right by the entry with a woman in his arms.

Back then, Clive always had a woman by his side, and at the time, Jake speculated on how long this one would last. Clive went through women like there was always one waiting in the wings, which was usually the case for his friend.

But all thoughts of Clive disappeared when Jake approached. The woman was small, not tall and leggy like Clive's usual choice. She was delicate, fine-boned, with long midnight-black hair that rested on her shoulders and seemed to shimmer in the sunlight. She looked like she could take flight at any moment.

He wanted her—no matter that she and Clive appeared to be a couple.

As if Clive sensed his reaction, he pulled the woman closer. "This is my Sophia." His voice, low and sensual, filled with pride as he showed off his latest possession.

Sophia took a step back, Clive's claim to ownership unappreciated, while Jake looked at his friend in surprise, shocked by the raw need he had felt. Stunned by how easily Clive had picked up on it.

It took one phone call for her to agree to have dinner with him. They'd been together ever since.

Their courtship had been short. They'd married—with no hard feelings from Clive—as soon as they graduated, Jake from law school and Sophia from Bennington with an art history degree. Their families were none the wiser until the ink was dry on their marriage license.

He still remembered the look on his father's face—as if he'd put something sour in his mouth when he'd been expecting a sweet—when he brought Sophia home as his bride.

During a private conversation, his father had choked out, "She's Italian?"

Nodding, Jake relished the old man's displeasure.

"I suppose she's Catholic?" Robert frowned upon any religion outside of the mostly Mainline Protestant elite that formed his opinion of the world.

Jake laughed out loud before offering reassurance. "She hasn't stepped inside a church in years."

It hadn't been any better at Sophia's. Just louder. Her family's concern had nothing to do with ethnicity or religion. Or even how young they were. Anthony had never expected his daughter to have a career and was shocked when she created a niche for herself in the art world.

His concern, and Rose Marie's, hadn't been about who their daughter had married as much as where they had held the ceremony.

"What do you mean you're married?"

Anthony's face turned red, and his chest puffed out like a rooster protecting his flock, while Rose Marie fluttered around as if he had stuck a knife in her heart.

"You're not married until I give you away in the church," Anthony said.

All these years later, her family still begrudged him the sacraments of the church and the elaborate wedding reception they'd never been able to give their baby girl. He'd worried that because he had wanted to keep things simple and fast, Sophia had missed an opportunity for a church wedding and might regret it. It had taken him months after their wedding before he'd finally asked.

Sophia's eyes had flashed. "The last thing I want is to troop down the aisle with every person my family has ever said more than two words to staring at me while I worry about tripping over a twelve-foot bridal train that probably cost enough to feed a family of four for months. My family will have to get over it."

She'd been reading the Sunday paper and flapped it in front of his face, stabbing her finger at a wedding photograph of a couple he didn't recognize. "Look at this!" *This* was a wedding that had taken place at St. Joseph's the week before. A high Mass.

"What? Do you know these people?"

She had practically snarled. "No, I don't know them. Look at the picture. Everything looks perfect, right? Now read this." Her fingernail jabbed at the newspaper as if it were the enemy and she was about to annihilate it.

He zoomed in on a small article slightly to the right of the wedding photo. The groom had tripped on the marble steps leading to the altar and passed out. Broken his two front teeth. His groomsmen had held him up during the service while the priest droned on as if passed-out grooms were the norm. The bride's mother insisted they weren't married, yet the wedding announcement reflected a happy couple.

"If I'd been that bride, watching that spectacle before it was my turn to walk down the aisle, I'd have turned and run. No. I do not want a church wedding."

His laugh had been loud. "Do you think the band played 'All I Want for Christmas Is My Two Front Teeth' at their reception?"

He loved Sophia and never regretted marrying her. But sometimes, the responsibility of a family—living in the right house, the right neighborhood, sending Emily to the right schools so that when the time came, the right college would accept her, all under the watchful eye of his father, who assured him that sooner or later, he'd fuck it all up—was overwhelming.

Catching sight of the world atlas that sat in its chairside stand between two windows, he imagined twirling the globe and taking off to wherever his finger landed. He grinned. *What man hasn't imagined the same thing? Hell, for that matter, what woman hasn't pictured taking off in the middle of the night and starting over?*

When he swiped his hand across his face, the stubble on his cheeks reminded him it would soon be twenty-four hours since he'd started his day, and he headed back up the stairs to bed.

Chapter 9

We Make Families confirmed the match with the Barclays, and Jake put his reservations aside. *Sophia knows what she is doing.* If these were her people, they were his people too.

Next were the fertility injections, which he hadn't given much thought to until he discovered it was his responsibility to inject Sophia with the required medication to prepare her body for the embryo transfer.

"In the butt?" He swore he felt the very last of his summer tan fading.

"*Yes.* In the butt."

He looked from the syringe she held to her butt. "You've already had a baby. Doesn't that count?"

"No. It doesn't count. Weren't you listening when Dr. Kelley explained this?"

The truth was, he hadn't been listening. He'd been thinking about the SNIPES deal, wondering when they would finally sign all the paperwork, while Dr. Kelley droned on about the transfer process. He recognized the look in Sophia's eyes. He was about to pay for his inattention as she detailed Dr. Kelley's words.

"Since it's not my egg, my body has to be built up to receive the embryo." She ended her lecture with, "I don't know what you're complaining about. You're *giving* the shots. I'm the one getting them."

"Are you having second thoughts?" The sudden flicker of hope that popped into his head surprised him. He wasn't even sure *why* he hoped she would change her mind.

"No. But I'm human. It won't be pleasant." She looked around the room and then back at him. "Hold on. I'll be right back." When Sophia returned a minute later, she carried two oranges. Handing one to him, she placed the other on her dresser. "Practice on this."

"And do what?" Jake held the fruit as if it were a foreign object.

Sophia pulled a needle out of her sewing box. "Use this. They do this all the time to practice giving shots."

"Maybe twenty years ago—on *television*, for Christ's sake. Not in real life."

"Don't be such a wuss. It'll work." And with that, she handed him the needle.

Rolling the orange in his hands once or twice, he placed it on the dresser next to the other. "You sure this is right?"

She nodded.

Jake shrugged then jammed the needle into the orange.

"Jake! Be gentle. Imagine that you're injecting *me*."

Heat rushed to his face. "Right."

He tried again. But this time, when he picked up the needle, he stood frozen as he imagined Sophia's naked butt on the burnished wood of the dresser, and they both watched as the orange rolled to the floor.

"This is ridiculous. Give me the syringe and drop your pants."

Sophia presented him with her upper buttocks. When several minutes passed and nothing happened, she asked, "Everything all right back there?"

Sucking in a lungful of air, Jake refused to admit that the thought of injecting Sophia made his stomach drop. "All good. Just give me a minute." He wished he'd studied to be a doctor instead of a lawyer.

"Honey?"

He felt a little lightheaded, a feeling he'd never once experienced at the sight of his wife's naked ass. Taking one final look at the syringe, he plunged it into her butt, doing his best to ignore her quick intake of breath.

Sophia completed the injections several weeks later, and it was time to schedule the embryo transfer. But by then, all he could think about was the senior partner meeting, where he would deliver the final report on the SNIPES deal.

Chapter 10

Jake kept his eyes on Stephen when he delivered his report, forgetting the five other men and one woman in the room. Stephen was the one to impress.

"All parties involved have agreed to the terms of size and location. After five years, we finally have a deal, and the first SNIPES store will open in Vermont by late spring of next year."

Amid the applause and congratulations, Robert's voice snaked into Jake's head. *"You're not strong like your brother. You'll never be the lawyer he would have been."*

Somehow, in the years following Robbie's death, Jake had become the scapegoat. His father had put aside his guilt related to his son's death and preferred to concentrate on what he believed were Jake's flaws.

After shaking his head to dispel his dark thoughts, Jake looked around the room again, hopeful for the future. He brought champagne home that night even though there had yet to be an announcement of his promotion.

Jake wore his new Burberry suit when he went into the office on Monday. He was that confident of his promotion. Afterward, he would call his father with his good news, finally accomplishing what Robert said was beyond him.

Amy tapped on his door, her face hopeful. "Stephen wants to see you."

This is it. Today is the day I've been waiting for. It took a few minutes to get from his hole-in-the-wall office to the plushest corner suite in the building, and the entire time, Jake tried to clear his mind so he would at least appear calm.

Linda, Stephen's secretary, nodded toward his door. "He's expecting you."

"Come in. Close the door, will you?" Stephen placed both hands on his desk and clasped them lightly, waiting for Jake to sit.

"Let's get started, shall we? You did a great job with the SNIPES account. Congratulations. You've proven yourself to be a fine team player."

Jake froze. *Team player?* There'd been no team. He'd managed that deal and brought it to the table himself. He looked directly into Stephen's eyes and waited, his heart thudding in his chest and his mouth dry as sand.

It took an eternity for Stephen to speak, and when he did, his words were muffled as if he were talking underwater. "As a courtesy, I wanted to let you know before I make the big announcement that I'm bringing Brian in as the next senior partner."

"A courtesy?"

"Yes. You have seniority and are an excellent lawyer, but it's Brian's time. But don't worry. I won't forget you." From there, Stephen barely drew breath, effectively cutting off any possible response.

Jake's mouth filled with the taste of ashes. He would never accept Brian's new status as senior partner. Remaining silent, he concentrated on keeping his face neutral and his hands still. *What was it my father always said? "If the deal's not in your favor, walk away."*

"So." Stephen cleared his throat. "I'll announce that Brian is our newest senior partner, and we can all move forward."

The meeting was over.

He drove home on autopilot after making a quick call to Sophia. When he entered the kitchen, the tangy aroma of honey-mustard marinade assaulted his senses, causing his stomach to surge into his throat.

"What are you doing?"

His voice was ragged. Filled with pain and humiliation and all the anger he'd managed to keep in check these past few hours, the sight of Sophia standing at the stove cooking his favorite meal gutted him.

Sophia turned from the stove. "I'm sorry. I thought... It was too late to cancel dinner when you called." She lowered the flame then concentrated all her attention on him, her words rushing forward like a tsunami.

"This was supposed to be..." She looked at him helplessly. "You have to eat."

Without responding, he headed toward the stairs.

"Jake?"

He stopped but didn't turn in her direction.

"I'm so sorry you didn't get the promotion. I know how important this is to you. Did Stephen tell you why?"

Why? Why the fuck does it even matter? "It's not my time, apparently. Brian is the new senior partner."

"Brian? The guy who's such a buffoon?" Her voice filled with fury. "What the hell is Stephen thinking?"

Those were the first words that made any sense to him. "Good question." Finally facing her, his entire body rigid, he changed the subject. "What time is the transfer tomorrow?"

The sun shot daggers into Jake's eyes the following morning when he finally opened them. He'd fallen asleep on the couch in his study, his legs hanging over the side and his mouth wide open, a thin line of drool running down his chin. Sniffing deeply, he coughed, spying an empty bottle of Macallan Single Malt in the trash. His eyes snapped shut but then flew open again.

"Jake?" Wrinkling her nose, Sophia tightened her robe more closely around her and opened every window in the room. "Honey?"

Jake squinted at the sun lighting a path across his desk then eyed his upturned rocks glass and the dregs of amber liquor puddled on the wood finish before he looked at Sophia.

"What time is it?" He looked around the room as if he didn't quite know where he was.

"It's almost nine. We need to be at the clinic in an hour. Will you be all right?"

"I'll be fine." And with that, he pulled himself from the couch, hit his shoulder on the doorjamb, and stumbled out of the room. Sunlight sent shimmery waves through his brain, forcing him to keep his eyes as mere slits as he felt his way up the stairs and into his bathroom, every step provoking an explosion inside his head. He ripped off his clothes and reached blindly into the cupboard for aspirin. *Stephen and his "team player." Brian no more deserves to be a senior partner than a first-year law student.*

Jake felt his anger well up again as he choked down the pills and twisted the shower handle to cold. "Jesus Christ!"

The water sprayed over his body, taking his breath away while he forced himself to stand still until the icy needles numbed him. He tilted his head back, letting the water stream through his hair before turning the faucet to hot and grabbing the soap, slowly focusing on his day. The embryo transfer. And if it took? Sophia would be pregnant.

Jake had never forgotten the day she had told him she was expecting Emily. For one second, he'd felt pure and unbridled joy. The emotion had come and disappeared so quickly that Sophia'd never had the chance to share in his happiness.

After turning the water off, he stood inside the shower stall with his hands pressed against the tiles and his head lowered, memories of his brother consuming him. Robbie pounding his head against the wall until his forehead was lacerated and blood ran down his face. Lying fetal-like on the floor with his arms protectively wrapped around his head while his father removed his belt, screaming, "What the hell is wrong with you?" *That* had been the old man's solution to Robbie's problems.

And every time it happened, Jake had stood silently while his mother begged his father to stop. Even though he'd been a kid, he should have recognized that his brother needed to feel something other than handcrafted Italian leather cutting through his skin. He should have done something besides be thankful *he* wasn't on the receiving end of that belt. They never knew what was wrong with Robbie because they didn't want to know. Not even after he died.

There's a difference between wishing you were dead and your own parent provoking you into killing yourself. That was the part Sophia didn't know.

The look on his brother's face—as if he were surprised even to find himself in the basement. His eyes were no longer navy blue but black as night. His finger turned white from the pressure on the trigger.

His father's strangled voice. "Just do it if you think that's the answer to your problems!"

Jake had stumbled backward at the sound of the explosion. And then... and then his father had thrown himself over what remained of Robbie's skull. Jake squeezed his eyes shut, but the words continued to scream in his heart. *Just do it. Just do it. Just do it.*

He'd been ten at the time, frozen until his father's voice broke through the screaming in his head.

"Don't just stand there. Get help."

Two cops and an ambulance had answered the call. One helped his father up the stairs and into a room that didn't contain his brother's dead body while the other secured the scene. His mother, thankfully, had been visiting her sister in Manchester.

The story had changed by the time he entered the room. His father told the police Robbie's death was an accident. He'd just been fooling around. He didn't know the gun was loaded.

Every word was a lie.

Robert shut Jake down before he could say a word. "There's no need for you to be here," he had said, informing the cops that Jake hadn't seen his brother kill himself.

So he had kept quiet, just like always.

He had never told Sophia the truth of that night. Had never explained the *accident*. Not even when she announced her pregnancy with Emily and he became consumed with the fear that whatever had been wrong with his brother would revisit itself in his child.

Chapter 11

Out of the shower, Jake wandered down to the kitchen in time to overhear Sophia talking on the phone. Queen of multitasking, she was also whipping up a batch of waffle or pancake batter. All he knew was that it was the color of oatmeal, and she was beating the hell out of it.

"What's up? Are you there already?"

Must be Marianne. Odd that they were talking an hour before they were due to meet—even stranger was the compassion that played across Sophia's face.

She glanced at him, pointed to the pot of coffee he needed desperately, then turned her attention back to her conversation. "Well, of course you can't come. Please. This is the last thing you should be thinking about."

The call ended with Sophia promising to call after the transfer was over.

Bypassing the cream he usually added to his coffee, Jake took his first cautious sip. "What's wrong?"

"Adam's mother passed away unexpectedly last night." Her voice held an edge of grief even though she'd never met the woman. But that was Sophia—she felt everyone's pain.

"What happened?"

"They're not sure. When the caregiver went into her room this morning, she was dead."

Jake danced away from the thought of *his* mother dying, even though there would come a time when he wouldn't be able to avoid that reality. All he could do was hope he would be ready to accept it when it happened.

"I know you were looking forward to meeting Marianne in person."

He eyed the toaster and loaf of bread sitting next to it, but then he thought better of putting anything into his stomach.

"It'll be fine. I shouldn't be feeling sorry for myself. Adam just lost his mother." She looked at the bowl filled with batter and poured the contents into the sink. "I don't know what I was thinking. There's no time for waffles this morning."

Emily arrived in time to watch as the thick cream-colored batter clogged the drain. "Is that my breakfast?" She dipped one finger into the batter and lifted it to her mouth.

"You can't eat that. It has raw eggs in it." Sophia sprayed Emily's finger with water while coaxing the remaining mixture down the drain.

"But so does cookie dough, and Nonna lets me eat that."

Sophia rolled her eyes. "Well, she shouldn't. If you're hungry, make yourself some toast."

Even though it hurt like hell, he chuckled at the exasperation that flitted across Sophia's face.

"I'm not that hungry. I can't wait to meet the Barclays."

Sophia shot her a look of sympathy.

"What?"

"Honey, they won't be coming. Adam's mom passed away unexpectedly early this morning."

"Unexpectedly?" Several emotions crossed Emily's face, but the one he found most surprising was fear.

"They think she died in her sleep."

"That really happens?"

Emily looked like she would never step foot in her bedroom again, but Sophia reassured her that age and preexisting health issues had contributed and that she had nothing to worry about.

"But we were all supposed to meet for the first time today. Go out for lunch."

And then, her disappointment morphed into confusion. "So we're not going today?" Emily had insisted on coming for the transfer even though it meant missing a field hockey game, and the Barclays not being there didn't seem to change her mind.

"Yes, we're still going. The Barclays don't need to be there for the transfer. The embryo is frozen. I know you're disappointed. So am I. We'll get together another time." Sophia hugged Emily and gently pushed her toward the back door. "It's almost ten. If we leave now, we'll just make it."

Before they walked out the door, Jake touched Sophia's arm and said in a low voice, "I'm sorry about last night."

"About that..."

"I know. Alcohol isn't the answer to anything."

"I'm going to remember that." She ran her fingers through his hair. "Your hair's still damp."

He grinned even though he was sure his face would crack from the effort. "It'll dry."

Emily's eyes swung from Sophia to him. "What happened last night?"

"Nothing." Their responses were simultaneous.

"Well, obviously something happened. And if you don't want me to hear what you're saying, you need to whisper. Dad looks like hell, and you were crying earlier. What's going on?"

Jake straightened his shoulders. "I don't look like hell. I have a headache."

"So *that's* what's going on. You got drunk last night."

"I didn't get *drunk*." His head was doing the two-step. Jamming his hands into his pockets so he wouldn't head toward the freezer and climb in, he added, "I may have had more to drink than I should have." He couldn't admit that he was hungover. That didn't seem like something a father should acknowledge to his child. Even if it was true.

He turned to Sophia and lifted her chin. "Why were you crying?"

"It's nothing. I was just being silly."

"It must have been something. You don't cry about nothing."

"It *is* silly. This is such a big step. It's emotional. And physical. And... and maybe I'm a little nervous." Visibly pulling herself together, she added, "We need to get going."

They were almost out the door when he caught sight of the camera bag slung over Emily's shoulder. "What are you planning to take pictures of?"

"Don't be a dork, Dad. Mom's face—what do you think?"

He didn't know what he was thinking, but his face felt warm when Sophia tossed him a sympathetic look. An embryo transplant wasn't a situation he had any experience in. "Right. Mom's face."

They weren't in the car long before Sophia started squirming.

Not taking his eyes off the road, Jake reached for her hand. "You okay?"

Sophia bit her lip. "I have to pee."

He flashed her a grin, hoping humor would help them get through the morning. "Didn't your mother teach you to go before leaving the house?"

"Dad! Don't you pay attention to anything? Mom needs a full bladder for the ultrasound."

Emily patted Sophia on the shoulder. "Just a little longer, and then it'll be over, and you can go to the bathroom."

"Em, I was joking." Jake barely recognized Emily since they'd started the surrogacy program. She was thoughtful and gentle, leaving her penchant for sarcasm out of most conversations unless meant for him. And apparently, she'd also lost her sense of humor.

Once they arrived at the clinic, Sophia signed in, and they took seats in the waiting room. He slouched in his chair, wishing he'd remembered a hat to hide behind. He'd give just about anything to close his eyes for a few minutes. But even if he could, Sophia's knee bouncing up and down like it was going to take flight still wouldn't have allowed him the chance to rest.

"I know you hoped Marianne would be with you, but I'm here." Jake squeezed Sophia's fingers, wanting to reassure her.

The bouncing stopped for maybe a minute or two but was replaced by the crossing and uncrossing of her legs. She flinched every time the nurse called out a patient's name.

"I'm fine!"

"I can see that."

Emily seemed almost as nervous as Sophia. "What should I do while you're in with Mom?"

The question came out like a whine, making him wonder if it was too early for more aspirin. "You're old enough to stay by yourself."

"I know that, Dad. But what am I supposed to *do*?"

Where they were sitting wasn't all that comfortable. He noted few magazines—*Motor Trend* wouldn't occupy Emily for long—and no television to entertain a teenager who could barely sit still for a minute, let alone one who was almost as anxious about this procedure as they were.

"Let me check."

A nurse stopped him before he took a step. "I didn't mean to eavesdrop, but there's a more comfortable lounge down that hallway." Pointing, she looked at Emily with the sympathy one gives a two-year-old coming off a tantrum.

Emily rolled her eyes and pleaded, "Mom, can't I come in with you?"

Sophia looked at him for an answer.

Fifteen was probably old enough, but then, Jake remembered how impossible it was for Emily to keep things to herself. He didn't want to hear her describing embryo transfers to her friends.

"The lounge might be a good idea. We'll come get you as soon as we can."

Emily swung from him to Sophia. "But, Mom, this is an advancement in fertility issues, and as a woman, I should be with you for support."

Even with his headache, he almost laughed. "Nice try."

Sophia looked torn but finally agreed that the lounge would be the best place for Emily to wait.

When they heard Sophia's name, they followed the nurse while Emily stomped off to the lounge, appearing a little happier after Jake handed her a twenty for breakfast.

The nurse, Stephanie, who didn't look much older than Emily but who was soft-spoken with a you-are-going-to-do-great smile, handed Sophia a gown—the kind that left your butt hanging out—and said she'd be right back. The room was a cross between a doctor's exam room and a bar, with dimmed lights and soft piano music playing.

"How you holding up?"

"Other than feeling like my bladder's going to explode?"

"Other than that."

He helped her slip on the gown, and within moments, Stephanie returned.

"You ready, hon?" Stephanie's demeanor seemed to put Sophia at ease, and he took his first deep breath since pulling himself off the couch that morning.

In preparation for the doctor's arrival, Stephanie confirmed pertinent information, such as name and birthdate, against the identifying data on the embryo. Jake did what he was good at—he held Sophia's hand.

By the time Dr. Davison arrived—the doctor who would implant the embryo—Sophia looked like she was sleeping.

"How are you doing, Sophia?" The doctor's voice was barely more than a whisper.

She never bothered opening her eyes but seemed to recognize his calming voice. "I'm well, thanks. Anxious to get this part over."

"Not much longer."

And then, in what seemed like minutes, the embryo was loaded into the transfer catheter and inserted into Sophia's body. She squeezed Jake's fingers hard, and he squeezed back.

"You did great, Sophia." Dr. Davison gently touched her shoulder then shook Jake's hand. Before they knew it, he was gone.

"Just relax," Stephanie advised, covering Sophia with a warm blanket. "I'll be back in a few minutes."

Sophia's eyes welled, and she released a huge sigh.

"Okay?" His voice filled with wonder. He hadn't expected to feel so emotional about the transfer.

She nodded as one lone tear slowly crept down her cheek.

"Hey." Jake wiped at the tear with his thumb. "What's going on?"

"Just a little weepy. This is probably the biggest thing I've ever done for someone else."

He crouched next to her so that they were at eye level. "This is huge, Soph. I can't tell you how proud I am of you." Curiosity finally got the best of him. "What did it feel like?"

"The transfer? Kind of like a pap smear."

"Babe. That's not telling me anything."

Sophia laughed and added, "It was slightly uncomfortable."

"At least if Marianne were here, she'd know what a pap smear feels like."

Sophia grabbed his arm and tugged him closer. "You did great. You did better than great. Thank you for being here." She kissed him gently. "I'm so sorry you didn't get your promotion."

He swallowed, unable to respond other than to grip her fingers. Maybe later, they could talk about it.

The transfer made everything real. They didn't know if it would take, but the possibility was there. Stephanie stepped back into the room, interrupting his thoughts. "When you feel up to it, you can dress and check out." She shook both their hands. "Good luck to you."

The door closed softly behind her.

"So. What happens next?"

Sophia sat up carefully. "Next, I get dressed. Then we wait to see if I'm pregnant." She looked wistful then gave him a small smile. "We should know in about two weeks." Buttoning her shirt, she shuddered slightly then sat perfectly still.

"You okay?" He'd think she was about to pass out if she wasn't mirroring the mystery of the Mona Lisa with her smile.

"I'm fine." She touched her stomach. "I had this amazing sensation, like the embryo is settling in—and I know that's ridiculous, so don't tease me." She looked like she'd just had a religious experience, and he couldn't remember the last time Sophia had entered a church. "And don't ask me what that feels like because I can't explain it."

Emily was flitting from one end of the lounge to the other when they stopped in to tell her it was time to go home. Before she noticed their presence, they watched as she picked up and put down magazines, fanned them into neat arrangements, studied the photos on the walls, and straightened any that looked the slightest off-kilter. They caught her plucking fuzz balls off pillows before he coughed to let her know she wasn't alone.

Grabbing Sophia's hand, she practically yelped, "Are you okay? Were you scared? Do you need to sit down?" Emily wrapped her arms around her mother like they hadn't seen each other in a week.

Sophia laughed, hugging her back. "I'm fine. There's nothing to worry about."

"When will you know if you're pregnant?"

"Maybe in two weeks. Grab your stuff so we can go home."

"Wait! Before we leave, I want to take pictures." She grabbed her camera and looked around the room. "Stand here. The light's good."

"Honey, that's not necessary.

"This will only take a second. I promise. Come on. Stand over here."

Once Sophia was in position, Emily took a couple of shots, and Sophia glowed in each of them.

Then, Emily handed her camera to him. "Take a picture of Mom and me."

"You know I don't take good pictures. Do a selfie."

"Don't be such a baby, Dad. This could be the best shot."

Chapter 12

When Sophia's alarm went off, she pounded on her bedside table until she finally hit the clock, knocking it onto the floor but blessedly stopping the racket. But she made no move to get up.

"You okay?"

Jake finally opened his eyes when she didn't answer and faced her. She was flat on her back, staring at the ceiling.

"Hon? What are you doing?"

"Trying to keep the room from spinning."

"Are you getting up?"

"Pretty sure I'm not. Can you and Emily get your own breakfast?"

"Sure." He kissed her forehead. It was cool. "Go back to sleep."

No sooner had he turned the water off from his shower than the bathroom door banged open. Wrapping a towel around his waist, he opened the shower door and found Sophia kneeling before the toilet, disgorging everything she'd consumed in the last twenty-four hours.

He knelt beside her, holding her hair away from her face and rubbing small circles on her back. "You think you have the flu?"

"Don't know." She drew in a ragged gulp. "Maybe I'm..."

He gave her a second then nudged. "Maybe you're...?"

Her face went gray. "Nothing." She flushed the toilet, pulled herself from the floor, and rinsed her mouth while avoiding the bathroom mirror.

"I can't be pregnant yet. Can I?" Sophia looked panicked. "It hasn't even been two weeks since the embryo transfer. The odds of pregnancy in the first transfer are about fifty percent in a woman my age. I was figuring on at least another round." Her words came fast.

"Slow down. It'll be fine. This month, next month—it'll all work out."

Still looking conflicted, Sophia crawled back into bed and turned her back to him, no longer interested in his calming words. That morning was the start of a pattern. Occasionally, she made it to the kitchen and saw him off to work and Emily to school. But just as frequently, she pawed at the alarm to silence it and left the two of them to their own devices while she battled nausea that started the moment she opened her eyes and didn't quit until her day was almost over.

They didn't mention pregnancy again until Dr. Kelley confirmed it a few days later. After hearing the news, they strolled back to their car in a daze.

"I'm pregnant." Sophia whispered the words distractedly, as if afraid that if she said them too loudly, the baby inside her would disappear. But something else was in her voice, something Jake couldn't pin down.

"You are."

He drew her close. But she just stood within the circle of his arms as if she were numb.

"Are you excited?"

She never responded. She didn't say another word until she pulled out her phone once they'd settled in the car. "I'm calling Marianne. She needs to know." She hit Marianne's number in her contacts and then looked at him. "Am I allowed to tell her, or is the news supposed to come from the agency?"

He had no idea.

Within a minute, she ended the call. "It went to voicemail. This isn't the kind of announcement I want to leave for a machine to convey. I'll call her later."

The remainder of the ride was quiet. Too quiet for Jake's liking. "You sure you're okay?"

"I'm fine."

Something was wrong, but Sophia wasn't sharing. He ran his finger along the curve of her cheek. "Don't worry, you'll get hold of Marianne later."

"That's not..."

"Gonna finish that thought?" He pulled into the driveway and was halfway out of the car before realizing Sophia hadn't budged.

"Soph?" When she didn't move, he closed his door, moved to hers, opened it, and knelt beside her. "Please tell me what's wrong."

Without answering, she pulled herself from the car and, with what looked like a great deal of effort, smiled. Suddenly, whatever dark cloud had settled on her shoulders disappeared, and her original enthusiasm returned.

"I can't wait to tell Emily." She started toward the door.

"I think she'll guess the minute she sees you."

"Why? Do I look pregnant?" She ran her hands over her concave stomach as if searching for a telltale bulge.

"Don't be silly." He grabbed her hands and pulled her to him. "You look absolutely ravishing. But do you think you should wait? You know, until you're a bit... more pregnant?"

"Maybe?"

When they knocked on the open door of Emily's room, Emily and Maddie were giggling, passing Emily's camera between them, apparently pleased with whatever pictures they were looking at.

"What's going on?" Sophia asked once they entered Emily's room.

Emily countered, "What's going on with you? You look like you've just won the big prize behind Door Number Two."

"Wait." Jake choked out a laugh. "What does that even mean?"

"It means Mom looks like she won a brand-new car. It's from a television show on Tuesday nights. You're still at the office."

Sophia wasn't even listening. She kept glancing in the mirror over Emily's dresser. "I guess I do look happy." She shot him a look.

Jake shrugged. This was her news. Finally, Sophia settled on the bed beside Emily without answering the question.

"Check out these photos." Emily handed her mother the camera.

Sophia looked into the LCD. "Oh! From the clinic." Her grin grew wider with each picture she saw. "I think this one's my favorite."

She held the camera out to him. "What do you think?"

The picture was the one he had taken of Emily and Sophia with their arms wrapped around each other.

"The photographer knew what he was doing."

"Very funny. It's our favorite too." Emily took her camera back and checked out the picture again. "I'll make a print—two prints—one for you guys and one for the Barclays. This will represent the beginning of your surrogacy if the transfer works."

Sophia looked at him again. They'd agreed not to tell Emily, but Sophia looked like she was about to explode. Instead of getting up, she slowly reclined until she was prone on Emily's bed, the glow in her eyes so bright she could make it available to land airplanes on dark and stormy nights. Whatever concerns she'd had earlier were seemingly resolved. Sophia was about to spill the beans.

Emily and Maddie looked at each other then at Sophia. "Mom? You're still grinning."

Sophia nodded. "I am."

Again, the girls exchanged glances. "You know you're acting really weird, right?"

"Yep."

Sophia pulled herself from the bed, grabbed his hand, and headed toward the bedroom door, her eyes still glowing and her blinding smile still in place.

"Are you sure you're okay?"

Sophia looked back at Emily. There would be no secret. No waiting to divulge her news. He chuckled.

Sophia drew in a deep breath. "Ask me again."

"Again?"

"Yes. If you ask me *again,* I just might tell you."

The three of them seemed to be playing a game.

"*Okay...*" Emily drew the word out like a piece of saltwater taffy stretched thin. Her eyes sparkling, she asked, "Why are you grinning like a fool?"

Bouncing on her toes, Sophia looked from Emily to Maddie, all thoughts of waiting forgotten. Nearly bursting with joy, she responded, "Because I'm pregnant!"

The girls looked at each other.

"*What?*"

They flew off the bed and wrapped their arms around Sophia. The look on Emily's face told him she was thrilled.

"Does Marianne know? What did she say?"

"She doesn't know yet. She wasn't home, and I didn't want to leave a message. Don't say anything to anyone before I tell her."

"Got it! I can't wait until she finds out."

"I know. I'll call her later. Right now, I need to start dinner."

They'd almost made it through the doorway when Sophia looked back. Both girls still had silly grins on their faces.

"Why are you both looking like *you* have a secret?"

The girls fell into a heap of giggles. "We *do* have a secret. You just told us you're pregnant."

Sophia glanced at him and shrugged. If something else was going on, she was too wrapped up in her own happiness to give it much thought. After following her into their bedroom, Jake wrapped her in a big hug.

"Congratulations! You did a great job of keeping your secret."

She didn't even bother to look embarrassed. "I know. I'm a failure."

Sophia was happy. This pregnancy was what she wanted, and Emily was thrilled. He couldn't help but grin.

"I need to tell you something." Sophia stepped away as if needing to put space between them, and her voice became serious so quickly that he felt uneasy. "I've thought about this for days and kept putting it off—but maybe this shouldn't be such a big deal anymore."

"Okay. Will this explain the back-and-forth moods you've been experiencing? Especially today?"

"Probably. I need you to listen and not react. Not until I'm done. Maybe it's time you put this to rest." Sophia moved closer as if whatever she had to say would upset him and she wanted to take the sting out of her words, but she was making him more than a little nervous.

"Maybe you just need to tell me."

"The baby's due in June." She glanced at him quickly and then looked away. "I'm sorry. I know how you feel about anything related to the entire month. I never expected the transfer to take the first time."

His chest tightened. He carried his briefcase to the bed, riffled through its contents, and tried to pull himself together.

"Maybe it's time to stop blaming the time of year your brother died and place the blame where it belongs. On Robbie's illness."

June. The word pulsed in his head. *June!* When he couldn't stand it a minute longer, he slammed his briefcase closed and faced her, forcing a smile that did nothing to lighten his burden.

"Sorry, I need to go back to the office. There's a brief I need, and since I'm going back, I might as well do what I need to do there. It'll be faster." He leaned into Sophia and kissed her forehead.

"Don't wait dinner for me. I'll grab a sandwich."

"Wait a minute. You can't just run away from this."

"I'm not running away." His entire body twitched with the need to escape. "You're right; it's time to get over it." He couldn't explain that his chest was on fire. He couldn't tell her any of it because he'd kept it all a secret for so long he wouldn't even know where to begin. "I'm fine. I really do need to run into the office."

They never went on vacation in June. They didn't socialize the entire month because he vacillated every time Sophia suggested an outing until she finally gave up. Fortunately, no one had a birthday that month except his father, and that barely counted since he was born on the first of June at 12:01 a.m.

Thoughts of Robbie clutched at his throat. Not the Robbie who'd taught him how to play football and tossed baseballs to him until he could smack the ball across the field but the Robbie with the gun in his mouth and the tears in his eyes. He couldn't get out of his house fast enough.

Jake had no idea where he was going when he backed out of his garage until he ended up at The Whistle Stop. After pulling into the parking lot, he turned off the engine and closed his eyes, but the image of Sophia grinning when she'd announced her pregnancy to Emily was as vivid as it had been an hour ago.

He called Matt. Then he went into the bar, grabbed a booth, and ordered a beer, keeping his eyes on the door. When Matt showed up, he waved him over.

Matt slid into the booth and reached over to straighten Jake's tie.

"Didn't realize this was a formal event."

Touching his collar, Jake remembered he'd left the house in such a hurry he hadn't bothered to change. "Yeah. It's not."

Before Matt had time to order a drink, Jake spit out his news. "Sophia's pregnant."

"Hey, congratulations." Matt reached across the table to shake Jake's hand, but he flinched as if Matt had waved a claw in front of him.

"Well, wasn't that the point? For Sophia to get pregnant?"

He could barely remember what the point was. "Yep, that was the point." He couldn't put his fear into words.

"So what's going on? You don't look like you called me here for a celebration."

Before he could answer, the waitress stopped by with a fresh beer for him and took Matt's order.

"The problem is…"

He glanced at Matt to see if he could look him in the eye. He quickly lowered his head. He couldn't look himself in the eye, let alone his best friend. "I don't know what the problem is." Swallowing a third of his fresh beer in one gulp, he tried again. "The problem is the baby's due in June."

"*Okay*. Is that not a good month? Do you have plans then? A vacation?"

The waitress dropped off Matt's beer, and he lifted the bottle to his mouth for a sip then placed it back on the table, never taking his eyes off Jake. "Work with me here—what's the problem?"

There was no way he could explain what was going on in his head when he couldn't explain it to himself. "My brother died in June."

Matt blinked. "I didn't know you had a brother."

Outside of the family, no one spoke of Robbie. "It was a long time ago. You didn't live here then."

"I'm sorry about your brother. But I still don't understand."

Staring at Matt, Jake hoped his confusion would clear. "Me neither."

Chapter 13

Jake still couldn't explain why a June delivery date devastated him when he returned to his house a few hours later. But food won out over his other worries. He'd never grabbed a sandwich at the office like he told Sophia. Because he'd never gone to the office.

Slathering mayonnaise onto two slices of rye, his hand jerked when he overheard Sophia's enthusiastic words.

"You're going to have a baby!"

He stiffened. She must have reached Marianne. Sophia might have recovered from concerns over the baby's due date, but he was nowhere near that point. He eyed the sandwich makings. What the hell, he still had to eat.

Sophia sounded happier than when she found out she was pregnant with Emily. *Of course she's happier. I'm not grousing that she broke our agreement not to have children.* He wanted to put it all aside, at least for tonight. Take his sandwich into his study and relax.

"Hello? Marianne, are you there?"

As Jake strolled into the library to let Sophia know he'd be in his study, she grabbed his hand, urging him to sit next to her.

"I probably scared her half to death," she muttered.

Speaking slowly and in a lower tone, Sophia tried again. "Did you hear me? *We're pregnant!*"

Marianne erupted into sobs that even he could hear. Sobs that sounded as if they came from the bottom of her soul. And then she started giggling before he could reconcile the depth of all that emotion.

"You're pregnant? I'm going to be a mom? Adam! Adam! We're having a baby."

The next sound they heard could only be the phone hitting the floor, and then they heard a few words from Marianne and Adam in the background. Finally, Marianne came back on the line. Still laughing but crying too.

"Sorry. I just... we're very excited. Thank you. Oh my God, thank you so much."

Sophia's eyes brimmed with unshed tears, and Jake wanted to be happy for her. He just didn't have it in him. Appetite gone, he kissed the top of her head and dumped the sandwich he'd been looking forward to into the garbage. The last thing he heard as he headed toward his study was that they were planning to meet for lunch in Morrisville—halfway between them so that Sophia didn't have to drive the entire way.

Dinner conversation the following evening was all about Sophia's lunch with Marianne.

"Tell us *everything*." Emily passed Jake the mashed potatoes and edged closer to her mother, waiting for what she called "the scoop."

"Well, she was there before me. She told me to look for a Jeep. I forgot to ask what color it was, but figured I'd look for a woman sitting in a Jeep. When I found it, I pulled in beside her. She was staring straight ahead with her fingers drumming on the steering wheel. I watched her, willing her to look my way, but when she didn't, I rolled down my window, lowered my voice, and asked her for a match."

"Mom!"

"I know. I was being silly. You should have seen the look on Marianne's face before she recognized me. Within seconds, we were standing in the parking lot with our arms wrapped around each other."

Sophia's face was flushed with happiness as she relayed her afternoon. "Marianne pulled back slightly to look down the length of my body until her eyes rested on my midsection. I burst out laughing. She was expecting a baby bump already. I told her she had to wait another month for me to look pregnant. Anyway, it was a great afternoon until I got sick."

That got Jake's attention. "Sick? You're just telling us now?"

She waved him off. "I'm fine. Marianne ordered a double bacon cheeseburger with onion rings and fries. I ordered clear broth and crackers. I didn't want to take a chance on getting sick, but then I did anyway. It was the rare meat. I used to love rare meat. But now? Not so much. I thought I'd be okay with the smell, but when Marianne sank her teeth into her burger, the juices dripped onto her plate, and the next thing I knew, my mouth filled with bile."

"Marianne ordered onion rings *and* fries?"

"Your mother was sick, and you are more interested in what Marianne ate?"

Emily looked sufficiently chastised, but then Sophia let her off the hook.

"Yes! I said the same thing, but she assured me she rarely eats fried food. Except when she's nervous. You should have seen her eyes light up when the waitress delivered her food, but as it turned out, she barely touched it."

"Why?"

"I had been telling her how I'd known I was pregnant almost from the beginning when I looked at her plate, and my stomach heaved. I looked away, hoping to draw a breath that didn't include the scent of rare meat, but instead of tables and booths filled with people enjoying their lunch, I pictured blood pooling on Marianne's plate. Next thing I knew, I was in the restroom. I was so embarrassed when I returned to the table and explained the problem."

Sophia's eyes sparkled as she related the story. "She did the sweetest thing. She called the waitress over, handed her the plate, and told her she'd have what I was having."

"Clear broth?" Emily's voice rose a notch as if the thought of anyone handing back a burger was beyond her.

Nodding, Sophia continued. "The waitress looked at the plate in her hand and the bowl on the table and must have thought Marianne was having a meltdown. But I felt better as soon as the smell of rare meat was gone. By the time lunch was over, we'd discussed everything from cloth and disposable diapers to crib versus cradle for the first month or so after the baby's birth. She's going to make a great mother."

Sophia reached her hand across the table toward Jake while Emily did the dishes.

"You didn't have much to say tonight. Everything okay?"

No. Everything is not okay, but there isn't a damn thing I can do about it. At least Jake kept the thought to himself. His smile was strained. Unsure where all the anger had come from, he responded carefully. "Everything's fine. Glad you had a good day."

He stood, and she grabbed his arm. "Sure?"

He couldn't get Robbie out of his mind. "I'm sure." He kissed her cheek and fled to his study.

Chapter 14

Sophia's pregnancy was the last thing on Jake's mind when he stuck his head into the laundry room before heading out for a run.

"Don't forget we're having dinner with Stephen and his wife tonight."

"Oh God, I did forget." Sophia set the washing machine in motion then turned back to him. "I don't know—I haven't been feeling great today."

He swallowed his groan. "It's on the calendar."

Putting her hand on her still-flat stomach, she gave him a weary smile. "This baby hasn't learned to read the calendar yet."

He was no more eager to appear at Stephen's dinner party than Sophia, but he didn't have much choice after Brian's smug look when he asked if he and Sophia were planning to attend.

Eager to get outside and feel his feet slap against the asphalt, a routine he'd been rigorously following the last few weeks, he came close to snapping, "You were never sick with Emily."

Sophia's eyes widened. "I know, but each pregnancy is different. This one is taking a lot out of me. I'm afraid I'll pass if I have to decide this minute." Gathering a few curls that had escaped from the loose bun on top of her head and twirling them around her finger, she offered him a little hope. "Let me see how I feel after lunch."

Shifting his feet back and forth, he remained quiet. That answer wasn't what he wanted. Jake knew he was being unfair—an ass—but he couldn't help himself.

When his feet hit the pavement a few minutes later, his thoughts automatically focused on that evening's dinner party. It would be difficult to have a polite conversation with the firm's partners—Stephen's consolation prize for Brian's promotion—but that was his job right now, to be a team player. He didn't want to think about the dark circles under Sophia's eyes or that the last thing she should do was get dressed up to attend a dinner party with him, but he kept returning to what he wanted. And what he wanted was for Sophia to attend the damn dinner with him.

Jake and Sophia strolled arm-in-arm through the front door of Stephen and Audrey's home right on time.

The staff served cocktails and small bites in the library. Jake had always admired this room where floor-to-ceiling built-in bookcases held leather-bound, signed first editions by authors like Alice Hoffman, Gay Talese, and Richard Condon. Books just waiting to be read by someone tucked into one of the wingback chairs scattered around the room.

After requesting a Manhattan for himself and a glass of Perrier for Sophia, he realized he'd never announced Sophia's pregnancy in the office. He'd been keeping a low profile, doing everything he could to prove he was a supportive member of the firm and hoping Stephen would soon acknowledge him as senior-partner material. But he couldn't bring himself to share the news he was struggling with.

Stephen clapped him on the back before he could warn Sophia that no one knew she was pregnant. "I'm just going to steal your lovely wife for a minute."

Whisking her away in the direction of the central hallway, Jake overheard him murmuring that he wanted to show her his latest acquisition by Luo Zhongli.

"A stunning piece featuring an old woman—her head bent, her aged arms reflecting every year of her long life. I want you to tell me what you think."

As Sophia was curator of the Shelburne Museum, everyone sought her opinion. She was missing out on a lucrative side hustle by not charging for her services, but she would never dream of accepting money from her friends. Or his boss.

Jake's plan to talk to Sophia on the way to dinner was again circumvented by Stephen when he led her into the dining room. Shrugging, he put it out of his mind. Sophia would never announce her pregnancy to a room full of people she rarely saw.

With Audrey on his arm, he followed behind his boss and Sophia. The familiar wine-colored wall panels gave the room the illusion of warmth, and the woodburning fireplace warded off the real chill of fall in Vermont.

This room, this entire house, reminded him of the house he grew up in. It exuded a wealth that reinforced everything his father thought was important. To Jake, it reminded him of all he was still struggling to attain. Stephen would see that he was worthy. His jaws clenched. Stephen *had* to know that he was a valuable asset to the firm.

Once seated, Jake looked around the table and caught a quick look of annoyance cross Audrey's face. When he followed her gaze, he found himself staring at Brian, who had flipped over his bread plate and appeared to be reading the markings. Brian would be that guy. He might wear his senior-partner status like a glove but was hopeless regarding social graces. Yet he had been Stephen's choice. A decision Jake would never understand.

Sophia was seated to Stephen's right, and he hoped she'd caught Brian being his usual socially awkward self. But she and Stephen had their heads together, talking about who knew what.

The first course, served amid the soft chatter of dinner guests discussing the approaching Thanksgiving holiday, was a cup of miso soup. Jake took the opportunity to glance at Sophia again while each guest was served. She was still chatting with Stephen.

Forgetting his earlier irritation, he couldn't help but admire how she'd pulled herself together. Her hair shone like silk. She had swept her curls into an intricate knot at the base of her head, holding it all in place by what looked like an old-fashioned hat pin. He leaned back in his chair, happy she was feeling better, optimistic that they'd get through the evening intact.

The soup was light and delicious. Jake generally preferred hearty soups—thick enough that a spoon could stand up in the bowl without support—but this was a perfect beginning to a meal that promised to delight even the most jaded appetites. After the soup, servers delivered plates of wild-caught Alaskan halibut, roasted tomatoes, artichoke hearts, and Mediterranean olives with miniature ravioli in a butter-and-lemon sauce. Stephen and Audrey had outdone themselves once again. Not that they had anything to do with the meal's preparation, but he couldn't fault their taste in caterers.

Jake was focused on his food when a startled gasp forced his eyes across the table in time to catch Sophia abruptly standing, nearly knocking down the server refilling wine glasses in her haste to leave the room. Before he could react, Audrey rose and followed. Everyone looked to him as if he could explain their hasty departure, but he had no idea what had happened. He pushed back from the table, intent on ensuring Sophia was all right, but Stephen motioned for him to remain seated.

"Just relax. If anything's wrong, Audrey will let you know."

He should have listened to Sophia earlier when she'd said she wasn't feeling well instead of guilting her into coming to the party.

Dinner conversation slowly picked back up while he toyed with his fish and waited for Sophia and Audrey to return. Regretting that he'd listened to Stephen, he was impatient to see that she was okay.

Maybe this is why Stephen passed me over. I'm too much of a yes-man. As soon as the thought took hold, he rejected it. It would take quite a bit to beat Brian in the ass-kissing department.

When the dessert course—individual maple hazelnut custard cups topped with maple cream—was served and the two women returned, Jake was sure everyone at the table heard his sigh of relief. They might yet get through the rest of the evening without further mishaps.

And then Audrey lightly struck her wine glass with the side of her knife—a peal of proclamation if he'd ever heard one. "Everyone! Sophia has permitted me to make an announcement." Audrey stood, her eyes sweeping over her guests and landing on Jake. "There's no need to be alarmed. Sophia isn't sick. She's going to have a baby. Nothing contagious here."

Before he could react, he caught a trace of a smirk cross Sophia's face as enthusiastic applause filled the room. He'd always admired a worthy opponent, especially when it was his wife. It surely hadn't taken Sophia long to realize he'd never announced her surrogacy at the office, and apparently, she figured it was high time everyone knew. He tipped his head in her direction. *Well played.*

Drawing in a deep breath, he acknowledged the announcement. "Sophia and I are pleased about this pregnancy. We've given this a lot of thought, but it's not what you're thinking."

"Sure it isn't," Brian mumbled, sounding like he'd had more than his share of wine.

Amid the laughter, a bottle of champagne appeared, and Stephen rose to give a toast.

The dinner conversation took a complete turn from corporate law—put a bunch of lawyers into any room, and they would soon discover their commonality was legal briefs and class action suits—to the surprising fact of how familiar most everyone was with surrogacy.

"My neighbor's done this three times for two different families," his dinner partner to the left commented. She was Todd's wife, but he couldn't remember her name for the life of him.

He nodded, but before he could say more, Leah, seated to his right, spoke.

"You must be very proud of your wife."

Of all the things Jake had felt since discovering the baby would be born in June, pride was not his primary emotion. But this wasn't the time to delve into his fears.

Audrey asked if they were keeping a journal.

"Our daughter, Emily, is. Well, really more of a photo album," Sophia responded, looking radiant. "We haven't seen it yet because she says she's keeping it for a special occasion, but I swear I'm not safe anywhere in the house. Emily's always pointing her camera at me."

Everyone had questions. "Have you met the people? The parents? What are they called?"

"Intended parents." Jake was determined to keep up with the conversation.

Several women surrounded Sophia, but she was glowing when one stepped away and he caught sight of her. Jake had thought he'd given her everything she could want, but he was beginning to see she could make her own happiness.

From the energy in Sophia's voice, she was getting her second wind on the drive home. "You never told anyone about the surrogacy." There was surprise in her tone and maybe a little hurt.

He gritted his teeth. "I know. I'm sorry."

"Are you ashamed that I'm doing this?"

The question was valid, but all he could do was grasp the steering wheel tightly and stare straight ahead.

"Or maybe you're ashamed of me. Or... or think it's unnatural. Or you're so worried about what your father will say that you can't think past that."

"Look. I just didn't. Don't make this into a big deal." He couldn't tell her he was too wrapped up in his own demons. That her pregnancy brought back past nightmares of standing on the basement steps of his family home, listening to his father egg his brother on because he thought Robbie needed to "man up" and get over what was wrong with him.

Man up. He fought the sudden pain in his chest. Robbie had been fifteen. He was nowhere near a man.

"Maybe I thought it was no one's business but ours."

Sophia wasn't buying it. "It would have helped Audrey to know I was pregnant when she walked into her perfect powder room and I could barely pull myself up from the floor."

He grimaced at the image.

"I had to tell her something. I took one look at that fish and... I can still smell it. Audrey was so understanding. She helped me clean up and redo my makeup. I couldn't very well *not* tell her."

He could do nothing about the hurt in Sophia's voice. He couldn't bring himself to tell her the truth of Robbie's death. Or how the memories of that night seared his heart.

"You were happy to tell her. I saw the look on your face. I get it. I'm a shit. I'm sorry you didn't feel well. I'm sorry I can't be excited about this."

"But you were thrilled. Remember when we had the embryo transfer? You were happy. I know you were. When did that change?"

"That was before."

"Before what?"

He opened his mouth. He wanted to tell her... but he couldn't. "Nothing." He only wanted to end this conversation, but Sophia was in no mood to let it go.

"Are you worried what your father will say when we tell him I'm a surrogate?"

He struggled to keep calm. "Don't bring him into this. He has nothing to do with it." *Who am I kidding? He has everything to do with it.*

"He will once he finds out."

"Is that what this is all about? Getting back at my family?"

"This isn't about your family. I've had every advantage in my life. I want to do something for someone else. Something that matters."

"Everything you do matters. You're Emily's mother. You're my wife. You're a renowned art specialist. Why can't you be happy with that?"

"Why can't you be happy about this pregnancy?"

"I was never happy—more like accepting." He pulled into their driveway, waiting for the garage door to go up.

"Are you saying I talked you into this?"

Did she talk me into it? Was I happy until I discovered when the baby is due? He didn't know when he'd ever felt more confused.

Chapter 15

Jake lay in bed long after he heard the front door close. No doubt Sophia had gone for a walk or was over at Christine's. *God knows what Sophia might say about our argument last night.* He tossed that thought aside in a second. That was not Sophia's style and never had been. If she had a complaint, she wasn't shy about calling him on it. He knew this as well as he knew it was Sunday morning and he should get his lazy ass out of bed.

Yawning, he rolled over, his thoughts still on last night. Audrey liked nothing more than to make a production out of almost anything, and Sophia knew that as well as he did. Just thinking about the sound of Audrey's knife tapping against her wine glass made him wince.

But maybe Audrey did him a favor. Everyone might cut him some slack in the office, assume Sophia's surrogacy was the reason for his foul mood rather than Brian's senior-partner status. Unfortunately, his short temper was leaking into his home life as well. That needed fixing.

He let out one long groan and hoped the fresh air would clear his head and rid him of his anger. After rolling out of bed, he threw on his running clothes then added an extra layer after listening to the weather.

Passing Emily's room, he paused then backtracked and rapped on her door. "Time to get up." When she didn't respond, he rattled the doorknob and opened it. "Hey. It's time to get up."

Emily pulled the blanket over her head, which irritated him for some reason.

"Get up!"

"What is your problem?" she mumbled. "It's Sunday. I get to sleep in."

"Not today, you don't. You need to rake the leaves in the backyard."

Seething, he slammed her door and headed down the stairs. *Now, I'm a jerk to my daughter.* It *was* Sunday. Emily *was* allowed to sleep in. *What is my problem?* Without coffee to fuel him, he stormed out the kitchen door and took off on his run, hoping he'd be calmer by the time he headed back home.

Later that day, he heard Emily and Sophia talking in the library. Intent on making amends after losing his temper earlier, he was about to join them when Emily's question stopped him.

"What's with Dad?"

Aware that he was eavesdropping, adding one more black mark to his name, he slouched against the paneled door where he had a clear view of the room.

"What do you mean?" Sophia looked confused.

"I don't know. He's been a pain in my ass. He made me get up early this morning to rake leaves. And it's Sunday. I get to sleep in today."

"Your father's fine." There was no hint of last night's argument in Sophia's voice as she defended him to their daughter.

He rolled his shoulders, trying to relax. He'd give just about anything to have Sophia's temperament these days.

"He's got a lot going on at work, and maybe you need to give him a break. And watch the language."

He could imagine Emily's eyeroll. Their conversation moved from him to the play Emily was trying out for at school.

Jake was about to join them when Emily mentioned the Barclays. "How do you think Dad will be when he meets them?"

"Dad? He'll be fine."

"I don't know how you can be so sure. The way Dad is these days, I never know what he'll be like."

"That's not true. Your father has a lot on his mind."

"That's what you keep saying. Don't you get tired of always taking his side?"

Sophia laughed, and his spine stiffened. He pushed away from the door and walked into the library as if he hadn't just heard her laugh—it was more of a snicker—as if his family hadn't been talking about him.

He was the bad guy. He couldn't deny it. He was short-tempered, had lost his sense of humor, and had trouble concentrating on anything Sophia or Emily said. But he was tired of being the bad guy.

"So! What's up with you two?" Neither of them even had the decency to look embarrassed that they had been talking about him. He plopped down next to Emily so they could huddle together on the couch.

"Who wants to watch a movie tonight?"

Sophia yawned. "Not me. I'm on my way up to bed."

His eyes narrowed. Sophia's voice had been filled with energy a minute ago, but he let it go. Masking his irritation, he grabbed Emily's knee, pinching it lightly. "Okay, kiddo. It's you and me. There's a couple of good ones on. You can pick."

"Ouch!" Emily scooted away from him as if he'd done serious damage. "That *hurt*."

"What? I barely touched you. Don't be such a baby." His voice rose, and he struggled to lower it. His intent was to be mellow. *Isn't that what I used to be?* God, he barely remembered what he used to be. Calmer, he asked again, "How about it? What movie should we watch?"

"I'm spending the night at Maddie's. Mrs. Lawrence said it was okay."

His shoulders tensed. This was not going the way he had hoped. "Hey," he coaxed, "I thought you liked spending time with your old man."

He swore Emily looked at him like he was scum. Lower than scum. And when she spoke, he was sure of it.

"That's when you were the dad you used to be. You're not so nice anymore."

Still trying, he did what he did best—he punted. "What do you mean I'm 'not so nice'? I'm always nice."

He turned to Sophia. "Tell her, Soph. Tell her I'm the best dad ever." He was determined to stay calm. To be the dad he'd always been.

But Sophia chuckled. "I'll see you two in the morning. Try not to kill each other down here."

When Sophia had left the room, Jake pulled himself up from the couch and poured a drink, hoping he and Emily would both calm down. They'd eat some popcorn and watch a movie. Remember that they loved each other.

"See? Even Mom agrees. You've been acting like a jerk."

A jerk. So now I'm a jerk. Jake's fingers tightened around his glass, and his anger barreled toward Emily. "Guess what, sweetheart? You're staying home tonight." His breath caught in his throat, and no matter how much he tried to relax his chest muscles to force air into his lungs, they remained taut until he heard a buzzing in his ears and felt lightheaded. Yet he kept going. "And don't go crying to your mother. She needs her rest."

Emily jumped up from the couch, her face red and distorted. "Since when do you even *care* how Mom feels?"

They stared at each other until Emily looked away then stormed out of the room and up the stairs.

Jake winced when Emily's bedroom door slammed. *What the hell just happened?*

He walked back to the bar to pour a fresh drink and caught sight of his image in the mirror hanging over the bar. He had always considered himself a good man but barely recognized the face that stared back at him.

Chapter 16

Several days later, Emily still wasn't speaking to Jake. He had his work cut out for him when he found her at the kitchen table, shoveling in a bowl of cereal, her camera next to her. She didn't look up when he headed to the coffeemaker.

"Morning. Surprised you're up already since you're on fall break."

Scooping up the last bit of cereal, she remained silent. Undeterred, Jake kissed the top of her head.

"What's with the camera?"

Again, silence. He should apologize for losing his temper, but he needed coffee before entertaining that thought too seriously.

He was so intent on getting coffee and making amends with Emily—pretty much in that order—that he hadn't noticed Sophia until he heard water running.

"I'm glad to see you've made up," she commented, filling the kettle for tea. She looked from him to Emily. "You are speaking to each other, right?"

Emily snorted.

"Look, whatever's going on between you two needs to stop. The day before Thanksgiving is hectic, and this year, that might be a major understatement. I don't need you *both* acting like children."

Her eyes zeroed in on him with that last statement, but he saw no point in defending himself when his temper had gotten the best of him. Again.

Ignoring the escalating tension, Emily made her intentions for the morning known. "I want to take your picture for the albums I'm making. Before you get crazy with all the holiday stuff."

Sophia looked frazzled already.

"Mom has enough on her plate without taking time out for pictures this morning—maybe do that over the weekend." He purposely kept his voice mellow.

"I wasn't talking to you." The acknowledgment was the first Emily had given him since he'd come into the kitchen.

Sophia looked up from her tea preparations. "Really? Didn't I just tell the two of you to stop?"

"I was... never mind." He was sorry he'd even decided to get up that morning.

"We can take pictures, but first, you need to help me peel apples."

Emily shot him a victory smile. "I thought you always make pumpkin pies for Thanksgiving?"

"I do. But this year, I'm making apple too."

"That's a lot of pies."

"Yep. I want everyone to have their favorite."

As if that will help when she announces her pregnancy. Jake poured himself a cup of coffee as he listened to their chatter, amazed at how close they had become while he resided in an alternate universe.

Finished with her breakfast, Emily rinsed out her bowl and glass and stacked them on the counter. "You want everyone to be happy when you make your big announcement."

Clutching the apple peeler in one hand and an apple in the other, Sophia grinned. "That too."

"Did you invite the Barclays?"

Even Jake thought that would be like tossing the Christians to the lions, and he broke his silence. "I don't think the Barclays need to witness the hysterics that will likely take place when Mom announces to your grandparents that she's a surrogate mother. Besides, I haven't even met them. It's not fair to any of us to do it over a holiday."

He could have been speaking into an abyss for all the response he got from Emily, but Sophia nodded in agreement.

Once the apples were peeled, Emily staged her photo. "Stand sideways over here where the light's good." Moving back a foot, she muttered, "Perfect." After fiddling with the lens, Emily looked through the viewfinder and framed Sophia to her satisfaction. "You don't look any different than the last photo I took of you. Pull your shirt up."

"No. Take the picture."

Before pressing the shutter release, Emily added, "You need to eat more."

"Don't you start. Christine was just lecturing me. I'll eat more as soon as I feel better."

"Deal. This is *our* baby. You need to take care of yourself."

Jake and Sophia gaped at each other. "Sweetie, you know this isn't our baby, right?"

"*Yes*, Mom. I know! But this is the most important thing you've ever done—except be my mom—and you need to feel good. Mrs. Lawrence said not to worry about the morning sickness because it disappears when you are twelve weeks pregnant. Also, it means the baby will have lots of hair. Isn't that cool?"

"That can't possibly be true."

But Emily looked convinced. "Mrs. Lawrence said she read it somewhere. And that's what happened with her, and no one has better hair than Maddie."

Again, he caught Sophia's eye, waiting for her to set Emily straight. But Sophia stayed silent, and he wondered if she was possibly considering this idiocy.

"You don't believe me."

"I think Mrs. Lawrence gets a little... a little overzealous with her opinions," Sophia said.

"But you have to admit, she's almost always right. She told Maddie you were pregnant before you got the results from the clinic."

That got Jake's attention. "She did?"

Ignoring him, Emily again directed her comments to Sophia. "Maddie made me swear not to tell because her mom made Maddie promise not to tell, but Maddie can never keep a secret from me."

"So something *was* going on between you two the day we told you I was pregnant! You already knew."

"Well, yeah, but we never told anyone else." Emily grinned. "Let me take another picture. Stand over here, and this time, lift your shirt."

The knot at the back of his skull throbbed. Anticipating his father's reaction to Sophia's surrogacy made him wish he were out of town. Or sick. Or that there were some reasonable excuse for not sitting at his dining room table tomorrow when Sophia shared her news. Yet Sophia and Emily had no trouble moving from what a disaster Thanksgiving would be to nonsensical pregnancy myths.

He wanted them to be as stressed as he was. Slamming his mug on the table, he shouted, "You heard your mother! She is not lifting her shirt."

Both Sophia and Emily looked at him like he'd lost his shit, but Emily was the one who responded. "What is *wrong* with you?"

Emily's eyes filled with tears. Surprisingly, she yelled at Sophia instead of turning on him. "Can't you see what he's like? Everything makes him angry. I can't stand to be in the same room with him." Face red, she glared at her mother, waiting for a response.

But Sophia just stood there, silent, her lips stretched thin, eyes dark, as Emily stormed out of the room.

He wanted to do the same. Maybe take it one step further and storm out of the house.

Fingers twitching, Sophia wiped up the spilled coffee that had spread across the table and dripped onto the floor.

"I don't even recognize you anymore. Are you going to tell me what's going on?" Sophia's voice shook as she knelt to wipe up the mess he'd made.

"Let me do that."

He reached for the towel, but she threw it across the room.

"You're not answering my question. Why are you so angry all the time?" Her eyes begged for an answer.

But he still couldn't tell her. When he looked at it from a distance, his anger, his fear—whatever the hell it was—seemed pathetic. He should be able to move on. But he couldn't.

Chapter 17

The last thing Jake wanted was a repeat of yesterday's argument. But it was Thanksgiving morning, and Sophia sat at the kitchen table with her hands wrapped around her mug of tea, looking like the holiday dinner and her big announcement to their families weren't even on her radar.

"What's up?"

At first, she didn't acknowledge his presence, but finally, she muttered, "Nothing."

He got it. She was still pissed. He wasn't so happy with himself either, but their families were coming for dinner, and they should at least appear as if they liked each other. "Look, can we start over and not continue yesterday's fiasco? I'm sorry I lost my temper, okay? Can we move on?"

Her eyes blazed. "What would you like to move on to? Will you answer my questions about why you've become a man I barely recognize?"

There was only so much Sophia knew about his childhood, about the night Robbie died, and he could not bring himself to tell her more. He could not tell her that the date the baby was due was ripping open wounds that he'd spent years trying to heal. He could not break his promise to his father. No one would ever know how Robbie died.

"Don't you think I know I've been an ass?" His voice rose with every word that erupted from his mouth. The last thing he needed was for Emily to come barreling down the stairs and side with her mother, but instead of lowering his volume, it grew louder. "Do you think I like it when our daughter looks at me like I'm something that needs to be scraped off her shoe? I'm doing the best that I can."

"Your best is not good enough. Working all these crazy hours is not good for you. It's not good for us. You need to think about another job."

"Don't be naïve. Cranston, Clark, and Cunningham is the most prestigious firm in Burlington. Probably in all of Vermont. Do you think it would be easy to find another position at a comparable firm? I deserve to be a senior partner at the firm where I've been busting my balls for the last fifteen years."

"Now who's being naïve? You know as well as I do that *deserve* has nothing to do with it. Your job isn't worth more than your family." She reached out to where he stood, but neither moved toward making a physical connection. "Will you at least think about that?"

She was right. Jake wanted to think about family first, but his insides curdled every time he walked past Brian's new office. It should be him selecting new artwork to decorate the walls, him with "Senior Partner" stenciled on the door under his name.

He forced himself to breathe slowly. It was Thanksgiving. When he was a kid, it was the one day of the year when everyone was happy. His mother prepared all his favorite foods while his father relaxed in his leather recliner, watching the game on television with whatever friends and family they had invited for the day. Even Robbie was content, tossing a football to him in the backyard.

Heart beating normally once more, he poured himself a cup of coffee and sat across the table from Sophia. "I get it. I swear things will get better. Give me a year. I'll resign if Stephen doesn't make me a senior partner in twelve months." *Can I accomplish what I want in a year?* He didn't know, but he would kill himself trying.

"You've made these promises before."

"I know. Please, just trust me." He reached across the table for her hand, but the look in Sophia's eyes stopped him before he got anywhere close. He refused to dwell on her rejection. Things would get better.

His stomach growled when he spied the pies on the back counter. "A piece of pie would taste good right about now. What do you say we cut into one of those bad boys?"

"Don't look so damn smug. You've made a lot of promises. See that you keep them."

"I will."

She looked up as if questioning the truth in his words.

"I *swear.*"

When just a hint of a smile touched her lips, he added, "About that pie?"

"No way. There are muffins in the basket. That's the best you're getting this morning."

Nodding, he forced himself not to look at the empty butcher-block table that should have held at least the beginning of their holiday meal. "So, about Thanksgiving dinner? Would you like some help?"

"I'll get to it. I've got a lot on my mind. All I can think about is how to tell our families I'm pregnant with someone else's baby without chaos reigning."

The more he thought about Sophia's announcement, the more his stomach roiled. "You sure you want to do this today?" He poured himself another cup of coffee and grabbed a muffin and the newspaper to head to his study. Before leaving, he gave it one last shot. "Maybe you can email them later? After they go home? You know, an 'Oh, by the way' kind of thing?"

"Very funny." She patted her slightly rounded belly. "It's not like my family will take this well either. Besides, if I don't soon tell them, they will figure it out for themselves."

"Well, wait till the end of the meal, will you? Then, I can enjoy my dinner. Speaking of food, where's Emily? I thought she was helping you today."

"She is. I didn't get her up yet."

His face grew warm. He took a sip of coffee and glanced at the newspaper folded to the front page. Tried to focus on the retail section that was inching toward the floor. "You know, that's one of our problems with her."

Sophia looked up over the rim of her mug. If he had to guess, he'd say she was struggling even harder than he was to keep the conversation pleasant. "What's one of our problems with her? And why do I think you mean one of *my* problems?"

Before he knew it, they were in the thick of it again. "You're too damn easy on her."

Sophia pushed away from the table and started pulling food from the fridge and pots and pans from the cupboards as if he'd just ordered her to. If that didn't wake Emily, nothing would. "If I'm too easy on her, *you* never give her a break."

Struggling to reach the big roasting pan on the floor in the back of the pantry, she added, "Emily's right. You really have become an asshole."

Wishing he'd kept his mouth shut, he pulled her to her feet. "Here. Let me help." He lifted the roaster to the counter, adding, "I don't mean to bite everyone's head off."

"No? Well, for not even trying, you do a damn fine job. Go." Sophia was shaking from head to toe.

"I'm sorry."

"Saying you're sorry and being sorry are two different things."

He closed the door to his study and poured a good-sized portion of Macallan into his coffee. Instead of sitting at his desk, he stretched out on the couch, leaving the muffin on his desk, appetite gone. Lifting the mug to his nose, he inhaled deeply, enjoying the richness of the dark roasted beans combined with the malt of the liquor. *What the hell? It's a holiday.* He took a long swallow and let the scotch-laced drink warm him from the inside out.

Maybe it won't be so bad. Maybe the old man will let it slide and not feel compelled to tell me all the ways this is inappropriate. He let that thought roll around and snorted. Like that would happen.

He could not think of a way to keep the day from proceeding. More than once, he'd thought back to the first time Sophia had talked to him about becoming a surrogate. He'd been surprised. What with her responsibilities at the Shelburne and Emily, he thought she had plenty to keep her occupied. But she had convinced him this was important to her.

"There are people who desperately want babies and can't have them. I can give them one." He couldn't fault that argument, but still, he wondered why he hadn't said no. Not that she'd *asked* for permission.

Reaching for the bottle, he added another shot to his mug while the sound of Thanksgiving preparations slipped into the room.

The doorbell rang—it was time to smile. All Jake wanted was to get through the day.

Before everyone gathered around the table, the centerpiece caught his mother's eye. "I swear, Sophia does something different every year. This is beautiful."

It was true. This year, she had taken a collection of old hurricane globes he swore he'd last seen in the garage, added a pillar candle to each, and centered the candles with unshelled hazelnuts, walnuts, and pecans to keep them upright. He could see that Sophia was pleased his mother had noticed her arrangement. Her smile turned genuine. Hopefully, her changed mood would go a long way toward softening their early-morning rift.

"Wonder what happens if I grab a couple of these nuts?" Emily teased, pretending to reach into one of the globes.

Sophia lightly smacked her hand away. "Oh no, you don't. It took me hours to get those candles straight."

They might yet get through the day unscathed. His mother was right about the table. Even if he didn't recognize the china, it all looked great. Sophia must have been scavenging through the local antique shops again. Small cream-colored plates with a maple-leaf design topped large chargers with a pumpkin-colored swirl around the edges. On top of everything, she had placed tiny hollowed-out pumpkins that would soon be filled with cream-of-butternut-squash soup. She'd thought of everything.

No matter how much trouble she'd gone through, he wasn't willing to place odds on how peaceful the dinner would be once she announced her pregnancy. He had to hand it to her, though—she'd given it her best shot.

Once Sophia lit the candles and everyone was seated, his gaze settled on his wife and daughter. Emily's mood had lightened with the appearance of her grandparents, but one look at Sophia told him there would be no waiting until the meal was over. She'd be spilling her guts any second. He braced for the fallout.

"We have news." Sophia acted as if she planned to pull the table-cloth out from under the perfectly set table, hoping for no more than a flicker from the lit candles but willing to take the risk. She looked everywhere but at Jake as she handed his father a plate filled with turkey, stuffing, and gravy, suggesting he help himself to the side dishes scattered around the table.

Jake grabbed his wine glass and inhaled its contents while everyone gave their attention to Sophia. He thought she would lead by explaining why this was important to her.

"I'm pregnant."

The room went silent. The only sound accompanying her announcement was the mad thumping of his heart.

Emily's grin was huge. Sophia's mother opened and closed her mouth several times as if intent on objecting, oddly enough reminding him of a baby bird looking for breakfast, but for that moment, she remained quiet. On the other hand, his father lost no time zeroing in on what he saw as the problem and directed his question to Jake.

"I thought you were—"

"He is!' Sophia jumped in, apparently appalled that the subject of his vasectomy was close to becoming the topic of conversation at their dinner table. "I'm a surrogate."

Jake reached for the wine to pour another glass before the situation grew worse.

Sputtering, his father looked as if the world had gone mad. "What in God's name is a surrogate?"

"I'm having a baby for a couple that cannot have children."

Emily jumped in before anyone could say more. "Isn't this the coolest thing? I haven't met them in person, but Mom and Marianne went to lunch together, and we've talked virtually with them. Dad hasn't even *seen* them, but I know he'll love them as much as we do." She shot him a look, maybe more of a dare.

He and Sophia pulled in a deep breath simultaneously, most likely not for the same reason.

"Mom and Marianne talk on the phone all the time. The Barclays live in St. Johnsbury, and they've been trying to have a baby for years, and now Mom's giving them one. A girl."

Sophia swung toward Emily so fast she almost sent the gravy boat flying. "How in the world do you think you know that?"

"I don't." Emily giggled. "But I want it to be a girl. I'm pretty sure the Barclays want a girl too."

By then, Rose Marie had found her words. "You're giving away your baby? And it's a girl?" The look on her face bypassed disbelief and moved directly to devastation.

Jake had to bite down on his tongue to keep from laughing.

"No, Mom. I'm not giving away my baby, and we have no idea if it's a girl." Sophia glared at Emily before turning back to her mother. "We aren't having more children. This is Marianne and Adam's egg and sperm."

At the word *sperm*, Anthony stared at his wine glass, his coloring closely resembling the cranberry sauce that filled the small turkey-shaped crystal dish to his left. At the same time, Rose Marie's eyes widened as if she'd never heard the word before but was fairly certain Sophia should not have used it at the dinner table. And definitely not in front of her granddaughter.

Even Jake was surprised when he laughed. "Sorry, I've had more time to let this sink in."

"The Barclays made the baby," Sophia continued, refusing to ac-knowledge the look on her parents' faces. "I'm just carrying it until it comes to term." She looked around the table. "Like an incubator."

Jake's eyebrows nearly hit his hairline, but he remained silent.

Sophia, seemingly unaware of the havoc she had let loose, sat, re-moved her napkin from its ring, gave it a good snap, and announced, "Please, everyone, eat."

Thank God for his mother, who'd remained silent until then but offered her blessing. "I think this is wonderful."

His father's head shot up like someone had pulled a string at the back of his neck. "Fern! Do you hear what you're saying? Our friends are going to talk about this." Then, turning to Jake, he added, "Do you even know anything about these people?"

Emily looked from his father to him. "That's almost what Dad said when I told him I wanted to adopt a rescue puppy. What is it with you two and genetics?"

Sophia turned to Emily. "Not now, sweetheart."

"But I don't understand why everyone's so angry. You're doing a good thing. For good people."

Ignoring Emily, Rose Marie squeaked, "My God! The church. What would the pope say?" She let out a sigh that should have extinguished every candle in the room.

"I don't plan on telling him, Mom."

Hoping to calm her grandmother down, Emily added, "It doesn't matter, Nonna, we don't go to church."

Just as he hoped they could all move on, his father opened his mouth and snapped at Rose Marie, who looked like it would take some time to recover after discovering her granddaughter hadn't seen the inside of a church in God knew how long.

"Of course you would worry about the church. You Catholics are always on speed dial with your church."

The day was even worse than he had imagined. The food was cold, the gravy that Sophia prided herself on had become a gelatinous mass, and his father and Rose Marie were engaged in a shouting match that the neighbors in the next block probably heard.

And when Robert grew tired of shouting, he wiped his fingers on his napkin, tossed it onto his plate, and stormed out of the room, his wife following closely behind.

Before disappearing completely, Jake's mother added, "He's been on edge lately. Don't worry—he'll come around." She let out a small sigh as if to say, "You know Robert," took a few steps toward the closet to retrieve her coat, then came back. "It's a wonderful gift you're giving these people, Sophia. When's the baby due?"

"Sometime in May." Jake piped up, leaving Sophia and Emily with their mouths hanging open.

And then his mother was gone, her footsteps quickening as if she wasn't quite sure her husband would wait for her after he'd slammed the front door behind him.

Rose Marie and Anthony followed, the rustle of coats and scarves pulled from the closet a repeat of his family's exit.

The house was blessedly quiet. "Would it have been too much for you to wait until the end of the meal to make your announcement, like I asked?"

Emily had already started to clear the table. "Would it be too much for you to stop acting like an ass?"

Sophia beat him to a response. "Language! And if anyone's going to call your father an ass, it will be me." She turned to Jake. "And what's with telling your mother the baby's due in May? You know perfectly well the delivery date is the middle of June."

He did know that. Perfectly well.

Chapter 18

By *anyone's* standards, yesterday had been a clusterfuck kind of day, and Jake needed a break. From his job, from his family. From the baby that nestled in Sophia's belly. His entire body itched with the need to disappear.

Sophia was still huddled under the blankets. She never slept past seven, but the clock in the entryway had just struck nine.

"Hey, you okay? I need to go into the office." She didn't budge. "Soph?" He nudged her shoulder.

"I heard you." She rolled over and pulled the covers up to her chin.

She looked exhausted. She also sounded like she was still pissed. If Jake stayed home, they would have words, and none would have anything to do with scanning holiday catalogs for Christmas gifts like they usually did the day after Thanksgiving.

Jake leaned over to kiss her goodbye, thought better of it, and mumbled, "I'll be home later," on his way out of the room.

Pausing when he reached Emily's door, he remembered all the times he had taken her into the office so she could play lawyer at his desk while he caught up on upcoming cases. Granted, it had been years since she had wanted to spend her mornings with him because sleeping in was more attractive to a teenager than spending time with her dad—not because she couldn't stand the sight of him.

His entire world had changed, and he didn't know how to turn it back—he was pretty sure that sneaking out on a day traditionally spent as a family wasn't the answer. And yet, when he thought about the day before and all the anger that seemed to sprout like weeds every time he opened his mouth, he couldn't get out of the house fast enough.

Jake spent the day in his empty office catching up on paperwork. Anything that was mindless and kept his hands busy so he didn't obsess about the disaster of Thanksgiving and his father storming out of his house. His entire body stuttered when he thought about going home and facing Sophia.

He left when he could think of nothing else to delay his return home. But instead of the short drive to his house, he went in the opposite direction, and he didn't stop until he found himself in Lyndon, a few miles from St. Johnsbury. Which struck him as ludicrous until he understood that his intention all along had been to meet the Barclays. The intended parents of the baby Sophia was carrying.

He drove around Lyndon until he passed The Tap House three times. *What the hell? I'm driving in circles.* Pulling into the lot, empty except for one vehicle, he figured it wouldn't hurt to take some time to think about what would happen if he showed up at the Barclays' door.

The room was small and dark. Jake chose a spot at the bar, not realizing until his eyes had adjusted that a pit bull mix was perched on a stool on the other side, lapping water from a bowl before him. Even in Jake's dour mood, the dog made him chuckle.

When the bartender asked for his order, he had just pulled out his phone to call home or at least take a picture of the dog. Her voice was smokey and raw, and when he looked up, her eyes were the color of dark chocolate. They would have been gorgeous, except they were rimmed in red.

"I'll have whatever's on draft," he responded, pocketing his phone without making the call.

Silently, the bartender placed his beer in front of him. He couldn't help but comment, "You look like you aren't having any better of a day than me."

Her cheeks flushed, and he lowered his head, immediately sorry he'd said anything, so he was surprised when she laughed. The sound was sharp, like clapping hands together in the empty room.

"It has been one hell of a day. Week, for that matter." She seemed to think about that then added, "Maybe longer."

"Sounds about right." Jake took in the empty room and then glanced back at this woman who looked like she could break a man's heart without trying. "Slow night?"

She laughed. "Lyndon's a slow town. What you see here is about average for this time of night. Even if it is the Friday after Thanksgiving."

He nodded, refusing to think about his own holiday. "What's with the dog?"

"Mikie? He's mine. I bring him to work with me."

At the sound of his name, the dog gave his full attention to Jake. His eyes were different colors. One was dark brown, the other blue as a Vermont sky on a cloudless day. He reached his hand out for the dog to sniff, but Mikie growled.

"Not very friendly, huh?"

"Generally not." She seemed to hesitate for a moment then reached her hand across the bar. "I'm Marcie, by the way."

Looking warily at the dog, Jake lightly touched her fingertips. "I'm..."

Marcie shook her head. "No need to give me your name."

Nodding, he finished his beer and ordered another. Again, he thought about calling home. But he was comfortable, and he liked listening to Marcie talk. He liked that she was tall and lean and didn't talk about babies. He liked that he didn't feel like such a shit when she looked at him.

At closing time, Marcie locked up the bar for the night, poured herself a beer, and sat next to him while Mikie hopped down from his stool and settled at her feet. And they kept talking.

It was nearly midnight when he climbed into his car for the slow drive home. The thought of meeting the Barclays was far from his mind.

Jake could tell by the glow from the bathroom light that Sophia wasn't in bed. He hadn't noticed her when he'd gone through the kitchen and directly up the stairs, but he hadn't thought to look for her either. He peeked into the guest room and then made his way back down the stairs.

He found her in his study, sitting at his desk, her head resting against the back of the chair, eyes closed. "Soph?" He moved closer. She opened her eyes when he touched her shoulder.

"What are you doing in here?"

Sophia looked at the clock on his desk. "What are you doing coming home at two in the morning?"

"I was at work. I told you this morning."

Nodding, she stood. "Since when did they start serving beer in the office?"

He hadn't done anything wrong. "I stopped for a beer on the way home."

One of her eyebrows shifted upward.

"Maybe more than one. I meant to call." He didn't mention Marcie but still hadn't done anything wrong.

"And you forgot."

"And I forgot." She seemed to accept that. It was the truth, he reminded himself, feeling guilty anyway.

"It's late. Let's go to bed." She wrapped an arm around his waist and urged him back up the stairs. He was grateful that Sophia had put yesterday behind her. Unlike Emily, who thrived on anger and held on to it with a vengeance, Sophia was slow to anger and quick to forgive.

The next few weeks felt like a battlefield. Whenever he thought he'd made some headway toward a reconciliation with Emily, he would come home angry, tired, or discouraged, and she did something to piss him off. And their battle would start all over again. He could not control his wrath, and he swore she spurred him on just because she could.

"You know that's ridiculous, don't you?" Sophia assured him, but he wasn't so sure. "Emily loves you."

There was a time when he would never have doubted that, but he was no longer sure he deserved Emily's love.

Chapter 19

Jake could no more explain why he found himself driving to Lyndon instead of home after returning a day early from a business trip to Colorado than he could explain why he never let Sophia know about the change in his itinerary.

When he walked into The Tap House, there were a dozen customers and someone other than Marcie behind the bar. The space wasn't the quiet place it had been the other week. He almost left, but then, he saw Mikie on his stool, lapping water from his bowl.

He chose a table in a dark corner, hoping Marcie would wait on him since the other bartender had his hands full. As if his thoughts made it happen, Marcie, her eyes on her order pad, headed in his direction. She didn't look up until right before she reached his table.

"What are you doing here?" Her voice held none of the silkiness he'd played repeatedly in his head since he'd last seen her. Before he could answer, she added, "How did you even know I was working tonight?"

His decision had been rash. He barely knew this woman.

"I didn't know you'd be here. But I can't deny that I hoped you would be." His ears felt hot. He stood, prepared to leave, and then gave it one more shot. "I wanted to see you again." He glanced at the bar as if he thought Mikie might put in a good word for him. "I should leave."

Marcie motioned for him to sit. "You're here. You might as well have a beer."

Within minutes, Marcie returned with his drink, her jacket slung over her shoulder and Mikie's leash twisted through her fingers. She slapped his bill on the table. "I'm leaving now..."

Mikie took one look at Jake and tried to jump up next to him. "Mikie! No!" Marcie tugged at the leash until the dog sat by her side. "Sorry. If you plan on having another beer, go up to the bar. Henry will take care of you."

She started to leave, pulling on Mikie's leash.

"Wait!" He stood and reached out his hand but stopped short of touching her. Instead, he leaned down and scratched Mikie behind the ear. "Can we go somewhere and talk?"

"Talk?"

Jake thought about his request from her point of view. "Really. Just talk."

Marcie studied him as if she could determine his trustworthiness by the color of his eyes. "Follow me."

He took one long swallow of the beer she had just delivered, threw a twenty on the table, and followed her out the door. The parking lot was small. It didn't take much to jump in his car and trail Marcie's path as she and Mikie walked toward her car, and within minutes, he followed her out of the parking lot.

Fifteen minutes later, when he pulled in behind her onto a private driveway, he questioned what the hell he was doing. He wasn't even sure where he was. If it weren't for the security lights, he wouldn't have been able to see the dwelling set back from the road. Oak and maple trees framed the sides, making it almost invisible. He could make out an overly large log cabin with lots of glass and massive front doors—not what he was expecting. *How does a woman who works in a bar afford this place?*

Marcie slid out of her vehicle, and Mikie jumped down after her and headed into the dark. The dog was back by her side within minutes, and they entered the house. He could leave, forget he'd ever followed her home. He didn't know this woman. He didn't know what he wanted from her. He only knew he didn't want to feel so alone. Within seconds, he'd caught up to her and entered the house behind them.

"Here, let me take your jacket." She held out her hand, but he took a step back.

"I'm good." It would have been absurd to tell her he wasn't sure he was staying, so he chose to tell her nothing.

"Suit yourself." She spun on her heel and walked into what he supposed was the main room. Pointing to the leather sofa against one wall, she added, "I'll be right back. Make yourself at home."

Relaxing against the cushions, he took in his surroundings. He noted a pipe on a side table and a few hunting magazines. Marcie didn't live here by herself. No longer comfortable, he stood.

He was still standing when Marcie came back with two bottles of beer. "I think I should leave."

"You just got here."

He nodded toward the pipe. "Who lives here with you? And when is he expected back?"

Shrugging, Marcie placed both beers on the table near where he stood. She rubbed her hands up and down her arms then turned to the pile of wood by the fireplace. Adding a log to what was already there, she crumpled up some newspaper, tucked the pieces between the logs, and struck a match. "Sit. I don't bite."

Taking her own advice, Marcie sat in the middle of the couch. She patted the space next to her. He felt foolish—he had nothing to fear from this woman—and lowered himself beside her. He'd come here for a reason. Maybe he owed it to himself to discover why he couldn't get her out of his head.

"My husband lives here. Did I forget to mention him?" She stared at his ring finger. "Did you forget to mention your wife?"

His face burned. "I should get going." But he didn't move.

"We're not doing anything wrong. My husband won't be home until Monday. Besides, he's not sure he still wants to be my husband. That's why he's away. To figure things out. And your wife? When is she expecting you home?"

He looked at his feet. Sophia would be crushed if she discovered he had returned from Colorado a day early. And didn't come home. "Sorry." He took a long swig of his beer. "I don't normally do things like this."

Marcie raised her beer and tapped her bottle along the neck of his in a silent toast. "Things?" The word seemed to hold a depth of meaning he could only surmise when it flowed from her lips.

"I don't go to out-of-town bars and talk to female bartenders until all hours of the night. I don't come back because..." *Because why? Why the hell am I here?* "Because I can't stop thinking about her." He looked around the room again. "I sure as hell don't mess around with married women."

Marcie's head snapped back as if he had struck her. "I don't do any of that either. I just needed someone to talk to the other night. It's not like I'm planning to cheat on my husband. Even if he's not planning on being my husband anymore."

This was the second time she had mentioned the elusive husband.

"So, what's the problem? If you don't mind my asking?"

Marcie drew in a deep breath and shuddered it out. "Family issues, I guess you could say. He's not sure he *wants* a family. Even though it's all we've talked about for years. We're trying to work it out."

He understood family issues, but they were not a subject he wanted to discuss. Family issues were messing with his own life.

They sat in silence. Jake felt his anger and fear lessen. It was good to sit, shoulder to shoulder, hip to hip. He felt her warmth seep into his body. He didn't have to force himself to pretend to want something he didn't. "You don't even know my name."

She placed a finger on his lips. "Shh... I don't need to know your name."

He closed his eyes. Sometime later, he woke to find her looking at him. She seemed perfectly comfortable in her own skin, watching him. Leaning into her, he touched a tendril of her hair. He'd never seen hair that looked as if rivers of gold ran through it.

"What are we doing here?"

When she didn't answer, he cupped her face and looked into her beautiful eyes. And then he kissed her. He knew he shouldn't. But he couldn't help himself.

The night was a blur—everything he didn't want to think about and everything he'd never forget. And the following day, after he walked out those big double doors, he sat in his car and wept, his head resting on the steering wheel while hot tears coursed down his face.

Finally, he pulled himself together and started his car. Looking toward the front of the house, he hoped—he didn't know what, exactly—maybe to catch a glimpse of her face pressed against the window, but all he saw was sparkling glass.

Jake was in no rush to enter his own house and confront the family waiting for him. He was in no mood to look into a mirror and face himself. Tension centered in the back of his neck and twisted until the muscles between his shoulder blades knotted. He tried to convince himself that last night was Sophia's fault. One more reason to resent this pregnancy of hers. He would never have found himself in Lyndon if she wasn't pregnant.

Even the thought was ludicrous. He had never met a woman with a bigger heart than his wife. That left only him to blame for his sins.

He had no sooner pulled into The Wayside in Montpelier for coffee when his cell dinged with a text from Stephen.

LINE case exploding.

Come into the office.

Stephen had said he wasn't touching that case. *So what the hell is going on? Damn manufacturers and their careless polluting.* Jake glanced at his watch and then at himself in the rearview mirror. He saw bags under his eyes and stubble on his cheeks. And he was still wearing the same clothes from yesterday. But still, he texted back.

Be there soon.

Grabbing a coffee to go, he was back on the road in five minutes, headed toward home. He couldn't go into the office the way he looked. No matter how big the emergency.

Leaving his car parked in the driveway, he grabbed his bag, his mind going in a million directions at once. When he walked into the house, Sophia was curled up in the kitchen window seat, flipping through a catalog.

He bent to kiss her cheek, but she turned so that his kiss landed on her mouth. Her lips were soft and full. But they weren't Marcie's.

"Welcome home."

Unable to meet her eyes and refusing to think about the night before, he muttered, "Can't stay. Stephen's in an uproar—I need to shower and run into the office."

She grabbed his arm. "Wait a minute. Where were you last night?"

Heart pounding, he stopped, a death grip on his overnight bag. "I was in Colorado."

"I called the hotel when your phone went to voicemail, and they said you'd checked out."

He had clicked off his phone when he walked into Marcie's house last night—flipped it back on when he was on his way home. Never even noticed the missed call. "Why did you call?"

Sophia countered. "Why did you check out of your hotel?"

Forcing air into his lungs, he spoke slowly, retying a loose shoelace to avert his face. "I didn't check out. Whoever told you that was wrong."

Seconds felt like hours until she spoke. "That's what I thought. It must be hard to keep track of all the guests." She flipped a page in the catalog and added, "I knew you'd let me know if you were coming home early."

Loosening his grip on his bag, he shifted it from one hand to the other. Again, he asked, "Why did you call?"

"I wanted to talk about Christmas. We haven't even discussed what to get our families, and the holidays are just around the corner."

Christmas. "Everything's been so crazy at the office. I promise we'll talk tonight."

"That's what you said last week." Sophia tossed the catalog into the basket that held the rest of the holiday advertisements. "I will make you figure this out for yourself if you don't schedule some time soon. You are never home, Jake. Will you even be home for dinner?"

"Look, I'm sorry. I don't know."

Twenty minutes later, he bounded down the steps and slipped his arms around Sophia as she stood at the kitchen sink, stacking dirty dishes into the dishwasher.

"Love you," he murmured, continuing through the mudroom and out of the house.

Backing out of the driveway, his head filled with memories of the night before. He wanted to drive back to Marcie's house and bury his face in her body. Instead, he headed to the office. *Jesus. What is wrong with me?*

Chapter 20

Senior partners exempt, everyone else huddled around the conference-room table covered with evidence boxes. Amy rolled her eyes in solidarity when she spotted Jake, but he barely had time to acknowledge her. Instead, he kept his face neutral and headed toward Stephen.

"Where do you want me?"

Stephen took his arm and directed him to the back of the room. "You're in charge."

Jake almost choked.

"Don't look so surprised. I didn't forget you. Get this done right, and senior partner is yours. I need anything that even hints at when the LINE people knew there were contamination issues in the Winooski River. Any email the least bit off. And I need it fast."

Jake looked at the paperwork Stephen shoved at him.

"I thought we weren't taking this case."

"I changed my mind. And remember, this is your chance."

He couldn't help but wonder what Stephen would do when they discovered information that implicated LINE. And he had no doubt that they would.

The next few weeks were a blur of long-buried emails and correspondence unearthed by Cranston, Clark, and Cunningham staff regarding what the LINE people knew and when they started lying to the Vermont public. Jake was in a tailspin—with the chaos at his firm and with thoughts of Marcie.

They'd agreed it was a one-time thing. And yet he called her. He couldn't even say his name since she didn't know it. "This is…"

"I know who it is."

"I wanted to hear your voice."

He heard her suck in her breath. "My husband and I talked. We're trying to work things out."

Her words played in his head.

"I see." He finally recovered enough to add, "I wish you well."

Marcie breathed into the phone. He thought she'd hang up, but she held on, and he imagined her clutching the phone to her ear. He closed his eyes and drew his hand over his face as if he could wipe away his shame. His exhaustion. His confusion.

Finally, he added, "I'm sorry I bothered you," before gently disconnecting the call. Marcie was right. It was time to move on.

He devoted himself to the LINE case—even though by doing so, he made a mockery of his life. The blatant violation of the law was clear, yet his willingness to toss his marriage vows by the wayside was shrouded in mist. Only his resistance to Stephen's desire to represent one of the most disgraceful clients in Vermont convinced him he wasn't totally without ethics. If he did what Stephen wanted—found the evidence and destroyed it—he'd receive the promotion he'd been working toward since law school. *But can I do that?*

There was no escaping the decision Stephen was forcing him to make. There was no avoiding the case. Even on the few nights he made it home for dinner, the discussion centered around LINE and what he was willing to share.

"Mr. Cranston must have a good reason for taking on the case. Right, Dad?"

Emily hadn't said two words to him in days.

"You're speaking to me?"

He could have kicked himself when her eyes darkened with hurt. She squared her shoulders. "About the *law*."

The kid was tough. She was more like him than he wanted to admit. She respected the law. Loved it. She wanted to become a lawyer, and he wanted that for her too. But he worried how easily she could compartmentalize her feelings. She had no problem tamping down her anger when she wanted to know more about a case he was working on and then holding on to it fiercely when it suited her. She was fifteen. *What will she be like when she is my age?*

He hesitated in making his own beliefs known—that Stephen took this case for the money and nothing more—and instead attempted to divert the conversation. "How was school today?"

Emily shot him a look that should have required stitches.

He shrugged. "You ask me a question. I get to ask you one."

"School was fine."

"Do you care to elaborate on that statement?"

"No, Dad. I do not." Emily sucked in a deep breath as if he didn't already know she was losing her patience. "I want to know what you think of this case."

He knew that. Emily was still at the age where good won out over evil. And he was in no mood to dispel that notion. She would learn the truth soon enough.

"It's too early for me to decide."

"That sounds like complete bullshit to me."

Sophia looked up from the slice of meatloaf she'd just slid onto her plate. "Language."

Snagging the last biscuit and slathering it with jam, Emily muttered an unconvincing apology. And then she pinned him to the wall. "Am I right?"

Jake heaved a sigh and pushed away from the table. "Help your mother with the dinner dishes."

In bed that night, he toyed with walking away. From the firm. From Sophia. Even from Emily. It wasn't the first time he'd thought of escaping, and even though he was mostly sure his thoughts were just a reprieve from the constant stress and he had no real intention of deserting his family, he felt his shoulders loosen. He could start somewhere new. He didn't need to be a lawyer. He could do anything. Maybe he'd get into landscaping. The idea of planting trees made him happy. He loved digging in the dirt but rarely had time even to mow the lawn.

Sophia's voice broke through his reverie. "You were a little rough on Emily, don't you think?"

"Why? Because I told her to help you with the dishes?"

"You know that's not what I mean. Emily is interested in what you do. She wants to be like you."

That was true. And in the past, Jake had worn her goal like a badge of honor. "The last thing Emily should be is like me."

Instead of arguing, Sophia moved closer, burrowing into him. "When are we going to remember that we love each other?"

Jake froze. He could barely look at her and not see Marcie's face. Seconds went by, and she trailed her fingers across his chest when he made no move toward her. Then she moved her hand lower.

He grasped her wrist and gently placed it on the bed between them. "I've had a rough day, Soph."

"It seems like all your days are rough."

He could do nothing about the sorrow that coated her words, even though he was the cause of her pain.

"Aren't you going to say anything?"

"What do you want me to say, Sophia? *Yes*, all my days are rough right now, and I'm exhausted. I'm trying to do my best for all of us."

"Don't you *dare* put this on me. This is all about you." She sat up and flipped on the light.

Sophia could sit there and stare at him all night without saying a word, so if he had any hope of sleep, he knew he would have to finish the conversation. "What?"

"What is going on?"

He stiffened. She'd asked a loaded question that he couldn't begin to answer. "Nothing. Everything. This case is sucking the life out of me. I would think that's obvious. Stephen wants me to save these people, but they are guilty as hell."

"You've been in tough places before, and that's never stopped you from wanting me. I get it. You're not happy I'm pregnant. But I miss you. I need you."

She was right about all of it. But he couldn't tell her the truth. "I'm tired. Can't I just be tired?"

But she wasn't listening. Pain ravaged her face, and the words she spoke were so low he could barely hear them. But he didn't need to understand her words to know she was suffering.

"Am I that disgusting to you?"

It crushed him that he'd hurt her. "Soph! No!" He tried to pull her into his arms, but she refused to be comforted. "I'm sorry. It's not you. It's not you at all."

His words were honest, but they weren't the truth. Only he knew the truth—and Marcie—and he couldn't bear for Sophia to learn what he'd done. They sat silently, each deep in thought, until her body finally sagged with exhaustion. He wanted their lives back where they'd been. *Is that even possible?*

Jake had almost fallen asleep when Sophia's head dropped onto his shoulder. Carefully, he lowered them onto the bed and forced himself to slow his breathing until he felt her body relax and melt into his. Then he inched toward the very edge of his side of the bed.

Chapter 21

Jake was looking for any reason to feel good about himself again. "Hey, I'm taking Em to see about a beagle puppy in Water-ford—that Homeward Bound place she's so crazy about. Want to come along? We can make a day of it. It might be good to get out of the house."

The look on Sophia's face was no different than the one she'd worn for the last few weeks. A look he was certain had to do with him staying as far from her side of their bed as he could.

"I'll pass."

Swell. "Look, I'm trying to do the right thing here. Make up for the last couple of months or so I've been camping out at the office. The trip will be good for Em too. Who knows? A puppy could be good for all of us." He was grasping at straws. "What do you think?"

"You mean you're trying to do the right thing after your trip to Kentucky failed to sway Emily to adopt a dog with a pedigree? Or are you trying to do the right thing because you're never home, and when you are, you are so grumpy that no one wants to be in the same room with you?"

He couldn't argue with her accusations, but at least they weren't personal.

"Or maybe you're trying to do the right thing because you can't bear to look at me, let alone touch me? Which 'right thing' are you trying to do?"

So much for not getting personal. "Soph. It's not like that. I love you. I... I'm just drained." He sat on the edge of the bench where her feet rested and took her hand. "I don't mean to make you feel unwanted. I love you." *I can't make love to you. Not yet. But I will. I just need to forgive myself.* "Things will be different once this case is over. I promise." It was a promise he meant. A promise Jake hoped he could keep.

Running his hand through his hair, he searched for the right answer to her questions. "I'm trying to do all of it. Mostly, I'm trying to make up for being such a jerk."

She nodded, which he took to mean that she agreed he was a jerk.

"What does Emily think?"

"She doesn't know."

Sophia put her knitting down and looked at him with what might have been pity. "You haven't asked her yet?"

It never dawned on him that Emily wouldn't want to go. "She'll come with me." Even he heard the uncertainty in his voice.

Sophia returned to her knitting, increasing his self-doubt.

"You don't think she'll come with me?" There was a time he could easily have envisioned Emily throwing herself into his arms at the mere mention of Homeward Bound. *But today?* Contrary to what he'd said, he could only hope Emily would come with him.

When he suggested the trip, Emily studied him as if he were a laboratory specimen on a glass slide that, if released into the atmosphere, would be the cause of total annihilation of the human race.

"You haven't mentioned Homeward Bound *once* since we got home from Kentucky. Why, suddenly, do you have time to make the trip?"

He had always admired Emily's ability to stand her ground, but it didn't seem like a great quality when she used it against him.

"Look, I get it. Right now, you don't like anything that comes out of my mouth. I'm trying to do something nice. For you."

He expected her to say something. Anything. But she continued staring at him.

"Because I've been so busy at work. Short-tempered." Still nothing. "Because I've been an asshole."

Maybe he imagined her smirk. But still, she said nothing. Just kept staring.

"Look, if you don't want to go, say so."

They glared at each other. Jake hoped he didn't have to admit he was bluffing.

"Fine." Her response came without a shred of excitement. She headed toward her bedroom then spun around. "Wait a minute. Is this some ploy to get on my good side, and even if we go to Homeward Bound, there's no way in hell we are getting a dog?"

"First, language. Second, this is not a ploy. I'm suggesting we go because if we're getting a dog, it should be a rescue."

"We're getting a dog?"

Finally, he had her attention.

Jake had hoped the drive to Waterford would help them loosen up with each other. Instead, Emily kept her nose in the brochures she pulled from her backpack the moment he started the car. Her initial agreement to spend several hours with him didn't seem to include conversation.

"Must be some interesting stuff in there."

She never looked up, and a response was apparently out of the question. But he'd gone this far—he might as well go all the way. "I'm asking because I want to know more about Homeward Bound."

As if just realizing he was in the car, she shot back, "You've read these brochures. You know what's in them."

He lifted both hands off the steering wheel and brought them back down with a light tap. "You caught me. I'm trying to make conversation. *Now* will you talk to me?" He waited. After five minutes, he was certain she wouldn't respond. The entire trip would be silent. Maybe she would never talk to him again. *Jesus, I'm going off the deep end.*

But then, she relented. After riffling through the mass of brochures, she selected one and started reading. "Homeward Bound is one of the world's leading organizations for rescuing beagles used in experimental testing. Most of our staff are volunteers. We all believe animals should be loved and respected."

She continued reading, and they seemed to coexist peacefully for the first time in months.

"I could totally work for this place," she said.

He turned onto I-89 S. "Finish college first. Then think about working for a nonprofit."

She laughed—a sound he hadn't heard in what seemed like forever. "Maybe I'll finish high school first."

Almost two hours later, they pulled into a kennel that was also the halfway house for animals rescued from laboratories before they went to foster homes or were adopted.

The manager's office was right inside the building. Jake knocked on the open door and introduced himself. Putting an arm around Emily, who still held a handful of brochures, he added, "And this is my daughter, Emily."

"Name's Tom," the manager responded, shaking Jake's proffered hand. Nodding to Emily, he said, "I see you've been reading up on us."

"Yes, sir. I found your website when I was looking for beagles. We're interested in adopting a rescue. A puppy if you have any. Or an older dog."

"Sorry, little lady, we don't keep puppies here. Let's see if I can get you the names of people with what you're looking for." Turning to his laptop, Tom stabbed at a few keys while Emily watched with what Jake feared was a look of expectation.

Waiting for a file to load, Tom looked through the window over his desk, muttered, "Be right back," and strode out of his office. Hustling down the sidewalk, moving faster than a man with that much weight around his middle should, he yelled, "Hey! Hold up a minute! I've got some people here interested in a puppy."

A man spun around at the sound of Tom's voice, and Emily's face burst into a giant grin.

"What?" He looked from Emily to the stranger. "You know that man?"

Emily shot out of Tom's office and ran after the people he didn't know before the words were fully out of his mouth.

Jake took off after her. "Emily! Wait up!"

Finally, she yelled, "Dad! It's Adam!"

He didn't consciously stop. He just did. At the same time, the woman with Adam turned. He closed his eyes for a moment then opened them. Prayed that what he was looking at was someone's idea of a bloody travesty. But she was still there. Marcie. And as soon as she spotted him, she looked as green as he felt. *What is Marcie doing with Adam?*

"Marianne! Adam!" Emily rushed toward the couple, and Adam returned her greeting as the woman stumbled, saving herself and the puppy she held when she grabbed Adam's arm.

He had the strangest desire to laugh. This was no better than what he deserved.

"Dad!" Emily yelled, turning back to him. "It's Marianne and Adam! The *parents* to Mom's baby!"

As if he wasn't already aware of that. Marcie's words from that night came back in a jumble: all they'd ever wanted. Family issues. Not a word about surrogacy.

"I see you all know each other," Tom commented, turning from Emily to Adam and Marianne.

"Emily here, and her father, Jake"—Tom looked back in the direction where Jake stood frozen—"are looking for a puppy. Looks like you can maybe help them out." And with that, he headed back in the direction of his office.

Emily wore the biggest grin. Adam looked pretty pleased himself. Marcie—Marianne, whatever the hell her name was—looked like he felt. Like there wasn't a hole big enough to crawl into.

"Dad? These are the parents. To Mom's baby. To *their* baby."

Yes. These were the people he had planned to introduce himself to that first night—the night he ended up at The Tap House. The night he met Marcie, who also happened to be Marianne.

He reached toward Adam's extended hand while Marianne held the puppy close to her heart and averted her eyes.

Adam gave Jake's hand a healthy squeeze. "Small world."

"Hell of a small world," Jake agreed.

Chapter 22

The last time Jake had driven this road, he hadn't even known where he was. It had been so dark that he could only follow the taillights of the car in front of him. But he still remembered every turn, every word they'd spoken, every kiss they'd shared.

Knuckles white from clutching the steering wheel, he followed closely behind the Barclays' Jeep to their home, where Adam had insisted they come for lunch. When Jake looked at his reflection in the rear-view mirror, his color still wasn't back to normal, but considering everything that had transpired in the last thirty minutes, he figured he was doing well staying upright.

Emily, her arms wrapped around the puppy, kept glancing from the road to him.

"Do you feel all right? You look like you're going to be sick."

He sucked in his breath and let it out slowly. "I'm fine." Jake's words and actions were nowhere in sync, but he couldn't do a damn thing about that.

"Don't you want this puppy?"

Emily held the dog up until she was practically in his face. But instead of big floppy ears and a little pink tongue sticking out of her mouth, he saw the puppy nestled in Marianne's arms. He saw the color of Marianne's face fade to white then a strange shade of green.

When he didn't answer, Emily pulled the puppy closer to her.

"She's so adorable. I'm calling Mom to tell her about Adam and Marianne. She'll be sorry she didn't come with us."

"Your mother's resting." His heart thumped so loudly that he was surprised Emily didn't hear it. "You can tell her when we get home." *Fuck!* He still couldn't believe Marianne and Marcie were the same person.

"She's going to want to know this." Emily reached into her pocket for her phone.

"No using the phone while you're driving." His words bounced off the windshield.

Emily dropped the phone between her feet. "Did you hear what you just said?" She picked up the phone and waved it at him as if he might not know what it was.

"*You're* driving. Not me."

He looked from Emily to the road.

Speaking as calmly as he could while his insides churned, Jake muttered, "Your mother told me she was going to rest while we were gone. There'll be plenty of time to tell her after we get home."

"You're acting weird—you know that, right?"

Weird... without a fucking doubt. Before Jake was ready, he followed the Barclays as they turned off the road onto the driveway he remembered so well. He pulled up alongside their car, opened his window, and drank in a mouthful of air. He would have sawed off his right arm for a drink.

Instead, he offered Emily what reassurance he could.

"Don't worry. We'll see what we can do about adopting this puppy." Jake hoped that was true. And then they could take this puppy home so that Emily and Sophia would forget everything but the dog, and he would be allowed to lick his wounds in private.

He held that thought as they followed Adam and Marianne into their house.

Emily stopped as soon as she walked through the doorway. "I've never been inside a log cabin before." She reached out to touch a wall but paused and looked at Adam. "Can I touch it?"

"Sure can." Adam laughed. "There's not much you can do to these logs."

She grazed a log lightly with one finger. "Now, I want to work for Homeward Bound *and* live in a log cabin."

"Sounds like a great plan." Adam nodded to Jake. "Come into my office, and we'll start the paperwork."

Jake hadn't taken a step when Mikie bounded into the room, barking loudly. "Mikie! No!" Adam lunged for the dog's collar and missed, leaving Mikie free to leap toward Jake and Emily. "Sorry! Mikie's trained to protect Marianne."

Mikie ran past Emily and sat peacefully before Jake. Then offered his paw.

"Would you look at that?" Adam stared at Mikie as if he'd never seen the dog before then said to Jake, "What are you, some sort of dog whisperer?"

Holding his arms stiffly at his sides, Jake ignored Adam's comment. He refused to look in Marianne's direction. Not all that long ago, he had tossed dog treats to Mikie from Marianne's bed.

Adam turned toward Marianne. "Mikie might need more training."

If possible, Marianne's face was paler than when she'd first seen him striding toward her that morning.

She ignored Adam's comment and addressed the dog. "Come, Mikie, let's go fix lunch." After hearing the command, Mikie reluctantly moved from Jake's side.

Still shaking his head, Adam led Jake and Emily into his office, explaining that Marianne occasionally worked as a bartender for a friend. Mikie went along to dissuade the rare customer who had too much to drink from making a pass at her.

Turning to Jake, he offered, "Beer?"

Uncertain he could speak, Jake nodded his thanks and wrestled with the cap until he could finally take a long, deep pull while Emily struggled to hold on to the puppy, who seemed to decide it might be fun to make a run for it.

"My mom will be so disappointed she didn't come with us today."

"I bet she will. We sure are disappointed. Hopefully, we can all get together soon."

At the sound of Adam's voice, the puppy made a giant leap from Emily's arms and flung herself at Adam.

"Whoa, little girl!" Adam held the puppy toward Emily. "Why don't you take her outside for some fresh air? Here," he added, rubbing one of the puppy's ears, "let me put a collar on her."

After clipping a leash onto the collar, Adam opened a door that led directly to the backyard while Jake silently sought an excuse to leave. The thought of swallowing food with Marianne sitting across from or beside him made his throat close. All he could think about was the night they'd spent together in this house.

Adam offered Jake another beer, but as much as he needed it, he couldn't afford to let his guard down. He watched Emily through the window as she chased after the puppy. She hadn't been this happy in a while. That was his fault too. *I've been a jerk to both her and Sophia.* He turned from the window when Adam spoke.

"Normally, there's an extensive vetting process in place when adopting one of these dogs, but I talked to Tom on the drive home, explained how we know you and Sophia, and he agrees to take our word that you will provide a good home for this little girl. We—"

"Excuse me." Jake was having difficulty concentrating, and it didn't help when Emily returned with the puppy, babbling a mile a minute. So he asked a question he knew the answer to. "Bathroom?"

"Oh, sure, down the hall. Second door on the left."

Jake barreled out of the room, but instead of to the bathroom, he headed to the kitchen, a room he was familiar with since Marianne had made him breakfast after he'd spent the night.

When he found her, Marianne was standing at the kitchen sink, staring out the window, a glass of water in her hand.

"What the *hell*?" Jake blustered, unable to control his rapidly escalating temper.

Startled, the glass slipped from her hands, sending water and fragments of glass flying. She whipped around to face him, grabbed a towel, and bent to clean up the mess. "Be *quiet*!"

"You told me your name was Marcie."

She nearly choked. "That makes us even. You—" Marianne winced as she cut herself on a sliver of glass. "You never told me your wife is a surrogate. You never told me she thinks the sun rises and sets on you."

He didn't understand. "Why would I tell you anything about my wife?"

"Dad?" His heart sank at the sound of Emily's voice. She stood in the doorway, the puppy in her arms, confusion etched across her face. "Why are you yelling?"

"I'm not..." Jake forced himself to lower his voice. "I'm not yelling. Marianne dropped her glass. I was helping her clean up the mess and then we need to get going."

Emily held her ground. "I know yelling when I—"

Marianne interrupted from where she still knelt on the floor. "I'm sorry, sweetheart. It's one of my migraines. I need to lie down, but we'll have lunch soon."

Before the conversation could go any further, Adam came into the kitchen. "Well, here you all are. I must have been boring everyone with my spiel on rescues."

"Not at all." Jake never took his eyes off Emily, hoping she would forget whatever she might have heard in the excitement of adopting the puppy while Marianne filled Adam in on her migraine.

"We need to get going." He directed his comment to Adam, ignoring Marianne, who continued picking up glass fragments while sucking on her bleeding finger.

"Of course. Let me get that paperwork." Seeing that Marianne was still on her knees, Adam reached down to help her. "Hon, I'll finish that as soon as I get what I need from the office. You go and rest."

Jake and Emily stared at each other until Adam and Marianne left the kitchen.

"What's going on between you two?" Emily looked around the empty room, all her earlier joy gone. "It's like you hate each other, and you've just met."

"Don't be silly, we don't hate each—"

They heard Adam before he entered the room. "As I said earlier, we don't have room for another puppy, and Tom doesn't keep puppies on site. We both agree that you showing up today is a godsend."

Jake nodded. *Godsend—not by a long shot.* He forced himself to listen to the instructions Adam spewed as if he would be tested on them later, the whole while fighting with himself not to think of the way Marianne had smelled or that spot on the side of her neck that caused her back to arch when he touched it with his tongue. He had to forget everything that had happened between them in those twelve hours he had known Marcie with no last name. That was what she'd said. "What good are names? It's not like I'm going to see you again."

Once Jake signed all the necessary papers, he could get out of there, and hopefully, Marcie or Marianne would keep her mouth shut. Looking at Emily, he thought again how happy she had looked playing outside with the puppy. He forced a smile, hoping to erase the scowl she still wore.

When they were ready to leave, Adam loaded him up with puppy paraphernalia and called out to Marianne to say goodbye, but when she didn't answer, he laughed. "She's probably on the phone with Sophia."

Jake's heart sank at what that conversation might be like.

They hadn't been in the car five minutes when Emily resumed her earlier attack. He'd been expecting it but had foolishly thought she'd be too busy with her puppy to sink her nails into him.

"Do you want to tell me what that was all about between you and Marianne?"

He kept his eyes on the road. He needed silence. He needed to breathe. He needed a fucking drink. Why had he ever thought adopting a puppy was a good idea?

Emily stared at him. "Dad?"

"I heard you, Emily. I'm going to tell you this once—nothing was going on in that kitchen, and even if there was, I do not answer to you."

The rest of the ride was silent. The motion of the car lulled the puppy to sleep. Emily put her earbuds in and listened to music, and he concentrated on getting as far from St. Johnsbury as he could.

Chapter 23

Emily scooted past Jake while he struggled to carry dog food, a bed, and a box with the word "crate" stenciled in bright-blue ink, all provided by Adam.

"Mom!"

He dropped everything on the kitchen floor, waiting to see what Emily led with while his insides churned.

"Mom! Guess what? You are never going to guess!" Emily was babbling a mile a minute while holding the puppy close.

Sophia took one look at the squirming ball of fur and asked, "What's this?" As if she didn't already know what it was and how it came to be in her home.

Ignoring Sophia's question, Emily blurted her news. "Guess who the foster people are at Homeward Bound?" And before Sophia could hazard a guess, Emily told her. "Adam and Marianne!"

Sophia looked to him for confirmation. He shrugged then dug crate parts out of the box, pretending to sort through the different pieces while praying to whatever deity oversaw husbands who should be flayed within an inch of their lives that none of their conversation would have anything to do with what Emily had heard in the Barclays' kitchen.

"You should have come with us! Adam and Marianne are the foster people. Well, one of the families who foster rescues. I wanted to call you, but Dad said you were *resting*."

Turning to Jake, Emily added, "We don't need the crate. Lilly's sleeping with me."

He dropped the front panel on the floor and reached into his shirt pocket for a cigarette, remembering too late that he'd quit years ago.

Sophia looked like she was still trying to wrap her head around Emily's news. "Why didn't we know they fostered puppies?"

He questioned the same thing himself.

"Probably because puppies that need fostering take a back seat to babies? Besides, they *volunteer* at Homeward Bound; they might not need to list volunteer jobs on all the forms along with—what is it Adam does, Mom?"

"He owns his own company. He's a roofer."

Since Jake no longer needed to put the crate together, he flopped onto the window seat next to Sophia, his insides still twisting.

"I remember now!" Sophia looked like she'd struck gold. "I *did* know they were somehow involved with a dog rescue organization."

"You *knew* the Barclays volunteered at Homeward Bound?" No way could Jake keep the exasperation out of his voice.

"I didn't know it was there. When we went to lunch, there was a sticker on Marianne's Jeep about a dog rescue organization. The name was scribbled out. I was going to ask her about it, but we were so busy discussing the pregnancy that I forgot all about it."

Jake had followed Marianne's Jeep home that night not so long ago but hadn't noticed any stickers. And even if he had, it had been dark, and his mind had been busy wondering what the hell he thought he was doing.

"I need to call Marianne." Sophia reached for her phone.

"I think they're busy today. Maybe wait till tomorrow."

Emily did a double take. "I didn't hear them say that." She shook her head as if she could shake him off. "Dad's been acting bizarre all day—I don't know what his problem is—but I walked into the kitchen, and he was *yelling* at Marianne."

"Jake?" Sophia's voice rose. "What in the world?"

He shot one glance at Emily, who had mastered the look of innocence years ago, so it was practically a work of art.

"I wasn't yelling. Marianne broke a glass and cut her finger. I was trying to help."

When Sophia pinned Emily in her sights, she looked right into her mother's eyes, ignoring his.

"I don't know. Maybe he was just speaking loudly."

And then, as if she hadn't tried to stir up trouble, she added, "The Barclays are so cool. They live in a log cabin with lots of land and trees everywhere. It will be perfect for a kid to grow up there."

Sophia hung on to every word. Even he could see how sorry she was to have stayed home. He refused to think of how close he had come to his entire world imploding.

"They have a dog named Mikie who's trained to protect Marianne because she works at a bar sometimes, but instead of barking at us, Mikie sat in front of Dad and gave him his paw. As if he already knew Dad."

Jake cringed at the memory, glad that Emily had so much to say she didn't pause before moving on to her next topic.

"One entire wall of their house is windows. Living there must be like living in the woods."

Reaching out, Sophia touched the puppy on the tip of her nose. "I get it, sweetie. It all sounds wonderful, and I could kick myself for not going along. Let me look at this little girl."

"I named her Lilly. Isn't she awesome? She was born into freedom. If you can call her pregnant mother being dumped at a kill center in Virginia 'freedom.' Homeward Bound rescued her."

Jake looked confused. "How do you know this?"

"Adam told me while you were in the kitchen with Marianne—you know, helping her pick up broken glass."

"She is beautiful." Sophia held Lilly so that they were eye-to-eye. The puppy was so small she practically fit into her hands. "And Lilly's a perfect name." Sophia touched each paw and rubbed the puppy's ears—ears that looked too large for the rest of her—then handed her back to Emily. "Why don't you take Lilly outside and show her the backyard?"

They watched Emily and Lilly disappear through the French doors leading to the patio. He wondered how long it would take before Sophia zeroed in on Emily's comments.

"So, what is it that Emily is trying to tell me?"

Jake thought he was ready to defend himself, but he wasn't. The truth would have to do—part of the truth. "I have no idea. She seems to think I don't like Marianne."

"What about the yelling?"

"Like I told Emily, when Marianne dropped a glass in the kitchen, she cried out. I was headed for the bathroom and asked if she needed help. That's when Emily showed up." Shrugging, he added, "That's all I know."

Sophia grabbed her phone off the table. "I guess she's in one of her dramatic moods."

"I guess." Relief and regret fought for first place in Jake's emotions.

Sophia scrolled through her phone contacts while he filled Lilly's water bowl and carried it into the mudroom.

"I know they're busy, but it will only take a minute to tell Marianne how sorry I am that I didn't come along today." After a few seconds, she left a message. "I can't believe I missed you today. Why don't you come to Burlington next week, and we can do some shopping for the baby? Call me back."

His hand spasmed at Sophia's words, causing Lilly's water bowl to skitter across the mudroom floor, splashing water everywhere. "Why would you invite Marianne to go shopping? You barely know the woman." Irritated, Jake shot the question at Sophia when she rushed into the room.

She grabbed some towels and knelt to help clean up the mess. "That's not true. We're friends. I thought picking out some things for the baby would be fun, and Burlington has more shops than St. Johnsbury. I'm hoping we can make a day of it."

He wondered if this day would ever end and if he'd still be sane when it did.

Chapter 24

The thought of Sophia and Marianne "making a day of it" would be funny if it were happening to someone else. But for Jake, the situation sure as hell wasn't funny.

The following day, he crammed all the dog-crate parts back into the box while thoughts of what a mess he'd made of everything gnawed at him. All he had wanted was to make his daughter happy. To make up for being a bastard these past few months. And what did he get for trying to be a nice guy? A mess he had no idea how to get out of.

Matt was the one person he could talk to, and when he picked him up for a late-afternoon racquetball game, they never even stopped at the club. They headed instead to their favorite bar, where they grabbed a table in the farthest corner so he could spit out all the gory details—the first trip to Lyndon, when he had no illicit intentions, and the second, when he had become consumed with desire for this woman who called herself Marcie.

Matt's face turned to stone by the time Jake finished. "Well?" He swallowed. "Are you going to say anything?"

"What do you want me to say? That you're not the man I thought you were? I can't believe you'd do this to Sophia." The look on Matt's face was cringe-worthy. "Have I said enough?"

Matt stood as the waitress showed up to take their order. When the bar grew unexpectedly silent, Jake noticed that all eyes were on them.

"Will you sit?" Jake hissed. He should have known better than to talk to Matt. He loved Sophia like a sister. Hell, everyone adored her. He rubbed his hand over his face. This day was going no better than yesterday.

The waitress put her hands on her more-than-ample hips. "I don't have all day, boys. What'll it be?"

Jake ordered two shots of Johnnie Walker and a couple of beers to wash them down while Matt reluctantly pulled out his chair again.

"Look, I know this is bad. I know I've fucked up. I've never done anything like this before." He would have made that statement with his hand atop a stack of Bibles. "You have to believe me."

"I'm not the one you should be trying to convince. Go home and tell all of this to your wife."

"I can't." Jake imagined confessing his lies, his betrayal. Watching the color drain from Sophia's face as he admitted his sins. Their marriage, always strong until recently, would be destroyed. He would lose everything that mattered to him. And Emily? How would he ever face her again? He could never tell Sophia.

"She's pregnant." At his lowest, Jake looked to Matt for an answer, adding, "She probably shouldn't get upset."

Matt leaned across the table until he was in Jake's face. "She *probably* shouldn't get upset? Maybe you should have thought about that before you fell into bed with Marianne."

The waitress had barely stepped away from delivering their drinks before Jake lifted his glass, downed a shot, and then picked up his beer. "She told me her name was Marcie."

"Jesus Christ! What difference does that make?"

Jake stared at the table—his shot glass empty, Matt's untouched.

"It doesn't. I wanted to support Sophia with this surrogacy. It means so much to her. I told you the baby's due in June. And my brother died in June. Nightmares I haven't had in years wake me—I'm drenched in sweat, and I can't fall back to sleep. I go into the office trying to show Stephen what a great lawyer I am, and I can barely see straight. Christ! I almost fell asleep in the last partners' meeting."

The waitress was within shouting distance, and Jake ordered another round.

"I needed to get away. To talk to someone who doesn't talk about babies all the time. I wanted to forget..."

"Wait a minute. I thought you two were on the same page. That's what Chris said."

"I am. I was." Jake shook his head. "I want to be, but I hate that she's pregnant."

It was the first time he had put that thought into words. But it didn't make him feel any better. "Every time I look at Sophia..." He couldn't go on. Couldn't tell Matt about the night Robbie died.

He started talking nonsense. "She keeps getting bigger."

"Well, she's pregnant..."

"I *know* she's pregnant. Don't you think I know she's pregnant?" His words seemed to bounce off the walls. Lowering his voice, he tried to make sense of it all. "It's hard to explain. It brings back so much of the past."

"You know you aren't making any sense. I thought you were smarter than this."

The truth of Matt's words, even though he hated hearing them, hit him like a punch in the face. "I thought I was smarter than this too."

They each downed a shot with one hand and gripped a bottle of beer with the other.

"It'll soon be over, and then everything goes back to normal," Matt said. "Sophia will have done something wonderful." He looked Jake in the eyes. "You need to forget this nonsense and move on."

Jake downed his last shot too fast, and the room tilted. He ignored Matt's advice. "What the hell am I going to do? And the worst of it is, I can't get her out of my mind."

"Sophia?"

"Marianne."

"Wait a minute. You're *serious* about Marianne? A woman who, according to you, you spent a single night with?"

Even Jake was surprised by his answer. He didn't *want* to think about Marianne. He could barely breathe when he thought of her. Was he prepared to throw away his entire life for a woman he'd spent one night with? "I don't know what I want."

The bar was nearly empty. The only sound came from the guy across the room throwing darts. Every time he hit the board, he expelled a hearty burst of air as if he were tossing axes and aiming for his arch-nemesis instead of a wooden board hanging crookedly on the wall.

When Jake entered the library later that night, Sophia and Lilly were snuggled together on the sofa with a quilt wrapped around them, a book dangling precariously from Sophia's fingers. She would be appalled to learn she had been the subject of his conversation with Matt. Not just horrified but destroyed. He could never let her know.

Lilly opened her eyes, whimpered softly, and went back to sleep. Several minutes later, Sophia looked up and offered a sleepy smile. "I never heard you come in."

Nothing startled Sophia. "I just got home." He'd been hoping she'd be asleep so he could avoid everything for one more day, but that didn't seem to be how his life worked these days.

"Come. Sit." She closed her book and patted the space next to her—one more attempt on her part to mend the distance that continued to grow between them.

"I'm beat. Going to bed." The house seemed too quiet. Before he could ask where Emily was, she told him.

"She's spending the night at Maddie's."

Was it his imagination, or was there a yearning in Sophia's voice? Not so long ago, he had loved when Emily was gone for the night so he could make Sophia scream with desire, but those days seemed like a lifetime ago. Before his night with Marianne. Before he could barely stand the thought of touching Sophia. Did she remember? Was she also questioning, like he was, if they would ever get back to the people they once were?

She looked at her watch, the desire he thought he heard in her voice gone. "I'll be there soon. I want to try Marianne again."

He stiffened. "Maybe she doesn't want to talk to you."

Sophia looked up from her phone. "Why would you say that?" Her question was tinged with hurt.

He wanted to soften his words, but he was simply stating the facts. "You're the carrier for her baby. That's all."

"That's not all. We're friends."

"If she were your friend, she'd return your calls."

Sophia shook her head. "She's probably busy. I'll come to bed as soon as I make this call."

Jake lay in bed wondering what he would do when Marianne told Sophia about their night together. He almost laughed. *Maybe Christine will beat her to it.* Every time he closed his eyes, he saw the disgust on Matt's face.

The bedcovers rustled when Sophia crawled in next to him.

"Get hold of her?"

Her voice filled with disappointment. "No."

"Did you leave a message?"

"Yes, I left a message. Marianne's not returning my calls." Creeping closer to the edge of her side of the bed, Sophia added, her voice calmer, "I'll try again tomorrow."

Within minutes, her breathing deepened into sleep.

If he were Marianne, he wouldn't want to talk to the wife of the man she'd slept with either, but something had to be done. Sophia was not letting this go.

Chapter 25

The following day, the LINE files were ready for review, but Jake opened another browser and typed in the Homeward Bound website instead. Then, he hit the *Donate* button and charged $500 to his credit card. *What the hell.* It was for a good cause.

The site's home page announced a large rescue in California, big enough that they sent some of their foster family volunteers from all over the country to collect the animals the labs were releasing. Were Adam and Marianne part of the release? Maybe Marianne not answering Sophia's calls had nothing to do with him. He was grasping at straws but had to find out what was happening.

At Amy's desk, he handed her a piece of paper with the Barclays' phone number and asked her to place the call.

"Is this in reference to a case?"

"No. It's where we adopted Lilly. Just call the number—use your cell phone. If anyone answers, hang up."

"Seriously? Hang up?" She flipped her strawberry-blond hair over her shoulder and grinned. "Are you in high school?"

His request was insane. Jake was almost sure the Barclays were on that rescue, and Amy would get no further than a recorded message. And then he'd know why Marianne wasn't returning Sophia's calls. Because the alternative—that she was searching for the right words to confess their transgressions—was more than he could handle.

Instead of agreeing with Amy that the demand was immature, he went for hard-nosed, which seemed to be an attitude he couldn't shake. "I don't pay you to question my instructions."

Amy looked him up and down, from his custom-made Hendrix wingtip oxfords to his Ralph Lauren silk tie, and obviously found him lacking. "You don't pay me, period. Stephen does."

Seething, Jake reached across the desk to retrieve the paper and make the call himself, hoping that Sophia had never given them his number, when Amy spun her chair around and placed the call. She whirled around again and grinned while the phone rang. And then he heard Marianne's voice.

"Good morning," Amy responded, her voice filled with laughter. "A friend told me about your puppies. Do you still have some? I'd love to come see them."

His eyes bulged. Although he motioned for her to hang up, she shrugged one shapely shoulder and continued talking. He paced frantically in front of her desk, not at all sure she wouldn't blurt out that he'd asked her to hang up if anyone answered.

Finally, Amy ended the call. "I understand completely. Next week will be fine. Thanks so much."

His chest was on fire when she placed her phone back on her desk.

"What? I want a puppy, and you're always going on about Lilly." Her casual response did nothing to ease his pain. Crossing her legs and allowing her shoe to dangle from the tips of her toes, she added, "Mr. Barclay's off on some big rescue mission, so Mrs. Barclay asked me to call back next week. She doesn't have time to show me puppies right now."

He spun on his heel and headed back into his office, angry at Amy and confused that Marianne had been home all this time but hadn't returned Sophia's calls. *Is she planning on confessing?*

Marianne had as much to lose as he did. She was as much to blame as he was. *She was the one who stood behind the bar with those big brown eyes, looking like she'd give anything to be spread wide by me.*

He shook his head in disgust. *It wasn't like that.*

Within minutes, Jake flew past Amy's desk, muttering, "I have an appointment," on his way out the door. After retrieving his car in the garage parking lot, he headed to St. Johnsbury, and before he'd even had time to calm down and think about what he wanted to say, he knocked on the Barclays' front door.

Prepared to lash out at her for ignoring Sophia, his anger disappeared the moment Marianne opened the door. Her cheekbones were more pronounced than the last time he'd seen her, and the shadows under her eyes testified to sleepless nights.

"Are you all right?" What stunned him even more was the stirring deep inside him. He wanted to wrap his arms around her. Instead, he held them straight against his sides, his fingers twitching with his need to comfort her.

Ignoring his question, she tried to close the door, but he stuck his foot on the sill, stopping her.

"What are you doing here?" Her voice stretched tight, she pleaded, "I don't want you in my house."

"Why aren't you answering Sophia's calls?"

"What am I supposed to say?" she barked, a wild animal in its death throes. "The thought of even looking at Sophia turns my stomach into knots." Her eyes swept beyond him as if she were looking for help. "Please. Just leave. I don't want you here."

"I don't want to be here. But I do want to talk to you. Return Sophia's calls. If you don't, she will start wondering why, and I don't want her wondering why."

"I can't," Marianne mumbled, clutching at her robe. "How can I talk to her? I made *love* to you. She will be devastated if she finds out. And no matter how much I regret it, how ashamed I am, it happened. It was a mistake I will regret for the rest of my life." She looked down at her feet and then up into his eyes. "Please. Go."

Jake didn't know whether anger or pain—he couldn't erase their night together even if he wanted to—forced his knee-jerk response. "Maybe you should have thought of that before you jumped into bed with me."

Marianne sucked in her breath as if he'd slapped her. Her reaction devastated him.

Realizing what they must look like, with Marianne slumped against the doorway as if she might pass out while he stood tall and menacing with his foot planted firmly on the sill, he glanced behind him and caught sight of a man walking his dogs down the road. He recognized the dogs first—two stately Great Danes with their owner, Sam Albright. Jake had forgotten that Sam had moved to St. Johnsbury after his wife died.

"Let me in before your neighbors start talking."

But Marianne seemed oblivious to his request or his increasing anxiety. "I don't expect you to believe me, but I've never done anything like that before."

For the love of God... He turned toward the road again in time to see Sam raise his hand in greeting. Having no choice but to wave back while Marianne's admission seeped into his soul, he still wanted to punish her for regretting their night together.

"Isn't that what everyone says?" It had been the first time he had done anything like that, but he still didn't regret it. The one thing he was certain of was that he didn't want to hurt Sophia.

"Whether you believe me or not, it's true. Adam and I had a horrible fight that night I first met you. Everything we've ever wanted was coming true with Sophia carrying our baby, but the more I talked about what we needed to prepare and how our lives would change, the more silent he became."

He felt her words in the pit of his stomach. "Adam doesn't want the baby?"

She nodded. "That night, when I left the house for my shift at the bar, that's all I could think about. That Adam would divorce me if I kept the baby, and I'd be alone."

Jake's voice grew harsh. "Sophia's carrying your baby, and now you don't want it?"

"Please! Be quiet!" Finally, she opened the door wider, allowing him to enter.

"*I* want the baby. Adam doesn't." She backed up to the newel post and sank to the bottom step. "He's gone."

"What do you mean, 'he's gone'?" Jake's voice was like sandpaper. "He was here when we picked up Lilly." His eyes shifted left and right as if Adam might suddenly appear. But instead, he saw what was missing. The pipes. The hunting magazines.

"He came back the last time he left you. He'll be back again." Jake sounded like he knew what he was talking about, but how well did he know Adam?

"I don't think he will."

Jake leaned against the front door, relieved, at least, to no longer be on display. This was a mess of his own making, and he needed to fix it. "Look. We both need to take responsibility for this. Sophia thinks you are her friend, and she's upset. We need to play this out, and once the baby's born, you find some excuse never to see her again. I don't care what it is. Just do it." Even as he spoke, he thought of what it would be like never to see her again. To never push his hands through her hair and hold her to him.

He swallowed. The ache inside him throbbed. "But... but until then, return Sophia's calls. She wants to take you shopping for the baby, for Christ's sake. Tell her you didn't return her calls because Adam left you. If we're lucky, she will never find out about us."

Marianne hadn't moved from the bottom step. Her eyes, pools of sorrow, never left his face. "Why do you even care if she finds out?"

How could he not care? "Because Sophia is my wife. And I love her."

The entire drive home, he wondered how he'd gotten himself into this mess if that were true.

The grin on Sophia's face when he walked into his house was like a beacon offering to help him find his way home. Guilt consumed him. Even Lilly, clamoring for attention with her whining, made him want to check over his shoulder to ensure Marianne hadn't followed him home.

"You look like you won the lottery, and I know you don't play. What's up?" Jake made a point of keeping his voice light and even.

Still smiling, Sophia returned to chopping vegetables while Lilly sat at her feet, waiting patiently for a carrot to hit the floor. "I'm just glad you're home."

"Uh-huh. What's going on?" He tossed his briefcase on a chair and wrapped his arms around her waist, forcing himself to melt into her, nuzzling his face into her neck. Trying to forget where he'd been.

This was what it used to be like when he came home. He remembered these moments. Sophia hummed in contentment until he froze when his fingertips brushed against her belly. His quick intake of breath was barely perceptible, but Sophia stopped humming, and except for Lilly's quiet whine, the room was silent. He forced his hand to remain where it was and exhaled slowly through his mouth.

"What's wrong?" Her words were stretched thin.

Everything. Is that what I want to say? "Nothing." They stood silently, stiffly, until finally, he moved his fingers gently over the hard mound of her stomach. He breathed deeply and swallowed the bitterness in the back of his throat.

Sophia began to hum again. So softly that at first, he thought it was the sound of her breathing, but then he recognized the melody as the first song they'd ever danced to and felt the notes flow through all the parts of his body he feared long dead. He could do this. He could be the man he had been. This life he had built with Sophia could be enough. It had to be.

"Why were you grinning like a fool when I came home?"

"Did you call me a fool?"

"Hmmm. I did." Again, Jake nuzzled her neck.

"Marianne called me back. We're getting together next week."

He was expecting this but hesitated before turning to the fridge and pulling out a beer. "Glad to hear you two have gotten past whatever the problem was." And then, feeling as if he were pushing his luck but doing it anyway, he added, "So why did it take her so long to return your call?"

"Adam was away on some big dog release with Homeward Bound, and she's been busy with the puppies they're fostering. He just got home, so life is back to normal."

"Is it?"

"Is it what?"

"Back to normal. Is life for the Barclays back to normal?"

"I guess so. You always take things so literally, but from what I could tell, their lives are fine."

"Good. Glad to hear it." *Why hasn't Marianne told Sophia that Adam is gone?*

Chapter 26

Sophia's absence was evident the moment Jake walked in the door as if all the energy in the house had been sucked out. Loosening his tie and shrugging out of his suit jacket, he checked her calendar. Ultrasound. And lunch with Marianne. This must be the second ultrasound. *Of course they're together.* Between the two of them, they would give him a heart attack.

Jake didn't want to think about Sophia lying quietly on the examining table while the technician located the baby inside her and reported on its progress. He didn't want to think about Marianne sharing that experience with her. The same one he'd shared with Sophia when she'd been pregnant with Emily.

Looking at that monitor almost sixteen years ago had been the first time he'd accepted that he was about to become a father. He and Sophia would be responsible for a baby who would need love and support. A baby who, even then, had the slightest smile. Pure joy emanated from Sophia while he could barely swallow. And when he looked again, instead of the vague shadows and movements from a moment before, he imagined a fully developed baby with a gun in her mouth.

Even the memory caused him to break out in a cold sweat. He had choked on a sob, startling Sophia, who had clutched his hand while the technician looked at him like he was some typical man who couldn't handle the business of pregnancy. But she hadn't seen what he'd seen. How could she? She hadn't been there the night his brother died.

The vision he'd experienced during the ultrasound had stuck with him for months. That was how convinced he'd been that whatever had been wrong with Robbie would carry over to his baby. But Emily had been perfect. Was *still* perfect. And when he held her for the first time and she looked up at him with the absolute trust that infants offer, he had fallen in love with her so fast the fear he'd felt when Sophia had first told him she was pregnant vanished.

Jake's head was still filled with memories when the sound of the garage door pulled him back to the present, and by the time Sophia entered the kitchen, his heart was beating normally.

Sophia seemed startled to see him. Not startled—something Jake couldn't identify. But he let it slide.

"You're home early," she said.

"You're home late."

"I am. I had my—"

"Second ultrasound. I saw your calendar. Everything good?"

"Everything's fine with the baby."

"That sounds like you want to add a 'but.'"

"But Adam left Marianne."

"Oh?" Each beat of his heart pounded in his head. *Will I know when my heart stops, or will I be dead by then?*

"He decided he didn't want to be a father. He no longer wants to be married to Marianne."

Jake had thought Adam would change his mind. Maybe not about the baby. But Marianne. *How can he leave her?* He pushed the thought away. It was none of his business. Keeping his eyes on Sophia, he waited for more. He wasn't sure what the more might be. He just hoped it wasn't about him.

"The man's an ass." Sophia hissed bitterly. "He just *left*. Told Marianne he'd handle the financial end but doesn't want anything to do with the baby." She poured a glass of water and drank deeply. "I know we had our problems when I was pregnant with Emily, but at least you didn't leave me."

It always amazed him that Sophia's memories of that time differed from his. She had radiated hope and well-being while genetic landmines tortured him.

"Is she all right?"

"Well, of course, she's not all right." She shook her head as if he understood nothing. "She's devastated. But she's prepared to raise the baby alone. She wasn't herself at lunch, and she practically fell apart when I asked what was wrong. I'm amazed that she's managed to keep so much to herself for so long."

Her hand crept to her belly as if that simple act would protect the baby. "I forgot to tell you—it's a girl! Emily was right when she predicted the Barclays were having a girl. I can't wait to tell her."

After washing her hands, Sophia pulled a fresh swordfish from the fridge. "I had no idea how difficult it's been for Marianne because I'm carrying her baby."

"Oh?" He had begun to believe that Sophia's tone held no bitterness or underlying accusations when he heard it again. "Like what?"

"Like she thinks I am the luckiest woman alive. I have you. I live in a beautiful house. I can get pregnant." She looked up from scrubbing potatoes. "She said she would hate me if she didn't love me so much. And then she started to cry because she was afraid she'd ruined our relationship, but I assured her that would never happen."

"Was that the end of it?" He grabbed his suit jacket, turned to head up the stairs then tripped over a pile of Emily's dirty gym clothes when Sophia's response stopped him.

"Mostly. I told her if she still feels this strongly after the baby is born, we never have to see each other again, but I'd hate for that to happen. I want Marianne in our lives forever."

Chapter 27

Several weeks later, Jake still couldn't concentrate after Sophia's announcement that Adam had left Marianne. Even though he had already known, he couldn't help but wonder how Marianne was coping.

Like most nights after dinner, Jake planned to go through the mail that sat in a neat pile on his desk. But after opening the third charity request, he threw the letter opener across the room. He started ripping the envelopes open by hand and tossing the contents onto a pile.

But the heft of the Visa bill made him pause rather than add it to the mound of rapidly accumulating bills. The balance was eight thousand four hundred fifty-two dollars. And change.

Certain there was an error, he returned to the first of four pages of itemized charges and reviewed each retailer. On page two, he came across a store he'd never heard of: Once Upon A Child. Grabbing the receipts he rarely looked at but insisted on keeping until he paid the bills each month, his eyes drifted to the charges—crib, dresser, changing table, rocking chair. Baby stuff. *What the hell is Sophia doing? And why didn't she mention buying all this stuff?* And then he remembered the odd look on her face the day she came home from her second ultrasound. *Apprehension?* He had no idea.

He ran different scenarios through his mind, trying to find a reason for her not to tell him, and when he couldn't figure it out, he found himself storming into the kitchen where Sophia was watering her plants.

"Why in God's name are you buying baby furniture?" The bill clutched in his hand, he added, "I thought you understood that this is not your baby."

Sophia's eyes touched briefly on his face before settling on the bill. "Don't be silly, Jake. Of course I understand this isn't my baby."

"Good," he all but snarled. "Then tell me what the hell *this* is?"

She glanced at the bill again. "I can explain."

"I doubt it, but go ahead—give it your best shot." He paced before her, trying to calm down. He knew he was being unreasonable, but his blood pressure skyrocketed every time he looked at the bill. *Did she take it upon herself to buy the furniture? Did Marianne ask for it?* The money didn't bother him. It was the thought that Marianne was taking advantage of the situation to get what she wanted. That thought brought him to a halt.

Is she taking advantage of me? Of Sophia? The idea that Marianne intended to fleece them made him furious. *Make up your mind. Is she the kind of woman to do that?* He didn't know, so he let his anger slam into Sophia. Crushing the bill in his hands, he faced her. "Well?"

"Will you calm down? Marianne doesn't have the money to buy nice things for the baby now that Adam's gone. He gave her a ridiculous budget for baby furniture. It's barely enough to keep Mia in diapers... Isn't it charming? It means 'mine.' Marianne picked the name after Adam moved out."

For one second, he pictured this baby that would look nothing like Adam and everything like Marianne. The image baffled him, and he momentarily lost hold of the anger that had consumed him the moment he saw the outrageous bill for baby furniture.

"So, what did you do? Give her your credit card?" He waved the balled-up bill in front of Sophia, and when she didn't respond quickly enough to suit him, his frustration skyrocketed. Only a supreme act of willpower kept him silent while he waited for her response.

"Of course not. We went shopping after lunch the day of my ultrasound, and I saw what she liked. So I went back and ordered everything. As a surprise."

"Congratulations! I'm surprised. Did it not occur to you to let me know you'd spent thousands on baby furniture? We never spent that much money on Emily's furniture when she was born."

They'd picked out furniture and put it on layaway, planning on bringing home one piece at a time as he could pay for it. Then, he'd come home one night, and the whole damn nursery had been furnished, right down to pictures on the walls and curtains on the windows. Anthony had taken it upon himself to pay the layaway off so Sophia could have everything. So she didn't have to wait.

"Things were different when Emily was born. We weren't making the kind of money we do now. My father..."

Jake held up his hand. "I know what your father did."

"Why are you in such an uproar? It's not like we can't afford it."

It was true. It wasn't the money. Jake wasn't sure what it was. But the idea of them providing *anything* for Marianne and Adam's baby made him feel like Marianne had somehow tricked him.

His head pounded from everything he couldn't afford to think about. "We're giving her a baby, for fuck's sake. You tell her it's all going back. And then, you call the store and have everything returned."

"I can't do that."

"You most certainly can. And you will."

Jake's eyes bored into Sophia's, but she didn't even blink.

"I'll pay you back."

That stopped him. The only way she could pay him back was to take the money out of their joint accounts and write a check, no different than what he would do. They had combined their money since the day they married, but they'd always discussed big purchases before making them. *How is Sophia writing a check out of our joint account "paying me back"?*

He let that slide for the moment. "Why didn't you tell me about this?"

"And when was I supposed to do that? Maybe I should make an appointment to discuss household expenses?"

"These are not household purchases."

"No. They're not." She poured the remaining water into the last plant and put the watering can back in the pantry, giving them both a few seconds to regroup. "I should have told you about the bill. I'm sorry. I'll pay you back."

He was intrigued. "You already said that. How you will do that is what I want to know." If Jake had to guess by the look on her face, Sophia was about to tell him something that would make the previous ten minutes look like child's play.

She looked him square in the face. "I have my own money."

"Your own money?"

"Yes. My father gave it to me on our wedding day. I've never touched it. I rarely think about it. It's just there."

Jake had known from the beginning that he was not the husband Anthony would have chosen for his little girl. "So let me guess, your father gave you escape money."

Sophia at least gave him the satisfaction of looking embarrassed. "Yes."

"And you've kept it all this time. And never mentioned it to me."

"Yes."

In seconds, he had gone from so pissed he couldn't see straight to eerily calm, regretting he had ever questioned the bill.

Chapter 28

Sophia handed Jake a check the following morning.

"What is this?"

"Don't be coy—it doesn't become you. It's the money I owe you."

"I can see that." Meeting her eyes, he tore the check into little pieces and let them flutter to the floor at her feet. "I don't want your escape money."

Before the confetti-like pieces had even settled on the floor, the back kitchen door opened, and Christine walked in, flashing a smile. "Good—"

"Jesus Christ!" Jake whirled toward the door. "Don't you ever knock?"

Christine took in the situation, hugged Sophia, and glanced at the floor. "I see I missed the party." Giving Jake a look, she added, "What's got your panties in a twist so early this morning?"

"Nothing. Not a goddamn thing."

His body tensed under Christine's gaze, and he fought the urge to look down at his feet, ashamed of his outburst but unwilling to apologize.

"You know, they say women get all emotional when they're pregnant, but I think men are even worse. What do you think, Jake?"

Not waiting for an answer, Christine bent to pick up the mess on the floor then stood quickly without touching any of it. "What *is* your problem? Matt and I were just talking about the mood you've been in."

"My mood?" He swore his heart was going to beat right out of his chest.

"Yes. Your mood. Matt says you're confused and strung out, and he hopes you get your act together."

He waited for more, and when none was forthcoming, he nudged. "Anything else you care to share?"

"*Should* there be?" Christine taunted, which answered his question about what Matt had told her.

Not that he'd expected otherwise.

"Don't know how this got here, but I'm happy to clean it up." Turning to Sophia, she added, "Sorry. Guess my timing's off. How about a walk?" She continued talking to Sophia as if he weren't still in the room. "You must be going crazy." Discretion wasn't on her mind when she added, "Anytime you need a break, come stay with us."

Christine busied herself around their kitchen as if it were her own, gathering mugs, filling the kettle, and lifting a plate of cookies from under the glass dome that kept them fresh. "Sit. Tea's almost ready."

Sophia smiled with gratitude as she settled in a chair. "What would I do without you? I'll be so happy when this baby comes and we can get our lives back to normal." She looked at him as if hoping to wipe out the last few days of fighting about that damned baby furniture. "Right, Jake?"

He was too angry to answer, and the way Christine acted as if he were invisible pissed him off more. "I'm going for a run." Looking at Christine, he added, "Do me a favor and don't be here when I get back."

He didn't know about Christine, but he'd definitely pushed Sophia too far. "Jake! Apologize this minute. Blowing up at me is one thing, but do not be rude to our friends. Honestly! What is wrong with you?"

Everything is wrong with me. How can she not see it? And even though he was wrong, he'd cut out his tongue before apologizing.

Christine looked as if she'd achieved her goal. She placed two mugs of tea on the table and turned to him. "Everything will be fine once the baby comes. I'm sure of it."

He slammed the door on his way out of the house. No matter how far he ran, he could never outdistance his problems.

They tiptoed around each other for days. Jake quietly paid the Visa bill, and Sophia rarely mentioned Marianne or the baby.

And then, days later, he came home from the office and heard Marianne's laugh. He froze. She laughed like she made love—like there was no tomorrow. What was she doing here?

Before he could move, his chance to flee disappeared.

"Jake? We're in the kitchen. Come join us."

They sat at his kitchen table. Sophia and Emily wore big smiles, but Marianne dropped her eyes to the mug in her hands at the sight of him.

"Dad! Isn't this great? Marianne's staying for dinner!" He didn't understand how Sophia couldn't hear the snark in their daughter's voice.

Before he could respond, Lilly came racing into the kitchen, running in circles around his legs until he bent to greet her. Grateful for the brief reprieve, he straightened. "What brings you to our neck of the woods?" His words sounded hollow. He felt ambushed. *Is Marianne's presence payback for ripping up her father's check? For my rudeness to Christine?*

Kissing Sophia on the cheek, Jake wanted to ask why she thought this was a good idea. Instead, he kept his smile in place while ruffling Emily's hair, forgetting how furious that made her.

"Dad!"

"Sorry." He grabbed a much-needed beer, twisted off the cap, and raised the bottle to his mouth in one fluid motion.

As if reading his thoughts, Sophia explained. "You'll never guess. I ran into Marianne on her way out of the courthouse this afternoon and invited her for dinner. She insisted she couldn't, but I wouldn't take no for an answer."

Sophia looked like someone had given her an unexpected gift. It was beyond him that she couldn't see that Marianne was melting into her chair.

"Wonderful." He took another long pull from his beer and jerked his tie loose. "If you will excuse me for a minute, I'll just get out of this suit."

Once upstairs, he headed first into the bathroom and grabbed the bottle of aspirin—he had a son-of-a-bitch of a headache—and downed four with a gulp of beer. Glancing in the mirror, he saw a man he barely recognized, eyes hooded as if he had something to hide. His mouth grim. When was the last time he was happy?

Within minutes, he'd finished his beer, pulled off his suit, and grabbed a pair of jeans and a sweater.

Dinner was in the kitchen where typically only family ate—Sophia clearly considered Marianne family—but Marianne evidently thought otherwise. She kept her head down, her eyes on the food she moved from one side of her plate to the other without putting any of it into her mouth, and rarely spoke.

Jake focused on the bowl of fruit in the center of the table with an occasional glance at Marianne. Even when her fragrance drifted across the table, making his memories turn from shades of gray to colors so vivid they hurt his eyes, he did his best to ignore her.

Meanwhile, Sophia blathered on about how the pregnancy was progressing, still oblivious to the tension in the room.

Was Marianne playing him? At this point, he had no choice but to join the conversation. "From what I read in the newspaper, that last release must have been brutal."

Marianne grabbed at his words. "It could have been devastating." Her voice was strained, as if she'd been screaming into a pillow for days and finally came up for air. "Thankfully, Homeward Bound stepped in and saved a lot of dogs from being butchered."

Nodding, he returned to scrutinizing the fruit, looking up when he heard the hitch in Emily's voice.

"Butchered?" Her face devoid of color, Emily looked from Marianne to him.

Marianne's cheeks flamed. "I'm so sorry! I have no idea what's suitable to say in front of children. That story's inappropriate for dinner conversation."

"No need to apologize. I brought it up." He came close to feeling sorry for her but then reminded himself that he couldn't afford sympathy, not when he didn't know why she was in his house.

Dinner conversation came to a halt soon after, and Sophia and Emily stood to clear the table.

Marianne rose quickly. "Let me help."

But Sophia wouldn't hear of it. "Stay where you are and talk to Jake. You two need to get better acquainted."

Their eyes skittered toward each other at Sophia's suggestion, then they quickly glanced away.

Emily and Sophia chatted as they rinsed dishes, which gave him the chance he had been looking for.

"You couldn't have come up with an excuse to turn down Sophia's invitation?" He worked hard to keep his voice low, but the intensity behind his words seemed to startle them both.

"I'm sorry. I didn't know how to say no."

He snorted, pouring himself more wine without bothering to offer any to her. "You rarely know how to say no, do you?" He winced at the crudeness of his words while Marianne's eyes welled with tears.

"Do you think I *want* to be here?"

That was what Jake was afraid of. "I don't know what you—"

"Dad! Look what you've done."

His hand shook at the sound of Emily's voice. Beads of the ruby-colored liquid in his wineglass stained the tablecloth like drops of blood from a wound that would never heal.

Emily looked at him as if he were a stranger. "Marianne's crying." Her reproach brought Sophia to the table before he could backtrack his words.

Sophia looked from Marianne to him and Emily. "What in the world is going on?"

Marianne wiped her eyes with her napkin. "Please. Everything is fine. I get a little emotional these days, what with... with Adam gone." Checking her watch, she stood. "I really do need to go." She looked around the table, skipping quickly past him. "This has been lovely. Really."

"Seriously?" Jake lashed out at Sophia as soon as the front door closed behind Marianne. "You invited Marianne for dinner?"

"I did. I'm tired of your attitude about her. She's the mother of this baby, and she's my friend. And I won't pretend she doesn't exist because you're still angry about the baby furniture."

"Wait. What baby furniture?"

"Not now, Emily," Sophia said.

"She is not your..." Sophia's feelings for Marianne shattered him. The truth would crush her.

"What? She is not my *what*?" Sophia's voice rose to match his.

Refusing to engage, he muttered, "Don't let it happen again."

Sophia rolled her eyes, but Emily went on the attack.

"This is Mom's house too! Why are you so angry all the time? And what baby furniture?"

The God's honest truth was that he couldn't begin to explain. "This doesn't concern you. Don't you have homework? And will you forget about the furniture?"

Ignoring him, Emily stalked out of the kitchen, leaving Sophia and Jake to stare at each other.

Later that night, Jake walked past Emily's room and overheard a conversation that forced him to retrace his steps. Emily was repeating the evening's events to someone on the other end of the line—most likely Maddie—including his rudeness to Marianne and his anger at Sophia.

She knew this was against the rules. Family conversations stayed in the family. Without thinking, he pushed the door open just as Emily spoke, the headache that had been building all night spiraling out of control.

"I don't know why he was acting like such an ass."

Jake grabbed her phone and stabbed mindlessly to end the call.

"What the hell?" Emily jumped off her bed and grabbed for the phone, but he held it out of her reach. Then, Lilly started barking, the sound piercing his eardrums.

"How often have I told you not to repeat family business?"

"Family business?" Emily's hands were shaking. "Is that what you call acting like a dick?"

He raised his hand, stopping its trajectory mere inches from her cheek. His entire arm quivered with its need to continue. Emily's eyes bulged. Did he stop because he'd never hit a human being in his life—let alone his daughter—or was it her look of terror that brought him to his senses? Would he ever know?

Emily recovered faster than he did. "Go ahead. Slap me."

"I wasn't going to slap you." His stomach churned with disgust at what he'd almost done.

"No? Could have fooled me."

He had to regain control of the situation. "Calm down. I wasn't going to slap you. But you need to respect me. Do not call me a dick."

He could barely see straight, the memory of his father raising his hand to him so vivid he wanted to throw up. He shook his head as if he could easily dislodge his childhood memories. He was not his father.

"I'll calm down when you give me my phone." Emily held out her hand, and when he made no move to give it to her, she threatened, "I'll tell Mom something weird is going on between you and Marianne."

He swallowed hard. "You don't know what you're talking about."

"I may not know what it is, but ever since we got Lilly, there's been something off with you. It's like you hate her, and you barely know her. She's a nice person. And Mom is having her baby. And she's Mom's friend!"

Sophia came into the room while they were still staring at each other. "Who's Mom's friend?" She looked from him to Emily to Lilly, who had finally stopped barking and was cowering beside the pillows on Emily's bed.

"Honestly! Sometimes, I think I have two kids instead of a husband and daughter. Are you two still arguing about Marianne? I can hear you all the way downstairs."

Turning to Jake, Sophia added, "I know you are unhappy I invited Marianne for dinner. As we all saw, it didn't go well. I plan to call her tomorrow and apologize for your boorish behavior.

"And the two of you"— she eyed him and Emily as if they were five-year-olds in the midst of a name-calling contest—"need to get over whatever you're fighting about. I'm going to bed."

Once Sophia left the room, he handed Emily her phone. "I am giving you your phone back, but not because you think you have something to tell your mother."

A fifteen-year-old would not bully him.

Chapter 29

That night, he felt the warmth of Marianne's naked body next to his and couldn't help but respond. He knew he was dreaming when he spotted Emily leering at him, reminding him that Sophia was in the same bed.

He knew she shouldn't be there. But Marianne just laughed, rolled over, and started talking to Emily. They whispered and giggled until, suddenly, their words turned ugly. Emily screamed that she would tell Sophia, but Marianne smiled and snuggled deeper under the covers as if that was what she had wanted all along.

"Jake. Wake up!"

Half asleep, he confused Sophia with Marianne. "Stop yelling—you're not supp—"

Sophia shook him again. "Jake!"

When he opened his eyes, Sophia held the phone out to him. "It's your mom. She's crying."

After rubbing his hand over his eyes, he grabbed the phone, his heart beating rapidly, his moment's reprieve from the nightmare gone when Sophia's words registered. "Mom?" He listened for a few seconds then pulled the phone away from his ear. The bedroom filled with the sound of his mother's pain.

"Mom! Slow down. What happened?" Pulling himself out of bed, he grabbed at the jeans he'd worn the night before, hopping on one foot to pull them on while capturing a stray word or two from his mother. Words that made no sense.

"Where are you?" Listening as best he could, he tried to reassure her. "Okay. I'll be right there." His left leg twitched as if a nerve had gone haywire after he disconnected the call.

Sophia flipped the light on, climbed out of bed, and pulled on her robe. "What's going on?"

"Mom's at UVM. My dad's had a stroke."

"I'll get dressed and come with you."

He stopped her before she had taken more than a few steps. "No point in us both getting ripped out of bed. I'll go and find out what's going on. How bad he is. See if I can't get my mother to go home."

He leaned toward Sophia, meaning to kiss her, but the image of Marianne cuddled beside him resurfaced, and he brushed her shoulder with his hand instead. "I'll call when I know something."

The drive to UVM was fast and quiet except for the occasional ambulance with its siren blaring as it headed in the same direction. He couldn't imagine his father incapacitated by a stroke. The man was made of stone.

Mentally preparing himself for the bright lights and the cacophony that would greet him, Jake strode through the entrance. He hated hospitals. Bad enough in the daytime but damn eerie in the middle of the night—what with the well-lit hallways and staff scurrying on rubber-soled shoes from place to place no matter what time the clock indicated. He planned to get in and out as fast as he could.

He wanted nothing more than to be back in his bed—without the nightmare presence of Marianne or Emily—but instead took the elevator to his father's floor. Striding quickly down the hallway amidst the sounds of intercom codes, doors opening and closing, and the occasional moan, he finally stopped when he reached his father's room.

Framed images of local landscapes by one of Vermont's best-known photographers covered the pale-blue walls. The heavy drapes at the windows added warmth to the room, and the rich leather of the two recliners reflected a luxury available only in private rooms. This was definitely a room for the likes of his father.

Jake's heart faltered at the sight of the empty bed. He swayed, trying to take it in. Relief that the man who openly despised him was gone. Sorrow, maybe, that he'd never had the opportunity to prove to his father that he was worthy. He didn't know.

His mother's eyes were closed, her fingers thumbing her rosary. As he moved to her side, he wondered what he could say to address her monumental loss. He could almost see the last few hours of fear and confusion wash across her face when she opened her eyes and oriented herself. He reached for her hand, still searching for words, when she offered a weak smile.

"He's having an MRI. To determine the damage."

He almost laughed. Had he felt nothing other than relief when he'd thought the old man was dead? He loved his mother unconditionally and knew she felt the same for him, but what, if anything, did he feel for his father? He couldn't answer that question.

"I don't understand. A stroke? Dad's never even had high blood pressure." He looked around the room, still trying to orient himself. "How long have you been here?"

A lifetime of pain pooled in the depths of his mother's gray eyes. They revealed so much more than concern for her husband, but as quickly as the truth showed itself, it hid within the lies of his mother's life.

Finally, she answered. "I didn't want to call until I knew what was happening." She quickly squeezed his fingers three times, just as she had when he was a small boy—their way of saying they always had each other.

"Your father keeps everything bottled up. He drinks too much. And honestly, the only exercise he gets is golf, so he gets none this time of year. He needs to take on a partner." She pulled a tissue from her sleeve and wiped her eyes. "He's never been the same since..."

Jake stiffened. None of them had been the same since Robbie had killed himself. His father had destroyed the remainder of Jake's childhood that night, but he had never told his mother. She knew as much as the police—that Robbie's death had been an accident. Telling her otherwise would have destroyed her.

They sat in silence, and before long, his father was wheeled back into the room, ready to hold court once the nurses had him settled. Jake couldn't help but notice that instead of the thin, open-backed hospital gown issued to most patients, his father wore a pair of fine herringbone cotton pajamas in nearly the same shade of blue as the walls in his room.

When the nurses left, with warnings that their patient needed rest and they'd be back in five minutes to check on him, Jake approached the bed. "How are you doing, Dad?"

The timbre of his father's voice was as strong as ever. "I'm fine."

Robert rearranged himself in the bed until he was at eye level with Jake. "Your mother overreacted. I shouldn't be here, but I agreed to spend the night so they can run a few more tests in the morning. Women like your mother drive up the cost of health insurance."

Jake winced, knowing that his mother had heard every word.

She stood by the bed, smiling, impeccably dressed, her navy-blue wool slacks and sweater tailored to fit. Her hair was perfectly styled—the silvery strands of gray tucked neatly behind her right ear, the part in her hair as straight as he'd ever seen it. You'd never know she'd spent most of the night praying that her husband would live, and to have him disparage her while she stood by his side both saddened and enraged Jake.

He had never once heard his mother dispute her husband's claims. *Maybe she should let you die next time.* The thought shocked him, but he would never say the words aloud. Like his mother, he stayed silent. Just like always.

Chapter 30

The stress of Jake's fight with Emily, his nightmare with Marianne, and then news of his father's stroke clung to him like the web of a spider encountered on a brisk morning hike. When he wandered into the kitchen the following morning dressed for work, he still had the urge to scrub the stickiness away.

"Did you get any sleep?" Sophia's voice hinted at the drama from their argument over Marianne's appearance at their kitchen table the previous night, but there also might have been a touch of compassion due to his late-night trip to the hospital.

She probably hadn't gotten much more sleep than he had, although he'd envied the sight of her curled up and softly snoring when he crawled back into bed a few hours ago.

"Not much." Yawning, he wrapped both hands around the mug of coffee she handed him, Emily's threats to tell Sophia what she thought she knew not far from his mind. "Have you talked to Emily?"

"No. Are you still fighting?" This time, she didn't even try to hide the exasperation in her voice.

"Nope. We're all good." Nothing like a bald lie to get the day started. He couldn't even think about facing Emily but knew he'd have to. He also needed to apologize to Sophia for his boorish actions last night, but that would have to wait. "I told my mother we'd meet her at the hospital this morning."

"Fine." There was a definite chill in the air—nothing to do with the temperature—when Sophia headed upstairs to change.

As Jake had driven home in the early hours of the morning, he'd let go of his fury with Emily and hoped to smooth over the harsh words they'd exchanged. But the look she gave him when she showed up at the breakfast table suggested hell would freeze over before she was ready to forgive and forget.

He was the adult. He needed to act like one. "I just got home from the hospital a couple of hours ago. Grandpa had a mild stroke last night." He hoped to keep the confusion he'd felt when he'd thought his father was dead out of his voice. "He'll be there for at least another day."

With a forkful of scrambled eggs midway to Emily's mouth, Jake finally had her attention. "Grandpa's sick? Why are you dressed for work?" Judgment written all over her face, she eyed him across the table. "No one would guess you were up most of the night."

That was the point. Jake wore a gray wool suit with a white dress shirt and a red tie with tiny white polka dots, intent on showing his father he was more than competent for the proposition he intended to float to him later.

Emily's tone was accusatory, but he let it pass. "Thank you for talking to me."

She didn't bother to look up from her breakfast. "I'm asking about my grandfather." Emily could split hairs with the best of them.

"Don't worry, Grandpa's in good hands. Your mother and I are going to see him before I go to work." He poured himself another cup of coffee, his father's words about his mother overreacting still playing in his head.

"You're not going to spend the day with him?"

"No, I'm not." He bit down when his voice started to rise. "Your Grandpa wouldn't want me sitting around all day. If I know him, he'll be reading legal briefs from his hospital bed by the time I get there."

"Jesus," she muttered, "would it kill you to show a little emotion? Your father's had a stroke. Don't you care about that either?"

She grabbed a piece of toast and her backpack, opened the door, then turned back. "Did you tell Mom you hit me last night?"

"I didn't hit you." His fingers tightened on his mug, but Emily was gone before he could say more.

Robert looked as if he'd enjoyed a restful night's sleep. He had somehow managed to make his hospital room look like he was holding court in an executive suite with his laptop and briefcase resting center stage on the little table beside his bed meant for medication and meals. Just like Jake had told Emily.

His mother stood next to his bedside, holding his hand, which squashed Jake's hopes of having a few words in private with his father.

Slightly annoyed but unable to stay that way when it came to his mother, he kissed her, whispering, "Good morning," before turning to his father.

"How are you feeling, Dad?"

"I'm ready to get out of here, but that damn doctor said I have to stay at least *another* twenty-four hours so they can run more tests."

Jake forced down the smile that had come so readily. "It might be a good idea to listen to your doctor. You don't want to have a major stroke."

"I got a little dizzy. Everyone's making a big deal over nothing."

"Calm yourself, dear. You don't want to get overly excited." His mother offered a cup of water, but his father pushed it out of the way, and the cup, narrowly missing her, crashed to the floor.

Seeing an opportunity, Jake turned to Sophia. "See if someone can clean this up, will you, hon? Mom, why don't you two get coffee or tea? I'll visit with Dad for a minute, and then Sophia and I need to leave."

Once they left the room and an aide wiped up the spill, he took his mother's position beside the bed. "You really had us worried."

"I'm fine."

"Dad, the reality is, you aren't getting any younger. Maybe now's the time to start thinking about selling your firm. Or I could come on to help. You and Mom deserve to have some fun. You've worked hard all your life. Why not take it easy now?"

He wasn't pushing his father out. He was trying to help him.

Driving home early that morning, he'd finally figured it out. He'd wanted a senior partnership at Cranston, Clark, and Cunningham because he thought that was what it would take for his father to see he was worthy of being brought into Robert's firm as a partner.

Once he'd examined his goals, Jake realized his father's approval was what he'd always wanted. To be seen as an equal. But with his father's stroke, there wasn't any time left to prove himself. He had to make his father understand that he was worthy.

"What the fuck is this? You think I'm too old to run my own firm? You think I'm leaving my office to *you*?" His father's face turned an alarming shade of red.

Jake lowered his voice. "Dad, that's not what I meant at all."

Still blustering, his father attempted to sit up straighter and inadvertently hit the call button, bringing a nurse into his room in seconds. Seeing that her patient was not in danger or in need of anything, she spun on her heel and marched out of the room, but not before advising them to relax and remember where they were.

"I'm not asking you to *give* me anything. I'm a good lawyer. If you bring me on, I can see how you run things... make sure there's a smooth transition in, I don't know, a few months."

"The firm is Robbie's."

Jake exhaled. He thought his father had finally put this to rest. "Dad—"

"The firm is Robbie's. It was always meant to be his. When I die—when I retire—when I *quit*, so does the firm."

That will show everyone exactly what he thinks of his remaining son. He stared at his father, and the old man looked back with what Jake swore was hatred. He should have backed off and stayed silent, but years of keeping his mouth shut finally ended.

"Robbie's dead. You get that, right?" He cringed at the bitterness that coated every word. But he couldn't stop. "Surely you remember? He blew his brains out when you told him to get on with it."

Jake had never cried in front of his father. As a kid, he'd waited until he could get to his room before letting his emotions loose. As an adult, he'd learned to mask his feelings, but tears blinded him as he waited for his father to deny his accusations, and when he remained silent, Jake raged out of the room, his chest heaving.

But within seconds, he was back. "Think about this. You say Robbie was better than me. Smarter. More deserving of the firm. Of your love. But he was the one you beat."

Jake closed his eyes, trying to ignore his father's cold stare, but for maybe the first time in his life, he said the words that screamed in his head. "He was the one you killed."

It wasn't remorse he saw in his father's eyes before he looked away. It was hate.

"You swore you would never divulge what happened that night." His father's voice had an edge to it that could cut steel.

"I did. But I'm done keeping your secrets."

He had to get out of there.

Jake paced outside his father's room, checking his watch every few minutes, his entire body shaking, growing angrier with each passing second when he needed to calm down. When Sophia and his mother returned with a cup of coffee, he waved it aside.

"I need to get to the office." He kissed his mother quickly and led Sophia toward the bank of elevators.

"For heaven's sake. Let me say goodbye to your father." But the elevator arrived, and Sophia followed Jake into it, leaving his mother outside Robert's room with Jake's cup of coffee cooling in her hand.

Sophia waited until they were in the car to speak. "Are you going to tell me what happened in there?"

"Nothing." Staring straight ahead, Jake never bothered to turn the car on, just stared into space.

"I know that's not true. Something happened. Maybe arguing with your father right now is not a good idea."

Pulling out of the parking lot, he headed home, Sophia's comments fighting with the truth. His laugh, when it came, was hollow. "You're probably right."

Why can't I tell her what my father did? He didn't know the answer; he just knew that he couldn't break his promise even though he told his father he would.

Chapter 31

The sun shot arrows at Jake's eyes, pulling him from the continuous loop of his father's belittling words—which had played in his head since he had talked to him several days ago—to an awareness that it was Christmas morning.

He carefully crawled out of bed so that he wouldn't disturb Sophia and made his way downstairs, in dire need of coffee. Even though it would only be the three of them for brunch, Sophia had set the kitchen table with red-and-green Christmas dishes and miniature poinsettias positioned at each place setting. Tea light candles ran down the center. He guessed this was her way of starting the day with some fanfare.

They were working toward a truce in the aftermath of his father's stroke, and he appreciated her effort. He needed to make an effort too.

Once his coffee was ready, Jake settled at the table, careful not to disrupt Sophia's display as he warmed his hands around his mug and savored his first sip of the dark, rich brew. He tried to put the argument with Robert out of his mind, at least for the day, but the old man's words continued to pummel him whether he was awake or asleep.

Within minutes, Sophia wandered into the kitchen and headed directly to the tap to fill the tea kettle. Her robe hung open, barely able to close as her girth grew wider. She was small-boned and petite—that baby had nowhere to grow but out. It had been the same when she was pregnant with Emily. Underneath her robe, she wore something flannel he'd never seen before.

Pulling out a chair across from him, she poured tea into her mug. "Where's our girl?"

That tugged at his heart. Emily was their girl. Always would be, even if she was currently furious with him.

"Still sleeping." He grinned. "Remember when she used to wake us up?" Jake found it hard to believe there had been a time when Emily woke them on Christmas morning, her face glowing with excitement at all the presents under the tree from Santa and a stocking overflowing with gifts from Sophia and him. "I miss waking up to the anticipation dancing in her eyes as she begged us to get up."

He caught Sophia's hint of a smile, so he kept going. "Look. I know things are... strained between us. I know that we're working on making things better, and maybe we're not quite there yet. But it's your favorite holiday. What if we take a giant leap and pretend you and I are where we want to be and give Emily a nice day? Even if she isn't talking to me."

Sophia looked interested.

"Drink your tea, then I think it's payback time." He couldn't help but chuckle.

Jake put his ear to Emily's door and opened it slowly when he didn't hear anything. "Hey, sleepyhead, Merry Christmas!"

Lilly opened her eyes then settled in again while Emily squinted. "Oh, look. It's Scrooge."

His good intentions crumpled under her tone, and he was ready to turn around and leave when Sophia slipped into the room behind him.

"Your father's trying, Em. Be nice."

At first, the only sound in the room was Emily's alarm clock ticking, but then, she relented. "Sure. Why not?" Her words, tinged with sarcasm, revealed her hostility, but still, she pulled herself up, bracing on one elbow, and changed the subject. "Are Grandpa and Grandma coming?"

Bile rose in his throat at the thought of the man who could so easily dismiss him sitting at his dining room table as if they were one big happy family. "No. Grandpa's too weak."

His mother insisted she would spend the day at home with Robert since he'd been released from the hospital a few days ago and needed rest more than holiday festivities, but they would take food and gifts over later this afternoon. Soon enough, he would face him.

"It's going to be the three of us this year since Poppy and Nonna are cruising the Mediterranean."

Sophia grabbed Emily's hands and pretended to pull her up.

"Come on, up and at 'em."

But Emily tugged slightly harder, and Sophia soon joined Emily on the bed.

"Do we have time to open presents?" Emily's eyes never wavered from her mother.

"What? Presents?" Sophia looked at Emily in mock horror. "You know we don't open presents until after brunch."

Widening her eyes and looking soulful, Emily begged, "Just one?" And then, without waiting for an answer, she declared, "We have time for one." Reaching under her bed, she pulled out a glittery package and read the nametag with great fanfare. "Oh, look! It's for you and Dad. How in the world did this get here?" Giggling, she added, "There's more under the tree, but this one's for now."

Sitting cross-legged on the bed, the package in her lap, Sophia laughed. "Well, I suppose we can open one. What do you think, Dad?"

Ignoring Sophia's question, he pivoted to his daughter, hoping to bury the hatchet somewhere other than in his chest. "But what about you? Don't you want to open one?"

"Nope. I already know what I'm getting."

He laughed. "And how do you know that?"

The moment felt lighthearted, but the laughter in her voice came nowhere near the look on her face.

"Because I always get everything I ask for."

Sophia snorted. "I don't know, Dad. I think we've spoiled her entirely too much."

"Totally." Emily agreed. "Now, open your present."

Emily had wrapped the gift in shiny red paper with images of festive Christmas trees, roly-poly Santas, and a generous helping of glitter that moved from the package to her bed every time Sophia touched the paper.

"You will be picking glitter out of these sheets for the rest of your life," Sophia commented as she pulled the silver ribbon off the box.

"Or at least as long as I live here," Emily said. "Come on, open your present!"

Carefully undoing the paper, Sophia looked to Jake. "Want to do the honors?"

He didn't want to do any honors. This was Sophia's present, and he was an unwanted plus-one. No more than he deserved.

But Sophia kept encouraging him, and he felt he had no choice but to play along. He lifted the lid to find a linen-colored photo album nestled in layers of tissue paper. The book was titled *Our Journey*, with a picture of the baby's first ultrasound in the middle of the front cover. He held the box out to Sophia. Her eyes filled with tears as she took in the image.

Emily practically bounced on the bed while Sophia pressed the album to her chest.

"Open it!"

Jake would rather have rubbernecked at a five-car pileup than look at the damn book, but he did it anyway. The first picture was the one he had taken on the day of the embryo transfer, with Sophia and

Emily's arms wrapped around each other, both grinning even though they hadn't known at the time if the transfer had been successful.

From there, the pages chronicled the order of events from the day Sophia found out she was pregnant to just the other day when Emily snapped a photo of Sophia standing sideways in her bathroom, looking into the mirror with her shirt pressed closely to her belly, a glimmer of joy in her eyes.

"Oh, Emily!" Her voice thick with emotion, Sophia whispered, "Thank you so much!"

Emily glowed at Sophia's response. Then she shifted those shimmering eyes to him. "What do you think, *Dad*?"

Her smirk told him all he needed to know about how much she enjoyed pushing his buttons. He couldn't say what he thought. He couldn't even say what he felt—like he was standing in the middle of a forest fire with no way out.

So much had happened since he had snapped that first photo. He barely remembered the man he'd been then. But he had to say something.

"I think it's a wonderful gift, Em. Thank you." He doubted she even heard him.

"I made one for the Barclays, too, but I wanted to give you yours first. From now on, we can fill the pages in as I take pictures." She searched Sophia's face. "You really like it?"

Sophia answered for them both. "We love it. And it gives me a great idea. I'll keep a journal so that once I deliver the baby, I won't forget how I felt or what I was thinking."

"Great idea! But you've got some catching up to do."

"I know, and thanks to you," Sophia said as she leaned over to kiss Emily's cheek, "this album should jog my memory."

Later, after opening presents and spending the afternoon with Jake's parents, Sophia joined him in his study, where he sat at his desk, staring at that damn globe.

She sank onto the couch and sighed, slipping off her shoes. "You don't like Emily's album."

"I didn't say that."

"You don't have to. You have not been yourself for months. Are you ever going to talk about it?"

He didn't answer. He couldn't.

After several seconds of silence, Sophia changed the subject. "I thought you were going back to your parents after dinner?"

"There's no need. The old man doesn't want me there." The bitter words they'd spoken to each other came unbidden, but he couldn't repeat them. "It makes sense—he's never needed me."

"That's not true." Sophia moved closer and perched on one corner of Jake's desk. "What did you two talk about the other day?"

"Nothing."

"It looked like something when your mother and I found you pacing outside his room."

Jake stood, grasping Sophia's hands to bring her up with him. He decided he could tell her part of the conversation.

"We talked about his firm. I offered to come on. To help. To take over when the time was right."

Sophia looked like he'd suggested running away with the circus. "But what about your job at the firm? Becoming a senior partner? I thought that's what you wanted."

He put into words what he'd recently figured out. "Honestly? My entire reasoning for wanting to be a senior partner was so my dad could see that I was good enough to come into his firm. Besides, for whatever reason, I'm convinced Stephen doesn't think I'm promotion material."

"But you can't know that for sure. I thought that was the whole point of all of this." She swept her arms wide as if all the pressure of these past years was taking up space in the room. "The crazy hours. The stress. And lately, your anger with all of us."

"I know. I'm sorry. I honestly just figured it out for myself."

Sophia didn't say anything. Jake thought... he wasn't sure what he thought. That he'd apologize, and she'd forgive him? "I'm sorry."

"I heard you the first time. You can't keep saying you're sorry and expect me to forgive you, especially when you keep changing the game plan. You're supposed to let me know when you make decisions that affect Emily and me. You don't answer my questions. You don't tell me what you're thinking. I can't be a partner in our marriage if I don't know what the hell is going on."

There was a lot Jake couldn't explain.

"What did Robert say when you told him you wanted to help?"

He'd never forget what his father had said or how he'd said it. The look in his eyes. The sound of his voice. He had spoken with such certainty. With such venom. "He said... he said it was Robbie's firm."

Sophia looked confused. "But..."

Jake's laugh was bitter. "I know... Robbie's dead."

Chapter 32

Robert. Sophia. Emily. *Marianne.* How much could Jake handle? Instead of going to bed, he quietly pulled on running clothes and laced up his trainers. He was trying not to wake Sophia, but he jammed his shin into the side of his dresser. "Jesus!"

Sophia sat up. "What's wrong?"

"Nothing. I banged my leg." He leaned in to kiss her. "I'm going for a run."

"It's almost midnight. Don't you think it's a little late?"

Jake had no idea what time it was. All he knew was that he needed to run. "I won't be gone long. I just need some air. And before you ask, the roads are dry," he whispered then closed the bedroom door behind him.

He started too fast and hadn't bothered to warm up first. Forcing himself to slow down to a steady pace, he tried to think, but every time his feet hit the asphalt, his father's words exploded in his head— *"The firm belongs to Robbie"*—and his pace increased.

But Robbie's dead. He died when you taunted him to pull the trigger. Don't you remember?

Who knew that his brother would pull the trigger? His father should have known—should have protected him. But deep inside, Jake knew Robert wasn't wholly to blame. Robbie wasn't even responsible. Whatever had been wrong with his brother seemed to have come with birth and wrap itself around the heart and soul of Robbie. That was what killed his brother, no matter who pulled the trigger. An illness ignored and excused for so long that when it finally erupted, it destroyed everything in its wake.

His feet smacked the pavement. His chest hurt, and his breath grew ragged. Soon, struggling for breath, he forced himself to slow his pace again. Finally, he had to stop. Bent at the waist with his hands on his knees, he swallowed great mouthfuls of air, gasping. When he pulled off his gloves to swipe at his face, his fingers came back wet with tears. He'd never been enough. He'd never been his brother. Robert blamed him. And he blamed himself.

By the time Jake returned to the house, snow had filled the sky and covered the streets, trees, and the occasional parked car with a layer of purity. It was a white Christmas, even though Christmas was almost over.

"Soph? You awake?" The run had helped. Finally, he saw the truth.

When Sophia opened her eyes, he stood at her side of the bed, breathing hard, his ears filled with the sound of his beating heart. "I need to tell you something."

Groggy with sleep, Sophia murmured, "Are you sick?"

He felt sick, although a pill wouldn't fix what was wrong with him. "No. I'm sorry I woke you." He felt like he was going to pass out. "I need to tell you this now. Otherwise... otherwise, you might never know."

He moved from Sophia's side of the bed to his and back again. He wanted nothing more than to lie down but was afraid he would die if he did. And then no one would ever know.

"I need to tell you about Robbie. The night he died." Jake still wore his running clothes, and he shook with chills. Kneeling next to Sophia, he was close enough that her breath touched his cheek.

She caressed the side of his face. "Honey, I already know. Remember? You told me. He was sick." She ran her fingers through his hair. "There was nothing you could have done. Nothing anyone could have done." She made it sound simple.

"No. You don't understand. There's more. I've never told anyone. Even the police don't know. Even my *mother* doesn't know." His heart kept time with the alarm clock on her bedside table.

"Jake, you're scaring me." She pushed herself up and turned on her bedside lamp while he stood, stripped off his damp clothes, and climbed into bed.

She wrapped her arms around him. "You're freezing."

"I-I'll warm up." Even his bones were cold, and he knew he'd never get warm when he thought about what he had to say.

"Tell me what's going on."

Can I tell her? He'd never told anyone.

"My father killed Robbie. And no one knows what happened that night but me. That's why he hates me."

She pulled away, her voice filled with horror. "What are you saying?"

"Let me finish. My brother was sick, but my dad told him to pull the trigger."

The look of horror on Sophia's face stopped him for a second.

"I heard him. That's why he hates me. He *knows* I heard him. He remembers that night every time he sees me."

The pain he'd carried all these years felt alive in the room when he told Sophia the rest—the sound of the gun going off and, when he looked, the sight of his father throwing himself onto Robbie's body.

Robert never wanted anyone to know. In that respect, they were alike. And even though Jake had sworn never to tell, he couldn't live with that night any longer.

"I should have stopped him," Jake confessed, his guilt over Robbie's death as crushing as it had been all those years ago.

"Your dad should have stopped him. You were a kid." Sophia seemed determined to make him see that night differently. "There was nothing you could have done."

Jake wanted so badly to believe that, but he wasn't sure he could.

Nobody had ever said those words to him. Finally, he began to believe in the possibility. It was a start. *The old man should have stopped him.*

"Why have you never told me this before?"

When Jake was a child, the reason had been clear. The secret was between him and his father. Only as a father himself did he begin to understand that the promise was one he never should have been asked to make.

"I promised my father I would never tell."

"Oh, Jake."

Sometime in the night, he rolled away from Sophia. He lay curled on his side of the bed with the covers kicked away, awake, not ready to face the day even though sunlight slipped through the slight opening in the drapes. When Sophia reached to pull the blanket up to cover him, he opened his eyes and looked at his watch. It was later than he thought.

"Sorry." She yawned. "I didn't mean to wake you. I just wanted to keep you warm."

He grabbed her wrist and pulled her to him. "Don't be sorry. I'm the one who should be sorry."

"Why? Because you told me the truth? Now that I know, I can see why Robert is the way he is. He's not going to change. You need to live with what happened and accept that it wasn't your fault. You were ten years old. You couldn't have saved Robbie. I'm not certain your father could have saved him, but what he's done to you is unconscionable."

He absorbed her words, wanting to believe them.

"You've been carrying this pain far too long. It's good that you told me, but you must talk to a professional. I can listen and love you and hold you. But you need someone to help you overcome this or at least help you live with it."

He tensed. "What's a therapist going to do? Tell me I'm crazy? No one can force my father to love me."

"No. But a therapist may be able to help you learn to love yourself. Just think about it, will you?"

Jake stared at her. He'd been an ass for so long that he could barely remember ever being nice. Because Sophia was the most empathetic person he knew—she put everything on hold between them and offered comfort. Love. For the first time in what felt like forever, they sat together in shared silence without the need to explain themselves. He'd made many mistakes. He needed to beg for forgiveness.

The grandfather clock struck eleven, and Sophia jumped up. "I need to get moving so I'm not late picking up Emily. She's at the school for the play tryouts.

"Want me to come with you?"

"Nope. I've got this. Maddie's mom drove the girls to the school earlier. I'm in charge of pickup. You go back to sleep." Sophia pulled herself from the bed and grabbed her robe.

"Soph? I'm sorry." He reached out and grabbed her hand. "I'm so sorry."

"For waking me up? You don't have anything to be sorry about." She stood between his legs and cradled his face with her hands, his actions these past months seemingly forgotten. "We'll work this out. I promise. But right now, I need to get dressed."

Her forgiveness was too easy, and his apology seemed brushed aside when he tried to make her understand. "I'm not the man you think I am." The words were a start, but not nearly good enough.

"You're the man I love. The man I married. The father of my child."

She moved toward her closet, but he pulled her back.

"Wait." He held her gently as if she were made of porcelain and would shatter if he pressed too hard. "You don't understand. Look at me."

He was desperate for her to see his truth, but she pushed him back until his head touched the pillow.

"*I am* looking at you. You're not perfect. Your father is a man who comes closer to a monster than anyone I know. Do you need help? Yes. Undoubtedly. If there's more, you can explain it to me when I get home."

Sometime later, he rolled out of bed, determined to do better. To be the man Sophia thought he was, not the man who had slept with Marianne and was still hiding the truth from her. He needed to tell her. And he would.

By the time he was out of the shower, Sophia was home. She found him leaning against the island in the kitchen, his hands wrapped around a mug of coffee.

"Glad to see you're up."

He pulled her to him with one arm while holding his coffee in the other.

After grabbing his mug, she took a sip then made a face. "Why can't you drink tea?"

"Because I like coffee." He unwrapped the scarf around her neck and kissed the tip of her nose. "But I also like you, so get out of that coat, and I'll make you a cup of tea."

He hadn't felt this close to Sophia in forever. Telling her Robbie's full story had released a lifetime of stress. He didn't owe his father silence.

"What was it you wanted to say earlier? Something about not being the man I think you are? What's that all about?" Her voice was light and teasing. As if she couldn't possibly believe he was anything other than the man she had married.

They settled in the library by the fire, snuggled on the couch. Emily, home from the play tryouts, had immediately climbed back into bed. It was almost as if they had the house to themselves. This was his chance. His opportunity to come clean. To apologize. Beg for forgiveness. The words tugged at his heart. Jake could almost hear himself say what needed to be said, but he couldn't imagine Sophia's reaction. *What if I destroy everything we just found again?*

He lifted her hand to his lips and kissed her palm. "I don't remember. Maybe I'm getting old. What do you think? Am I an old geezer?"

"Hardly." She nestled even closer. "Speaking of old geezers, assuming your dad recovers fully from his stroke, your mother wants to throw him a birthday party. He turns seventy-five next year."

He wasn't ready to think of his father or his birthday. "That sounds like a lot of work for my mother."

"Yep. That's why she asked if I'd organize it."

The thought of celebrating anything for the man made his stomach sour. He'd get over his father's bitter words—or at least file them in an imaginary drawer he never opened—but he hadn't reached that point yet.

"Wait a minute, his birthdate is weeks from your due date. That sounds like a lot of work when you're almost nine months pregnant. Maybe my mother should wait until he turns eighty. I might be in the mood to celebrate the day he was born by then."

"I know. But this means a lot to your mom. And she never asks us for anything. I can get most of the organizing done now, well before I get big and fat."

"You won't get big and fat."

"Oh, I plan on it. How often does a girl get to eat all the ice cream she wants?"

"Good point. Maybe we need to feed Emily more ice cream. Think that would make her a little more compassionate toward me?"

"Don't worry about Emily. She loves you—adores you. Let her see you're back to being you, and everything will be fine."

He never mentioned Marianne or the sins he needed to atone for. But he would. He vowed to himself that he would.

Chapter 33

Jake's optimism about his reconnection to Sophia lasted until Adam's name appeared on his phone. Seconds passed before he accepted the call. They'd had Lilly for months—Adam should not need to contact him. The baby talk was between Sophia and Marianne. And the Barclays were separated. *So why is Adam calling?*

The pulse in his temple throbbed. "Adam! What can I do for you?" By the time Adam responded, he had poured himself a drink and downed it, his pledge to Sophia to cut back forgotten.

Adam's first words made Jake wish he'd never answered the call. "Emily's been talking to Marianne, so I guess I need to talk to you."

Jake's mouth went dry. He reached for his drink, but the glass was empty. He poured another, but his next swallow did little to alleviate the sensation of grit sliding down his throat. "Oh?"

"I gather Emily didn't mention it to you."

"Can't say that she did. Is there a problem?" He could no longer sit. Gripping his phone, he paced from one end of his study to the other, praying that this call wasn't what he thought it was.

"That's what I was afraid of. Why I'm calling."

Jake swallowed. *Not now. Not when I've finally found my way back to Sophia.*

"Marianne posted on the Homeward Bound website about an older dog, Miss Molly, that's being fostered and needs a forever home, although, to tell you the truth, forever won't be very long. The dog is sick and requires lots of attention. And, I'll be honest, her medical bills are off the charts. But kids don't think about money when they want to do something good."

With the wind knocked out of him, Jake sat, closed his eyes, and listened, still gripping the phone, but maybe not as tightly.

"Emily wants to adopt her. I'm not sure why Marianne didn't contact you herself, but since I'm over at the house fixing some loose roof shingles, I thought I'd give you a call."

Jake heard Marianne in the background, and his breath caught in his throat.

"Hold on a sec, will you? Marianne needs something." The next thing Jake knew, he was holding a phone with no one on the other end.

He chugged the rest of his bourbon and reached for the bottle. *What's so important Marianne needs to interrupt the call?* Not for the first time, he understood that Marianne had the power to ruin his life. She would always be in control unless he told Sophia first. By the time Adam came back on the phone, Jake was nearly numb.

"Sorry about that. Marianne's worried it will start snowing again before I finish with the shingles, so I'll keep this short. I know you aren't in the market for a senior dog, but Marianne believes this dog means something to Emily, so she asked me to call. You should be proud of that daughter of yours."

He'd always been proud of Emily—he was ashamed of himself. Leaning his head back against the chair, he closed his eyes. "I'll tell you what, these next few weeks are a killer for me, but I'll come at the end of January and look at this dog. Tell Marianne that if Emily calls again, not to mention that we've talked. I might make this a surprise."

He needed to make things right with Emily. *What did she call me? A dick?* He would have laughed, except the term was painfully close to the truth.

It was the middle of February before Jake followed up with Adam on Miss Molly, the beagle Emily had set her heart on from Homeward Bound. A few days later, he found himself driving home from Waterford with the heat in his car set to high, hoping the dog would still be alive when he pulled into his garage. His luck held, and he managed to get her settled in Emily's room while Lilly sniffed and hovered.

Emily arrived home first and, as was her current norm, went sailing up the stairs without a word. Just as quickly, she returned and threw her arms around him. "I can't believe you... how did you know? I didn't even tell Mom."

He laughed. At least he had fixed one part of his world.

Sophia's reaction to the addition to their family was less enthusiastic. "What do you mean we have a new dog?"

"Wait until you see her, Mom."

Jake chimed in. "Wait until you see her, Mom."

Sophia stared at him, apparently not in the mood for his humor. "Well, where is she?"

"She's in Emily's room. Tom said she's very timid, and we should confine her to one room at a time so she doesn't get overwhelmed."

"And the best thing is," Emily interrupted, "I didn't even *ask* Dad."

Sophia gave him the once-over. "But what about Lilly?"

Jake would need to fill in the blanks, but he had time. "Not to worry. I hired someone. She'll take Lilly for walks and help with Miss Molly." This was the beginning of getting his family back. He was sure of it.

Later that afternoon, Jake ran upstairs for a sweater and overheard Sophia talking. She wasn't talking to him, and Emily was on the phone with Maddie downstairs. He peeked in Emily's room. Miss Molly's bed was empty. He hoped the dog was house-trained, a question he'd neglected to ask. Sophia was on her knees, looking under the bed.

"So, there you are," she whispered, then she reached into her pocket and pulled out one of Lilly's dog biscuits. "What are you doing under there? You wait right here. I'm going to get help."

Feeling like a voyeur, he wanted to let Sophia know he was there without scaring her half to death, but before he could act, she pulled herself up from the floor and stood just inches from him.

"Jesus, Jake. Are you trying to give me heart failure?"

"Sorry, I heard you talking and couldn't figure out who was here. I see you've met Miss Molly."

"I have. And I'm assuming Miss Molly is your way of returning to your daughter's good graces."

He grinned, feeling the flush in his cheeks.

"We'll talk later about how I don't like surprises, especially those that require care. For now, bring Miss Molly's bed down to the kitchen. And see if you can't coax her out from under Emily's bed. Maybe carry her down? She's lonely up here."

"Lonely? Did she tell you that?"

Sophia grinned. "She did."

Carrying Miss Molly and her bed down the stairs, Jake found Emily curled up in the kitchen window seat with her phone glued to her ear. Jake placed the quivering dog in her bed in an out-of-the-way corner of the room and leaned against the island, waiting for Emily to get off the phone.

Sophia looked from him to Emily when she came downstairs. "Are you *listening* to her conversation?"

"No, I'm not listening. I'm waiting for her to hang up so we can take the dogs for a walk."

He hadn't been intentionally listening until Emily said, "My dad?"

Her voice had emphasized the question, and she zeroed in on him, causing the hair on the back of his neck to stand up.

The call ended soon after. "How often have you been to Marianne's house?"

Jake crossed his arms, striving for casual, but his eye twitched anyway. "Just the once, when we picked up Lilly."

"That's what I thought. But Maddie's Uncle Sam seems to think he saw you there a while back."

Uncle Sam. He had been so intent on getting into the house that day that he forgot Sam was Maddie's uncle.

"You remember him, don't you? Mostly bald with wire-frame glasses like no one told him it's no longer the hippie generation? He was always at Maddie's family birthday parties when the Lawrences still held them."

He made a point of acting like he had to think about it. "I guess, but there were so many people at those parties..."

"I know, right? He must be confused." Turning her attention to Lilly and Miss Molly, Emily grabbed their leashes. "Come on, you two lazy bones. We're all going for a walk."

Jake forgot the conversation as they worked their way slowly—in deference to Miss Molly—around the block.

The weather was mild for February, and the fresh air kept his mind off Emily's question. They were all moving closer, and he felt good about that, but his night with Marianne remained a secret. Whatever that night had been—an infatuation that burned out almost faster than it flamed, a mistake on both their parts that they equally regretted—it was over. Yet images from that night—her hands, her lips, her mouth—continued to torment him. No matter how much he regretted it, he couldn't forget it.

He had promised himself he would come clean, but Sophia still didn't know. Maybe not all secrets were meant to be told. But what if she found out anyway? Wouldn't that be worse?

Over the next few months, Jake easily ignored the need to confess. Sophia was deeply involved in organizing his father's birthday party, and his job was crazier than ever. The LINE case alone kept him at the office late every night. He didn't have the time to tell Sophia about Marianne. That was what he told himself.

Chapter 34

An invitation to a garden party at the end of May caught Jake's eye. "What the hell is a garden party?"

"Dad! It means the weather's nice, so the Lawrences plan to have their party outside. It'll be fun."

He wasn't convinced.

"Yeah, Dad, it'll be fun." Sophia chimed in, grabbing the invitation and sticking it on the fridge. "It's been too long since we've seen the Lawrences."

"Who all's invited?" What he meant was, *Is Sam Albright going to be there?*

The invitation reminded him of the day Emily questioned how often he'd been to the Barclays' house. And that reminded him of Sam waving to him while he and Marianne argued on her doorstep. And that reminded him that he'd lied to Emily about how often he'd been there. None of those things was good.

"You know it would be rude to ask, right?"

"Relax, Emily. I thought you might know. It doesn't matter." *It matters, all right. Maybe I can make an excuse to skip the party. Go into the office instead.* He played with that idea but finally decided it was safer to be there to control the situation. Jake had no idea what he would say or how he would explain why he had been at Marianne's. He couldn't think past avoiding Sam. Maybe he was worrying about nothing. Maybe Sam wasn't invited.

After all that worry, he discovered he liked garden parties. They allowed him room to steer clear of people he wanted to avoid—right up until he ran into Sam with Willow and George by his side. He remembered Sophia commenting a while back that the dogs were a great comfort to Sam after his wife died. He didn't know about that, just that Sam and his dogs were inseparable.

When Sam held out his hand, Jake had no choice but to offer his own. "Good to see you again!"

Sam congratulated Sophia on her surrogacy before she drifted a few feet away to talk to friends, and then he resumed talking to Jake and Emily, adding, "Haven't seen you in years and now twice in the last few months. Willow and George wanted nothing to do with a ride in the car, but I convinced them the fresh air would do us all good."

The tension in the back of Jake's neck moved toward his shoulders, making him want to put his head between his knees and howl.

"So how is Marianne? I was going to stop in the day I saw you at her house, but the dogs were intent on their afternoon walk." He shook his head as if to rid himself of disturbing thoughts. "It's a damn shame Adam left. We all hoped he'd get his head on straight, but it doesn't look like that will happen."

Emily's eyes looked like they were about to pop out of her head. "Dad?" The more Sam talked, the more determined she was to interrupt the conversation.

"Wait a minute, Emily." He hoped Sophia wasn't paying attention to what was happening a few feet behind her.

"Dad!"

Emily's voice continued to rise, finally catching Sophia's notice. "Emily!" Sophia chastised, moving closer to him. "Stop interrupting your father."

Jake and Emily stared at each other, and even though he prayed for her to drop it, she couldn't get her words out fast enough. "I guess you *were* at Marianne's more than once?"

"This isn't the time..." He slapped a smile on his face and took Emily's arm, intent on leading her away from Sam and Sophia.

But Emily wouldn't budge. "Stop. You're hurting me."

When he took his hand away, he saw faint red marks on her arm where his fingers had pressed into her skin. "I'm sorry, I didn't mean—"

"Jake?" Sophia's voice was low, but he knew her well enough to understand that she wanted to know what the hell was going on.

He kept his eyes on Sam, who looked like he wished he had listened to Willow and George and stayed home.

"I guess I forgot."

"Why did you lie?"

"I didn't *lie*, Emily. I forgot." His words were tight, with no room for argument. "Go find Maddie and grab your overnight bag out of the car. We can talk about this later."

Emily hesitated then stalked off. Sam seemed to think this was an excellent idea and traipsed after her, the dogs trailing behind, leaving Sophia and him alone.

"So, why were you there?" She sounded mildly interested, as if she were just making conversation, and his shoulders settled back into place.

He ran his hand through his hair. Within seconds, truths and nontruths raced through his head as he searched for an acceptable answer. "Look, Emily is making a big thing about nothing."

"That doesn't tell me why you were there." Doubt seemed to trickle into her voice, and he understood that an answer was required.

"It was a while ago. When Marianne wouldn't answer your phone calls. I was worried about you, so I called, but she didn't answer. So... I took a chance and drove over there. I didn't want you to know I'd interceded because you think so much of her. I wanted you to think she decided to return your calls on her own."

"Did she say *why* she didn't want to talk to me?"

"No. I guess this whole thing is hard on Marianne too. But it doesn't matter now, right? You two are good." Sweat trickled down the back of his shirt.

"You drove all the way to St. Johnsbury?"

"Jesus. What is this? An inquisition?" Jake was beginning to feel trapped. "I met with a client in Lyndon, so I stopped at Marianne's after the meeting."

They drifted away from the other guests until they stood near a three-tiered stone water feature that flowed into a small pond. "Why didn't you tell me you'd been there?"

"I don't know, Soph. You know everything's been crazy at the office. I guess I forgot."

She seemed to think about this, and again, he relaxed.

"That doesn't explain why Marianne never mentioned it."

He winced but forced himself to remain calm. Sophia wasn't making this easy. "You'd have to ask her, but I'm guessing with Adam gone, she had more than enough on her plate without worrying about you every second."

Regretting his choice of words when Sophia's eyes turned glassy, he moved closer, lifting her chin and shifting his gaze slightly, adding, "I don't know. Maybe she felt bad about ignoring your calls?"

"Maybe you're right." She laughed, moving even closer. Smiling like he was her knight in shining armor, she added so softly that he barely heard, "But you're lying."

He stepped back. Instead of a hair's breadth between them, they were now a foot apart, and Sophia's voice had turned to steel.

"When you speak less than the truth, your eyes flit from place to place. Did you know that? They can never settle on one thing.

Usually, when you lie, it's something small—how much you've had to drink or that you did not eat the last chocolate chip cookie. Even with the damn cookie in your hand and wearing a grin that makes it impossible to do anything but laugh, you try to lie your way out of it." She paused to catch her breath after the rapid pace of her words. "But this is different."

He had never seen this side of Sophia, although Anthony warned him once that he never wanted to get on the wrong side of his baby girl because even though she was not a large woman, she could take down a full-size man with just a look.

"I know you are lying about Marianne. About how many times you were at her house. What I want to know is why."

No one seemed to notice them, not that he could tell, but they would become the center of attention if this kept up. "Soph, let's talk about this at home. This has blown all out of proportion."

"*Stop*. You are doing it again. Tell me the truth."

Jake had waited too long. He had vowed he would tell Sophia the truth about Marianne. But when he had the chance, and he'd had more than one, he'd lied. To her. To Emily. He should have come clean instead of hoping for a miracle. But God wasn't handing out miracles. Not to him, anyway. "Can we go home?"

He followed her into their house and threw his car keys on the is-land. "Yes. I've lied. I never meant to hurt you. I never meant to hurt Emily. I'm sorry." Those few words exhausted him. He needed to sit but refused to give himself that small luxury.

He was guiltily aware that even a few hours ago, he hadn't been prepared to accept the enormity of his betrayal.

"We are way past sorry. Tell me what I want to know." Sophia's voice betrayed her words. He knew her well enough—she would give anything *not* to know. None of this could be good for her or the ba-by.

"You don't want to know this, Soph."

She picked up his keys and threw them, hitting him square in the chest where they fell to the floor, the sound rebounding in his head.

"Tell me!"

"What does it matter?" He rubbed his chest, bent to retrieve his keys, then thought better of it and left them on the floor. "I made horrible mistakes. Isn't that enough?"

"You won't be getting off that easily. Tell me."

Her eyes turned dark, but he told her what she insisted on knowing. Kept telling her even when she looked away. "I was in a bad place, and so was Marianne. Not that that's any defense." He looked at his hands, praying for absolution. "I have no excuse."

Jake looked around the kitchen as if someone would corroborate his story. But he was on his own. And even if he wanted to, he couldn't think of one damn thing that would make any of this better.

"I thought having this baby was brave and good, but then you told me when the baby was due. I... I freaked. It was a reminder of everything bad in my life. Nothing good has ever happened in June." He silently willed her to understand, but she just stared at him.

"You're telling me you slept with Marianne because this baby will be born in *June*?" Her question ended in a shriek.

Jake began to see the insanity of his logic, but it had all been real. His anger. His fear. The nightmares. "You know Robbie died in June. I told you how he died." Silently, he begged her to understand, but she gave no indication she was even listening. "Everything got mixed up in my head."

He kept talking. "I never thought I'd be this guy. I never thought I'd..." He looked for another word, any word. *Who am I kidding? There is no other word.* "I never thought I'd cheat on you."

Cheat. The word stretched between them, and Sophia's face crumbled. She dropped heavily into a chair, her face a mask of pain.

"Maybe you don't believe me, maybe you'll never believe another word that comes out of my mouth, but I've always loved you. From that crazy moment in Bennington when I first saw you. I love *you*. I love our family."

He knew her. She would never stop. Not until he had told her everything. Not until he broke her heart.

"Was it because she's prettier than me? Because I'm pregnant and fat?" Her eyes reflected her pain. "How could you do this to me?"

He wanted to tell her what he'd done had nothing to do with her. He wanted to say that he had needed Marianne just for him. But of course, he couldn't tell her that. What he'd done had everything to do with her. With their marriage.

"I don't know... I'm sorry."

That I was caught? He hadn't felt regret when he kissed Marianne for the first time or when he'd stripped off her clothes and run his hands over her body. Only later, when he sat in his car the following day, did he realize the depth of his infidelity.

Jake moved toward Sophia, wanting nothing more than to comfort her, but one look told him he'd be a dead man if he so much as breathed on her.

He tried to explain. "Thanksgiving had been such a shit show with both of our families storming out of the house, the dinner ruined."

His father's disdain when he'd wiped his fingers on his napkin and tossed it on his plate remained a permanent stain on that day.

"The next day, I just needed to get away. I went to work and kept putting off coming home. When I finally left, I drove to Lyndon instead. I didn't have anything on my mind except meeting the Barclays. I wanted to meet the people who were fucking with my life."

He had never forgotten the loneliness of that day. His footsteps had echoed through the hallways as he moved from his office to the conference room, a sad reminder that he had nowhere else to go on a holiday weekend.

"I felt that all of this... my nightmares, *everything*, was their fault. If you hadn't wanted to be a surrogate, there would be no baby. No Barclays. I knew what I was doing was crazy. I stopped at a bar to have a beer and rethink my plan before I made a complete ass of myself."

He never looked anywhere but into Sophia's eyes. He owed her that. "The bartender said her name was Marcie. The place was empty, and we talked. All we did was talk." He wanted to end the story there. Pausing, he closed his eyes then forced himself to continue, eyes wide open.

"Weeks later, I drove up there again. Went to the bar. Went to Marcie's house. Soph, please, don't make me say more."

Her face looked as if all the blood had drained from her body when she whispered, "You slept with both this Marcie person *and* Marianne?"

"No! Oh my God, no! They're the same person."

"How is that even possible?" She looked as confused as he'd felt the day he discovered the truth.

"She told me her name was Marcie. She said names didn't matter. I never told her my name." Nothing he said was helping.

He reached out to touch her, but she held up her hand before he even got close.

"You slept with a woman you didn't know?"

She looked at him like he was lying in the gutter and she had to step over him to avoid contaminating her shoes. She looked at him as if she had briefly considered tossing him a dollar but then decided he wasn't worth it.

"How did you spend the night away from home, and I didn't know it?"

He remembered the lies. All the lies. "It was the day before I came home from Colorado."

"The day *before*..."

"I came home a day early. I never told you."

Sophia blinked. She couldn't have looked more stricken if he had slapped her.

"I asked you why you checked out of the hotel early." Her emotions played across her face in a fury as she remembered the conversation. "You told me the desk clerk must have been confused."

"Yes." He had no excuse for any of it. It dawned on him—not for the first time—that maybe his father wasn't so far off in his low opinion of him.

"I didn't realize who Marcie was until Emily and I went to look at puppies at Homeward Bound."

"Marcie and Marianne are the same person." She said the words as if doing so would help her understand. He would never forget the pain that exploded on her face. "Why would she tell you her name was Marcie?"

He'd wondered that himself. He honestly didn't know if it would have made a difference. Would he have made the connection if she had told him her name was Marianne? If he had realized he was driving to St. Johnsbury instead of just following behind the car of a woman he had become infatuated with?

"I don't know." Taking a chance, he moved toward her again, but she stiffened when he reached out.

"Don't."

He backed away. "Soph, I'm sorry. I made a mistake!"

"You made a *mistake*?" Both Lilly and Miss Molly whimpered at the sound of her voice.

"A mistake is putting a quart of milk in the pantry instead of the refrigerator. A mistake is hitting the wrong contact on your phone. *This* is not a mistake. This was a *choice* that you made."

She bent over in the chair as if she were in pain, but before he could even think of reaching out to her, she straightened. "Were you ever going to tell me?"

"No. I wanted that night to disappear so you would never know." That was probably the most honest thing he'd said in months.

Sophia's face was red. The baby was due soon. This was not a conversation to have with someone about to deliver a baby. He just didn't know how to stop it. But Sophia had no intention of stopping it.

"Is that why you were so on edge when you came home with Lilly? Why Emily said you acted strange around Marianne? Why you blew up when I invited her for dinner?" The questions were sharp, with edges that drew blood.

"I was confused." He was afraid to speak, afraid not to. "I was angry. I'm not making excuses, but everything in my life was messed up. *Is* messed up. My job. My father. And you and Marianne were getting so close. I was terrified she would tell you. I wanted to tell you. And then..."

"And then?"

"And then I couldn't."

"You couldn't."

If anything, his words infuriated her.

"You lost your voice? Hit your head and developed amnesia?" Her face was a mask of tears when she looked at him. "Why did you let me find out this way?"

Sophia was bitter and hurt. Furious. He had no idea if they'd ever recover.

"I was terrified you would leave me. When I told you about Robbie, I realized how much I trusted you. How much I needed you. How much I love you. We got back to how we used to be, and it made me even more afraid to tell you."

Jake's heart thudded in his chest while he waited for her to say something.

"You slept with Marianne. She was my friend. Do you have any idea how I feel?" Sophia shuddered out a deep breath. And then, as if she'd only thought of it. "Have you two been *laughing* at me while I'm carrying her baby?"

He'd never thought past keeping his secret. All his focus had been on keeping himself safe from the truth—even when he'd realized he loved Sophia and didn't want to lose her, he just wanted to make his night with Marianne go away. He wouldn't blame her if she never spoke to him again.

"No! No, it wasn't like that. Marianne was mortified when she discovered who I was. I was telling the truth about why I was at Marianne's when Sam saw me. I knew you were upset and… and I wanted to fix it."

He stopped himself. Even that was a lie. *Can I do nothing but lie?*

"No. That's not true." He shook his head as if he could force all the lies to disappear while Sophia stared at him in horror.

"I didn't know why Marianne wasn't returning your calls, and I was afraid she was trying to figure out how to tell you, and I went there…"

He would never forget the pain that had crawled up Marianne's face that day. "I didn't threaten her, but I told her she had to return your calls and go shopping with you and be friends and that after the baby was born, she was never to see you again." He drew in a long, slow breath. "That's the truth."

"And you thought that then, you would never have to tell me?"

"Yes. No! I knew I had to tell you. I just kept putting it off. Soph, we can get past this. I know we can. We're a family."

Chapter 35

Days after the garden party, Emily still wasn't talking to Jake. He could barely look at Sophia without feeling remorse so profound it was burying him alive. On top of that, Stephen wanted an answer. Would he accept his first-chair assignment on the LINE case?

He needed to talk to someone, and Matt was out of the question. Their relationship had been kept alive simply because their wives were best friends.

Certain his head would explode, Jake pushed the button on the intercom and practically bit Amy's head off. "Don't put any calls through for the rest of the day."

"What's going on?"

"Please just do what I asked."

Exasperated, he swiveled his chair around to face the boxes of internal documents gathered months ago for the LINE case. Taylor. Moore. Johnson. They were guilty as hell and needed to be held accountable for their actions. But his job was to get them off free and clear.

As first chair, he was to present the evidence Stephen had deemed acceptable—proof that, no doubt, had been doctored—to reflect that no one was aware of any issues with the water until people started developing liver and kidney problems. His job would also be to note that LINE had launched an investigation *before* the first death. And of their own volition. *What a bunch of crap.*

The choice came down to presenting the case and being named senior partner or resigning. According to Stephen, he didn't even have to win, although there would be a helluva bonus if he did. If he left the firm, he'd have to start over. He didn't want to start over. What comparable firm would hire him after Stephen put the word out that he'd refused to get his hands dirty?

Christ! He rubbed the back of his neck and spun forward again. He had to talk to his father. He couldn't help himself. They'd barely spoken since their scene in the hospital when he'd raged at the man for not loving him. For not accepting that he still had a son.

He wanted his father to tell him not to take the case. Because then he would know he'd made the right decision.

Slipping his suit jacket on, he stormed through his office and stopped at Amy's desk. "Something's come up, and I need to leave. I should be back in an hour or so."

"Something with tonight?"

"Tonight?" He drew a blank. And then it hit him—the birthday celebration. "No. I... I need to do something. Everything's fine." He headed toward the door, bumping into the bookcase on his way out. Turning back toward Amy, he grinned. He was losing his shit.

"Are you sure you're all right?"

"I'm fine."

He considered calling rather than just showing up at his office, but he couldn't take the chance that he would be easily brushed off. It might be more difficult if they were face-to-face. At least, he hoped so.

Jake no sooner started the car than he remembered Robert wasn't in the office—because of the party—so he drove to the house, wondering how he had ended up with no one else to talk to.

His mother rushed out the front door to greet him before he parked his car in the driveway.

"Jake!" Her voice was a burst of sunshine amidst dark clouds of his own making.

"Mom!"

He picked her up and swung her around as if she were a child. His mother could make him feel like he'd made her day just by showing up.

"What a nice surprise. Is your father expecting you?"

"Afraid not. But I'm hoping he's home?"

"He is. He's in his study. Shall I set another place for lunch?"

"Can't." Forcing enthusiasm, he added, "No time today." They entered the house together, and he leaned down and kissed her cheek. "If I don't see you before I leave, I'll see you tonight." Then, he went to find his father.

"I thought I heard you." Robert stood to shake his hand when he saw him. "I don't see anything on my calendar..."

"No. This is spur-of-the-moment." The old man looked good—his color heightened by fresh air and sunshine, his posture as straight as always.

"Well, that doesn't seem like you." Waving his arm toward one of the two leather armchairs in front of his desk, he added, "Have a seat. What's up?"

Hedging, he asked, "Are you all ready for your big night?"

"Not much for me to do. Sophia's carried most of the burden for this shindig."

"She has. Emily will be my date tonight since Sophia's running the show. Can't wait to see her all dressed up."

"She'll be a beauty." Picking up his letter opener, his father rolled it between his fingers—first one hand then the other.

Jake recognized the action for what it was—boredom.

"I'm guessing you didn't come here today to discuss the party. What's really on your mind?"

Jake took it slowly. He didn't mention Stephen's vow of senior partnership. He'd relayed that promise too many times.

"I can't represent LINE when all the evidence points to their guilt. The company continued to convey to the public that there were no contamination issues with the river until the news outlets started reporting on the illnesses. Only then did they bring in specialists to research the issue. Conveniently, right before the first death."

Robert remained quiet while Jake talked but burst out laughing as soon as he'd finished.

Jake pressed back against the chair. "What's so funny?"

"You are a damn fool if you turn this case down. The fact that Stephen gave it to you is remarkable, but since he has, it is up to you to make the most of it. LINE can do a lot for your firm if you pull them out of this."

He closed his eyes briefly. Stephen had said nearly the same thing at the last partners' meeting. Giving his father his full attention, he waited for his final words. Every discussion with Robert ended with a closing statement.

"You want my advice? Take the case."

Jake didn't want to be a fool, but he also wanted to sleep at night.

After returning to the office, he asked Amy to see if Stephen had any free time for a short meeting. Then he barricaded himself behind his office door to create a winning strategy.

Amy knocked on the closed door and stuck her head into the office. "Stephen will see you at two. Is there anything you need me to prepare for you?"

"I'm good. Take the rest of the day off. Get yourself dolled up for tonight."

Her eyes widened. "You sure?"

He nodded. He didn't want any witnesses if things went south this afternoon. After Amy left, he reviewed his notes until he was confident he could convince Stephen to drop the case. At two, he knocked on Stephen's office door. Ready or not, this was his shot.

"Come in. Sit. I was surprised that you requested a meeting today. I thought you'd be helping Sophia with tonight's last-minute details."

"She's got everything covered."

"I bet she does. She's one of the most organized women I know. Speaking of tonight, I thought I'd announce your senior partnership after dinner. Think your old man will object to sharing his night with you?"

If he weren't so stressed, he would have laughed. No one shared the stage with his father. "About that. We need to talk. I think we're being shortsighted on the LINE case."

"We?"

Jake leaned forward. "I think there are other things to consider. If the firm takes this case, it will impact us negatively. There has been an uproar in the community. The contaminated water has ruined people's lives. Families have lost loved ones."

"Everyone deserves the right to representation."

"Yes. But maybe we could convince LINE to accept the blame and settle out of court. It would save them on court costs and be the right thing to do."

"But that's not what the client wants. The client wants to be found innocent of knowingly causing the tragedies that occurred."

They were clearly not speaking the same language. That they would never agree. But Jake gave it one more shot. "But the client is guilty."

Stephen smiled as if he were teaching the rule of law to a five-year-old. "But not until they've had their day in court."

He was getting nowhere. Standing, Jake held out his hand. "Thanks for your time."

"Hold on a second. Sit." Stephen swiveled to the antique sideboard behind his desk that took the place of a standard office credenza and picked up a box. Swinging back to face him, he handed it to Jake.

"Take a look."

Inside were what he assumed were business cards. He looked at Stephen.

"Go ahead. Pull one out."

Stephen was playing him for a sucker. He had no interest in considering his ideas and was wasting his time. Jake selected a card from the box and ran his thumb over it—triplex paper with gold foil stamping. His name was engraved on the card, with 'Senior Partner' underneath.

"All you have to do is accept the first-chair assignment."

Jake held the card in his hand. It felt substantial. It felt like everything he'd ever wanted. But the cost was too great. He moved to return the card to the box when Stephen stopped him. "Keep it." Returning the box to the sideboard, Stephen added, "Take the weekend. Think about it."

Chapter 36

Jake disconnected the call without leaving a message. He wanted to prepare Sophia, but she wasn't picking up. Pulling into his driveway, he drew in a ragged breath. How much more could he ask of her? He had until Monday to answer Stephen—he would either have his dream job or no job. He had to talk to Sophia.

With just enough time to shave, throw on his tux, and head to the hotel, he walked into the house to find Emily in the kitchen, wearing a pink strapless three-quarter-length gown that nipped in at the waist and flowed outward. She was the best thing he'd seen all day. And she was on the floor playing with the dogs.

"Em? I'll be ready in a minute." The last thing he wanted was to piss her off, but she was going to ruin her dress. "Maybe you should get off the floor."

There was more than typical teenage attitude on her face when she mumbled, "I wanted to go with Mom, but she said I had to wait for you."

He'd had enough. Between Stephen and his father, he had no time for Emily's snark. "Will you get up off the floor?"

Lilly growled, and Miss Molly whined. Emily stared at him.

He wanted to turn around, get back into his car, and drive until he ran out of gas. Instead, he held his hand out to help her up.

"That came out louder than I intended. I'm sorry. I've had a rough day, and we don't have much time. I get it. You're mad at me. But tonight isn't about you. It's your grandfather's night, and we are going to celebrate with him. Tomorrow, we can deal with what a jerk you think I am."

The ride to the hotel was silent, which was fine with him. He was out of words for the day, and the ones held in reserve were for Sophia. His mind set on finding his wife, they moved quickly through the ballroom until he caught Emily giving him the side eye. He stopped, nearly throwing them both off balance. Withholding as much of his exasperation as humanly possible, he addressed the situation.

"What? Why are you giving me that look?"

"Why do you keep patting your pocket? The noise is annoying."

He had no idea what she was talking about. "What?"

"That!"

When she pointed to his tuxedo pants, he realized he was continuously patting at his pocket as if his hand had a mind of its own, and sure enough, the rattling was irritating as hell.

"Sorry. I'm looking for your mother."

"So she can make you stop making a racket?"

He cracked a joke rather than tell the truth. Emily didn't need to know he could soon be out of a job. At least she didn't need to know tonight. She also didn't need to know that Sophia was considering leaving him and would decide as soon as the baby was born.

"I need to give your mother my car keys. See?" He pointed to the offending pocket. "The keys make my pocket bulge."

"They make you look fat? Seriously? I don't think you'd know what to do if you didn't have Mom." She looked at him as if she were twenty-five, not fifteen, and found him wanting. "And maybe you need to remember that."

He *wouldn't* know what to do without Sophia—that was the truth—but he wasn't about to explain that to Emily in the middle of a ballroom filled with his father's peers.

"Look, sweetheart, I'm human. It's not a crime to forget something, and I forgot that I'd been to see Marianne a second time. I explained all of this to your mother. She understands. Don't you think it's time for you to give me a break?"

Now I'm lying to Emily.

"It doesn't seem like she understands. It seems like you two have taken avoiding each other to a master-class level." Her eyes filled. "No matter how much I want to believe you, I don't. It's like I don't even know you anymore."

Jake wasn't expecting such honesty. Ignoring the guests moving past them, he pulled Emily to him and held her until she settled against his chest, her head nestled under his chin.

"Hey, I'm still your dad. I still love you. I know things have been crazy at home. They've been crazy at work, too, and with the baby coming soon and this party, Mom's been a little preoccupied. But everything's going to straighten out. Things will be better. *I* will be better. Give me a chance to make things right."

He stepped back and looked at her, praying he could make good on his promise. "You are a sight for your old man's eyes. I'm sorry I didn't tell you that earlier."

Emily opened her mouth as if... as if she would respond with a snide comment. Instead, she looked at her shoes, a blush blooming on her cheeks. He lifted her chin.

"Don't go shy on me now. You *are* beautiful. Inside and out. And I don't know how I got so lucky as to have you for my daughter. I guess I have your mother to thank for that too."

"You have Mom to thank for everything."

He laughed. This kid was tough. "You're right—I do. And speaking of your mom, let's go find her."

They caught sight of Sophia near the grand staircase. Once again, pregnancy had given her an inner glow that made anyone who saw her smile. Her dress bared one creamy shoulder, the shimmery fabric falling gracefully to her feet, almost obscuring her nearly nine-month pregnancy.

Watching Sophia greet Stephen and Audrey reminded Jake of the decision he had yet to make. Not that he needed reminding. Emily started in their direction, but he made no move to join her.

"Don't you want to say hello to the Cranstons?"

Before Jake could respond, Stephen and Audrey moved into the crowd quickly gathering near the bar, and he felt a momentary rush of relief, but then his parents made their way toward Sophia. There was no avoiding his father.

"Come on." He pulled Emily along as they headed in Sophia's direction. "Let's say hello before you find your friends."

He had hoped to talk to Sophia before the festivities began, but clearly, that would not happen. First, he had to play the doting son to the father who demanded so much yet gave so little in return.

He leaned in to kiss Sophia, but she sidestepped him, a reminder that she wasn't sure she still wanted to be married. Hoping no one had caught the exchange, he greeted his mother. Finally, he shook his father's hand, as he'd done earlier in the day.

Robert looked dashing in his tailor-made tuxedo. He seemed especially pleased with himself, as well he should. It had been months since his stroke, and for anyone who didn't know he'd been ill, there was no way to tell. And here they were, celebrating his seventy-fifth birthday.

"I trust you've made the right decision?"

Avoiding the question, Jake gazed at his mother. "You look stunning tonight, Mother."

Her eyes sparkled. "Not nearly as beautiful as your lovely wife and daughter. They are exquisite."

"They are." Sophia's gown complimented the dusty rose of the painted columns planted in each corner of the room and the architectural details on the ceiling so that no matter where people looked—at Sophia or around the room—they were dazzled by shades of rose and lilac.

Somehow, Sophia always managed to blend in and stand out at the same time, just like when he'd first met her in college. He hadn't been able to keep his eyes off her. He wished he'd never lost sight of her, and still, he continued to pat his damn pocket.

"Dad! For the love of *God,* will you give your keys to Mom and stop making so much noise?"

He grinned at how quickly Emily had regained her composure from their earlier conversation when she'd bared her vulnerability. Removing the keys from his pocket, he held them out to Sophia.

"Can you hold these for me? They are annoying our daughter."

"They are not annoying me. They're annoying everyone."

His parents laughed, and he hoped the levity would convince Sophia to react kindly. She took the keys and placed them in her purse but also managed to shoot him a look. Like he'd stepped in dog shit. There would be no playing nice in honor of his father's celebration from her end.

After Sophia left to greet the other guests, Emily went off with Maddie to join their friends, and he mingled on his own. Waitstaff passed through the room with trays laden with filled champagne flutes and small bites—baby beef Wellingtons enrobed in flaky pastry, brie-stuffed tartlets, arancini. Everything needed to whet the appetite before dinner.

The evening had been orchestrated within an inch of its life, ensuring it would be perfect. And perfection was what his father expected. Sophia had been right. The ballroom was the ideal place for this event. Its coffered ceiling, sixteen-foot columns, and spiral staircase offered the decorum his father demanded.

When Jake found Sophia again, she was reviewing the table settings with the head waiter. He waited until they'd finished then touched her arm lightly as she was ready to step away.

"Hey, I need to tell you something. It's probably not the best time..."

Sophia swung toward him with a momentum that surprised him. "You don't need to tell me anything."

Surprised—as if he would even dream of bringing Marianne's name into tonight's celebration—he muttered, "No. It's something else."

Her left eyebrow skittered upward. "You want to tell me about someone *else* you slept with?"

He stepped back as if she had struck him. "No." He looked around, mortified. "Let me explain."

"I doubt that you can." She stalked off, leaving him confused.

Not knowing what else to do, he did what he always did when he was in the same room as his father. He played the dutiful son, entertaining guests with stories of growing up in his father's house—not true stories—but funny ones. He grabbed a flute of champagne every time a waitperson came within reaching distance and hoped it would soon be time for dinner. If he kept drinking, he would be flat on his ass.

The next time Jake saw Sophia, she was at the top of the stairs, champagne flute in hand. Everyone quieted as soon as she raised her glass and addressed the crowd. She never understood how easily she captured the attention of both men and women, which was part of why he'd always loved her. She never recognized her strengths. He'd tell her that tonight.

"Good evening! I wanted to take a moment to thank you all for coming to celebrate Robert's birthday. The family hopes you have a wonderful time tonight as we honor Robert and share stories of his achievements." She took a sip from her flute and held it up to the crowd. "Apple juice!"

Everyone, including Jake, laughed, and she continued her speech. "You know Robert as your friend, your business acquaintance. Your partner."

Sophia focused on his mother, who stood next to the old man. "Your husband."

His mother's pride emanated off her like sunbeams glancing off a mirrored surface. It never failed to amaze him how she refused to recognize his dark side.

Sophia waited for the applause to die down. "Here's to Robert! The man of the hour."

A smirk crossed his father's face as he acknowledged Sophia, his entire body seemingly reflecting his delight as he accepted her accolades as his due.

Jake tried to catch Sophia's attention while the guests applauded, but every time their eyes met, hers danced away as if she couldn't bear the sight of him. He didn't like how she seemed to favor her left side as if she were in pain. But there was something else too. It was like she was burning up inside, not with fever, but something even more threatening. And when she stumbled, his heart nearly stopped, starting again after she caught hold of the railing.

She held up her hand to show that she was okay and then, without missing a beat, gave their guests the parting words they were waiting for. "I believe dinner is served. Please enjoy your evening."

We don't need to stay for the dinner. The evening is a success even by my father's standards. We can go home and talk. I'll tell her about my job. We can start over.

Sophia slipped off her heels, slowly straightened, and descended the stairs. Even from where he stood, he could see her teeth chattering. Refusing to look at him, she stepped back when he leaned in to kiss her.

"I'm leaving. Please give my excuses to everyone."

"Wait a minute. I'll go with you. We need to talk."

"We have nothing to talk about."

They were making a scene, but he no longer cared. "I'm not letting you go until you tell me what's wrong."

"What's *wrong*?" Her eyes brimmed with tears. Throwing her shoes at his feet, she whispered, "Do you really want to ask me that?"

"I... did Stephen talk to you? I wanted to tell you myself."

"Stephen? What does Stephen have to do with this?" Before he could respond, Sophia headed for the exit, walking right by Emily.

"Mom?" Emily reached out toward her mother, but Sophia appeared blinded by tears and anger.

"What's going on? Why's Mom barefoot?" Emily picked up Sophia's shoes, which were still on the floor at his feet. "Why were you yelling at each other?"

Before Jake could respond, Robert stopped him as Sophia disappeared through the hotel doorway.

"You just can't let me have my night without making a scene, can you?"

"Not now, Dad."

"Don't 'not now' me. I'm your father."

Jake grabbed Sophia's shoes from Emily and followed after his wife.

Emily, trailing closely behind her father, yelled, "Dad! Stop. What's going on?"

They reached the valet station in time to see Sophia slowly maneuvering his car down the circular driveway.

"What the *hell*, Dad?" Emily grabbed his arm. "Why's Mom leaving?"

Ignoring Emily, he kept his eyes on his car until it disappeared.

"Why is Mom driving your car?"

"Not *now*." Turning to the valet, Jake handed him a fifty and requested the hotel limo drive Emily home.

"No! I'm not leaving."

He grabbed her hands. "Look, I need you to go home and be with Mom. I can't leave yet."

"Come with me!" Emily looked as if her entire world was collapsing.

The pain in his daughter's eyes was heartbreaking, and it crushed him that he was the one to put it there. But he couldn't leave until he talked to Matt and Christine. He had to know what was going on before he faced Sophia again.

"I can't. But I'll be home soon. Please. Do as I ask."

His head was pounding. But Emily didn't budge. Frustrated, he grabbed the fifty back from the valet, shoved it into his breast pocket, and headed for the ballroom, Emily struggling to keep up with his long strides.

Jake had no sooner reentered the ballroom than Matt and Christine approached from the side. Matt grabbed his arm and spun him around.

"Where did she go?"

"She... she took my car. Said she was going home. What happened today? Why is Sophia even more upset?"

Matt turned away as if he could barely look at Jake then swung around, asking his own question. "Why did you wait so long to tell her?"

Thinking back, he had no idea. "I was afraid..."

Filled with remorse, Jake hoped he could appeal to Christine's compassion. "What's going on?"

Christine didn't look any happier to see him than Matt. "She went to see Marianne today."

"She did what?" Jake's chest burned as if Christine had thrust a red-hot poker into it. "Why would she do that?"

"She wanted to tell Marianne that she had loved her like a sister. That she couldn't understand how Marianne would betray her. She wanted to ask her why."

Matt refused to look at him while Christine talked, but Jake couldn't think about Matt, about how, along with everything else, he'd ruined their friendship. He could barely listen to Christine.

"I'm worried about her," Christine said. "She was in bad shape when she left our house this afternoon to get ready for tonight. I can't imagine how she drove home from St. Johnsbury and pulled off this event."

He knew exactly how she did it. Sophia needed to see Marianne's regret—her pain. She needed to know she wasn't the only one devastated by his sins. That was where she had found the strength to get home.

"Please. We're a family. We belong to each other."

"You need to go home, Jake. *You* need to talk to Sophia."

Christine opened her mouth as if she were on the verge of saying more, but Matt pulled her back before she could utter another word, the look in his eyes reflecting his unchecked anger.

"Family? You should have thought about losing your family before you slept with Mari—"

"Matt!" Christine's desperation-filled warning was too late.

Jake barely recognized the fury in Matt's voice. But he knew Emily's when he swung around to face her.

"You *slept* with Marianne?" The color had drained from her tear-stained face.

His mind spiraled from everything that had gone wrong. "It's not what you think."

They stared at each other for no more than a heartbeat. Then, Emily reached into his breast pocket and snatched the fifty peeking out of the top. And then she was gone.

"Jake!" Matt yelled. "Stop her!"

But he just stood there while Christine and Matt ran after Emily.

How did this day so quickly go to hell? He needed a drink. The hotel bar was empty when he slid onto a stool, and since he was the only customer, the bartender showed up quickly to take his order.

"Maker's Mark. Double. Thanks."

The bourbon was smooth. Jake intended to sip it then go home and try to clean up the mess he'd made. Instead, he finished his drink quickly and ordered another.

This time, the bartender stuck around. "Looked like a great party."

Jake was in no mood to talk. Instead, he lifted his empty glass. "I'll have another."

Chapter 37

Emily's tears fell like raindrops on Jake's face when she dropped to her knees beside him on the kitchen floor.

"Dad!"

The plea in her eyes was devastating. Jake twisted away, wanting to hide.

Finally, her voice wavering, she begged, "I need you. Mom needs you! The baby's coming."

She sounded as if she were submerged, her words garbled and burbling over. *The baby.* He struggled to listen. This was his daughter, and she needed him. He pushed himself upright and shook off the fogginess that threatened to envelop him. Shook off his pride that seemed so meaningless in the face of her need. He pulled her in close and hugged her tightly.

"Let's go," he told her. He was sure that was what he said.

But later—he had no idea how much later—when he cracked open an eye, he was still flat on the floor. The only thing he'd managed to do was rid himself of his jacket. Emily was nowhere in sight, while Lilly licked his face as if she could revive him. He wanted to tell her that it would take more than her tongue lapping at his cheeks to bring him back to life, but his eyelid slammed shut again before he could utter a word.

He'd had too much to drink. "I'll have another," he remembered saying. The memory made him want to vomit. And each time he'd uttered those words, another drink was set before him until, finally, the bartender told him to go home. He wasn't even sure how he got home.

The next thing he knew, he was looking up at Matt's face. And the man did not look happy. Jake swallowed, his throat a sandbox that stray cats had mistaken for a litterbox.

"What are you doing here?"

"Get up."

Matt hoisted him up the stairs and into the bathroom, where Jake collapsed on the floor. Faster than he cared for, Matt dragged him up off the floor and shoved him into the shower, where ice-cold water rained down on him. His tuxedo would never be the same.

"Jesus Christ!" Jake flung the shower door open and collapsed onto the rug, shivering. "What the hell are you doing?" Everything was happening so fast he couldn't think.

"Take your clothes off and get back into the shower. The baby's coming. And even if I would be happy to never see you again, your wife might want you to be there."

Sophia? He wasn't sure she would want him anywhere near her, but he did what he was told and struggled out of his tux, ripping his shirt off and sending his cufflinks skittering across the bathroom floor.

"Emily called after she couldn't get you up." Matt spat the words out as if his disgust was choking him. "Sophia was going to drive herself to the hospital. Luckily, she listened to Emily, and we took them. I said I'd come back for you. Don't make me sorry that I did."

Jake struggled into the shower again. He hadn't dreamed that Emily'd tried to revive him. He couldn't imagine ever facing her again. After letting the frigid water wash over him until he couldn't stand it any longer, he rotated the faucet to hot until his skin felt like it would blister. Matt threw him a towel when he opened the door.

He was sober but shaky when they backtracked through the bedroom. Sophia's gown was on the floor in a heap of silk, the contents of her beaded bag alongside it, lipstick, tissues, and a couple of crackers, scattered everywhere. It looked like she couldn't wait to shed the trappings of her evening.

The ride was quick but filled with Matt's disdain. "Sophia told Chris that Marianne loves you. Is that true?"

Jake winced. "No! We agreed it was a one-time thing that could never happen again."

Bile rose in Jake's throat. The look on Marianne's face when he'd glimpsed her through the rear window of his car the day he told her to return Sophia's calls—it hadn't been guilt or remorse. Her love had devastated him because he loved Sophia. That was the truth. No matter how many lies he had told, he had never stopped loving Sophia.

Barely able to keep up, Jake followed Matt into the hospital and down the long hallway to Sophia's room, every step shooting a knife into his head. Matt swung into the room quickly, eager to leave the stain of his proximity far behind, but Jake stopped in the doorway, unsure of his welcome.

When Matt suggested Christine and Emily join him for breakfast, Jake realized it was the next day, and his father's party was already relegated to the past.

Christine looked at her watch. "Sophia's just come off a contraction. They've slowed up quite a bit since we arrived. It should be okay to leave her for a few minutes. Em? Let's take a break."

"You go. I'm not leaving Mom. Take Dad. He probably needs to refuel." Emily didn't bother looking in his direction when she added, "I'm not sure a gallon of coffee will help him, but I suppose it's worth a try."

Jake flinched. He could have spread the derision in Emily's voice with a knife.

"Go," Sophia urged. "All of you." She kept her eyes on Jake but spoke to Emily. "I'll be right here when you come back."

Emily looked none too sure of that. "Promise?"

"On my honor." Sophia kissed Emily's cheek, adding, "Em? Let's keep this day venom free, okay?"

The room emptied, but he remained standing in the doorway. His head was on fire, and his insides felt like someone had ripped them out and danced on them. He still smelled the liquor seeping from his skin even though he'd showered until he stopped mumbling gibberish.

After the others left, Sophia closed her eyes. The easiest recourse to make him disappear, he suspected. If Jake was going to make this right, he had to do more than wish he'd never made it wrong. How much would he give for a chance to do it all over? *Everything. I would give everything.*

Jake moved closer to the bed. "I'm sorry. For sleeping with Marianne. For not telling you the truth. I'm sorry I've been such a bastard. I'm sorry you had to confront Marianne." His hands shook so badly that he shoved them into his pockets. "I'm sorry I was too drunk to take you to the hospital."

That was when the worst memory surfaced. Emily knew he'd slept with Marianne. The look on her face when he'd found her standing behind him at the hotel with Matt's words ringing in the air.

"I'm sorry that Emily knows about Marianne. She overheard Matt at the hotel last night."

Her eyes opened slowly. "She told me." Sophia was eerily calm, and it set his nerves on edge.

"What did she say?"

He wasn't sure he wanted to know, but he didn't deserve protection from Emily's scorn. He would never forget the pain and disgust that flashed across her face. His declaration of remorse would never make up for destroying his daughter's faith in him.

"She thinks you're a jerk. She says she no longer knows who you are but is pretty sure she hates you."

He bowed his head, taking Emily's revulsion as his due. "What did you say to her?"

"I told her I already knew. That you told me." Sophia's hands made circles on her belly—little loops that grew bigger until she had covered the circumference with imaginary spheres. The motion was mesmerizing.

"I wouldn't worry about what she says right now. Emily worships the ground you walk on—maybe not lately, but other than these last months, her only goal has always been to be just like you. I told her that you love her. That hate's a strong word."

Sophia gave him hope even though it was the last thing he deserved. "You are a better person than me."

"I know." She didn't even smile. "Teenagers think in black and white. Good or bad. They aren't old enough to see what might be in the middle. I told her I didn't think you set out to hurt us. What you did was wrong, but maybe it wasn't evil."

"What did she say to that?"

"She still wants me to leave you." Her voice was flat. Any emotion left in her squeezed out, a puddle to be wiped up and forgotten.

The words were barely out of her mouth when her belly tightened under the sheet that covered her. Jake was unprepared for the crazed look in her eyes and the wail that escaped from deep within her as she reached blindly for his hand.

"Christine said the contractions were mild?" His voice was shaky.

"Not anymore." She took slow, deep breaths, breathing through her mouth, staring at him.

Jake stabbed at the call button until a nurse appeared. "Help her!" He gripped Sophia's hand tightly while the nurse checked her progress.

"She's coming along nicely—don't you worry. I'll call the doctor, but she has a little way to go yet." And with that, she was gone.

Within minutes, Sophia took a deep breath, releasing her grip on his hand as if slime covered it.

He had to tell her everything, even if he confessed between contractions. "I know you went to see Marianne today." Remembering the pink sky he'd seen earlier, he amended, "Yesterday."

He couldn't imagine what it must have taken for her to confront Marianne. To listen as Marianne admitted the truth when he had dodged it to save his skin for so long.

"She loves you. I saw it in her eyes. In the way she spoke your name."

She was telling the truth even though it was the last thing he wanted to admit. "I know."

"Do you love her?" There was a bite to Sophia's question, and he feared she was building up to a confrontation that he was pretty sure wouldn't be good for either her or the baby.

"No! I thought..."

Her agitation continued to grow and was spiraling out of control. "You thought *what*?" Her voice rose, and her earlier calm was missing, as if that last contraction had finally knocked some sense into her. "That you can come in here while I'm delivering the baby of the woman you slept with, and I'd forgive you because you finally had the guts to tell me the truth?"

Before he could respond, the nurse charged in. "This is not the place for yelling!" She looked from him to Sophia to reassure herself that they understood she meant business. "Whatever is going on in here needs to stop." Turning on her heel, she pinned her eyes on him and added, "And you should be ashamed of yourself."

Suitably chastised, he hoped he wouldn't say anything else to incur Sophia's ire.

Ignoring him, Sophia concentrated on her breathing, but finally, she huffed, "Whoever thought natural childbirth was a good idea was a man."

Unlike the last contraction that had taken them by surprise, this one seemed to build slowly. The picture of Emily with Lilly and Miss Molly was nowhere in the room. But she'd been admitted as an emergency—three weeks before the baby was due. Most likely, the bag with the photo meant to help Sophia focus on something other than the contractions ripping through her body was still sitting in the corner of their bedroom.

Sophia rubbed the small of her back as best she could, her mouth a thin line of pain, and he risked moving forward.

"Let me do that."

She tensed when he laid his hand on her back, but he didn't move it, and when she didn't say anything, he gently applied pressure, moving his fingers slowly until he reached the base of her spine. She sucked in her breath, and he froze.

"Did I hurt you?"

"No. Don't stop." Her words were barely audible but gave him hope.

He rested one hip on the bed while he rubbed her lower back. Gradually, as she leaned into him, he deepened the pressure until he heard her sigh of relief. *Finally, I've done something right.*

"Don't think for one moment that I forgive you because you are helping me now."

Jake had hoped for that very thing even though he would cut out his tongue before admitting it. Fingers nearly numb from the repetitive motion, he strained to maintain the pressure and remain alert when, minutes later, Sophia spoke again.

"What were you trying to tell me in the ballroom?"

Struggling to get her to stand still long enough to tell her about Stephen, about his job, none of it seemed important at that moment. "This isn't the time, Soph."

"Unless you are sleeping with someone else, you might as well tell me now."

Her voice hinted at sarcasm. Maybe she didn't believe there hadn't been anyone else, but Jake still cringed when he thought about what he had done.

"Stephen has given me until Monday to let him know if I'll take the LINE case. If I turn it down, I'll most likely be looking for another job." He reached into his pocket for the business card with his name on it then remembered it was in his tuxedo jacket.

"I wanted to talk to you before I spoke to Stephen, but I couldn't reach you." That conversation seemed like a lifetime ago instead of yesterday. "The LINE people were aware of the risks and allowed the pollution to continue. They only brought in specialists when the public raised their concerns."

He laughed, low and bitter. "I'm not some goddamn saint, but I don't think I can do what Stephen wants, what my father wants. I had hoped I'd just be giving up my chance to become a senior partner and that I'd have time to figure out what I wanted to do next. But when I told Stephen how I felt, he wasn't interested in anything I had to say." Jake ran his hands through his hair, pushing the feel of the luxurious business cards with his name on them out of his head.

Sophia listened without interruption, separating this issue from everything else they faced. "I think you already know what the right thing is."

He did.

Dr. Kelley strode into the room just then and examined Sophia. "How long since your last contraction?"

Sophia bit her lip. "We were talking. I guess I didn't notice that it's been a while."

"No worries. It happens sometimes. Why don't you and your husband walk in the hallway and see if that doesn't get things going again?"

Dr. Kelley put his hand on Jake's shoulder on his way out of the room. "How about you? Holding up?"

He nodded even though he wasn't at all sure that "holding up" would adequately describe the fear running through his veins.

Jake handed Sophia her robe and helped her out of bed. They turned left on their way out of the room, planning to circle the entire floor, hoping that would get things started again.

"Maybe we'll run into Marianne when we pass the nurses' station."

He almost tripped over the IV pole they were pushing. "What?" Jake could barely hear her name without waves of remorse washing over him.

Sophia nodded. "She's coming to share the birth. I promised her."

Jake faltered. "Soph, she's not going to want to be here, not after... everything."

"Yes, she is. This is her baby. She'll be here."

Chapter 38

Jake and Sophia had no sooner returned to her room than the contractions revved up. Within minutes, they were nonstop, and he forgot about Marianne as Sophia writhed in pain, her face red with exertion, sweat running in rivulets into her hair. He had never felt so helpless in his life.

"What can I do?" He reached out to smooth Sophia's hair from where it stuck to her face, but this time, she recoiled from his touch. "I'm sorry! I was trying to..."

Her eyes were wild. "You want to help? Get this baby out of me." Her head twisted from side to side, and she squeezed his hand so tightly he was sure he would need X-rays. "Call the nurse. I need to push."

When Dr. Kelley arrived, he agreed it was time to meet the baby.

Two nurses wheeled Sophia to the operating suite. He followed along closely, stopping long enough to throw on scrubs. But then he halted, his eyes fastened on Sophia's.

"You coming?" the nurse at the foot of the bed demanded as if she doubted his ability to go the distance. He didn't blame her.

He'd missed Emily's birth, and he desperately wanted to be with his wife, but the decision wasn't his. But when Sophia nodded, he strode through the door as if he belonged there.

The bright lights forced him to squint. Machines beeped. Voices were fast and furious. People hurtled themselves through the room.

Dizzy, he closed his eyes to keep the room from spinning, wondering what the hell he'd gotten himself into.

Seconds later, the room went calm. The only thing moving at breakneck speed had been his imagination, maybe his heart. Humbled, Jake kept his eyes on Sophia, lying on a narrow OR bed with a sheet draped over her.

Dr. Kelley arrived within minutes. "Okay, Sophia. Let's do this."

Jake moved to the head of Sophia's bed. His job would be to support her when she pushed.

"Marianne's not here yet." Sophia tried to pull herself into a sitting position. Failing, she expelled a deep breath and laid back again, tears seeping into the sheet. "This is her baby."

He imagined Marianne in the room. There would be no need for him if she were here.

"Sorry. This baby's not waiting, Sophia." Dr. Kelley's voice was firm. "Push!"

Her face was red with effort, and the guttural sounds escaping from deep inside her reminded Jake of a deer he had encountered in the woods with its leg caught in a trap. Sophia pushed. In between, she asked for Marianne.

"She's not here, Soph." He didn't want her here, but he kept that to himself.

Dr. Kelley seemed even less interested in Marianne's arrival than Jake. "Push like you mean it, Sophia. No holding back."

She didn't hold back. She was strong, brave, and beautiful. He'd never loved her more. He pressed against her back to give her support while a nurse swiped at the sweat running down her face. He had no idea why women ever wanted children if this was what they had to endure to have one. In the overhead mirror, Jake saw the baby's head emerge, then her shoulders, then the rest of her, and when she loudly greeted them, he had never heard anything sweeter in his life.

Sophia burst into tears and lay back on the bed, exhausted, but still, her eyes searched the room. "Marianne?"

"I'm sorry, Soph, she's not here." After everything Sophia had learned about their deception, he didn't understand why Marianne's presence was so important. He couldn't bring himself to tell her that Marianne was the last person he wanted to see.

The nurse laid the baby on Sophia's chest while the doctor clamped the cord. Everyone hesitated slightly when they realized Marianne was supposed to cut the cord. They looked to him in her absence.

Jake looked around the room, even happier that Marianne was late. "Tell me what to do," he finally responded, accepting the surgical scissors.

Sophia grabbed Jake's arm when an orderly arrived to take her to her room. "Call Marianne. Tell her the baby's here."

"Soph, I don't think..."

"Please!"

His prayers were answered when no one picked up, and he left a message announcing the baby's birth.

Exhausted, he made his way to the labor room that Sophia had vacated not so long ago to discover a new patient pacing the floor. He found Emily, Matt, and Christine in a waiting room thanks to a nurse whose job was apparently to keep track of patients and their families.

His fatigue had disappeared. All he could think about was how formidable Sophia had been.

"Everyone's fine," he announced, moving toward Emily, who allowed him to hug her after a moment's hesitation.

"Mom's...?"

"She's good. So's the baby."

Before he could say more, a police officer entered the room.

"Sophia Trenton?" The man must have been six and a half feet tall.

"Can I help you, officer?"

"I need to have a word with Mrs. Trenton. Or her husband?"

Taking a step back, Jake was confused as to why the police would be looking for Sophia so early in the morning. "Sophia's resting. She just delivered a baby. I'm her husband, Jake. What's this all about?"

The officer held out his hand. "Cole Ellis." Pulling a notebook from his pocket, he flipped it open. "Adam and Marianne Barclay? Your wife is their emergency contact. With you as the secondary contact?"

"I... Yes."

He refused to think about why their names were on that card, how Sophia had begged him to add his name along with hers so the Barclays would have two emergency contacts. But he was still confused by the police officer's presence.

"Like I said, my wife's resting. This isn't a good time."

Scanning the room, Officer Ellis hesitated. "Is there somewhere we can talk privately?"

Jake's earlier euphoria from watching Sophia give birth disappeared, and he was in no mood to be sociable. Not with a stranger, anyway. "These are my friends and my daughter, Emily. You can say whatever you need to in front of them."

All eyes were on Officer Ellis when he delivered his news. "There's been an accident. We called the phone number on the contact form, and when no one answered, we drove to your house."

He rechecked his notebook and added, "One of your neighbors, Mrs. Johnston? She told us your wife was here."

Officer Ellis turned to Christine and Matt. When his eyes landed on Emily, he looked back to Jake. "Your daughter? You might not want..."

Emily was on her phone, most likely announcing the baby's birth to Maddie, and Jake's patience was wearing thin. The only thing he could think about was Sophia.

"Get on with it."

"Yes, sir. The Barclays were involved in a hit-and-run tonight out on Hardwick Road."

"What? Is everyone okay?"

When Officer Ellis didn't respond, Jake's chest grew tight. The air got stuck somewhere in the middle every time he inhaled, and his lungs shut down.

He no longer wanted to know how they were, but Officer Ellis told him anyway. "I'm afraid neither one survived."

He wasn't sure that he understood. The officer's lips moved, and his look of commiseration nudged Jake's brain that something tragic had occurred, but still, his words made no sense.

"*What?*" There was a buzzing in his ears.

Officer Ellis's mouth was still moving.

"What did you say?" Finally, the words slowly seeped in, and his heart slammed against his chest as if looking for an exit. Nowhere in his scenario of fixing his mistakes had he pictured a world where Marianne wasn't in it.

"The Barclays..."

Jake waved his arm in fury. He didn't need to hear it again. *What the hell is this?*

He hadn't paid attention to God since the night Robbie died, but instead of him, the Barclays had paid for his sins. For one moment, he thought this was a practical joke and the guy was there to sell tickets to the annual chicken barbeque. But the look on Officer Ellis's face assured Jake this was no joke. Hardwick Road. They must have been on their way to the hospital.

"What happened?"

"Drunk driver. Luckily, there was a witness. A woman lost control of her vehicle and hit the Barclays' car head-on. And she's barely got a scratch on her." He shook his head. "I hate drunk drivers more than anything."

Emily's phone dropped. She looked from him to Officer Ellis.

"Drunk drivers?" She threw herself at Jake. "They're *dead*? I told her I never wanted to talk to her again! I hung up on her when Mom made me call to tell her the baby was coming!"

Emily pivoted slowly around the room, but each face confirmed the words she'd heard.

Finally, she whispered, "And now, she's *dead*?"

Instead of beating wildly, Jake's heart felt like it had stopped. He held Emily's face between his hands, forcing her to look at him.

"Listen to me. Marianne knew you were upset. A lot was going on. She knew you were scared and mad. She knew... she knew you had every right to feel all of those things. The baby was the only thing on her mind."

Only seconds after Officer Ellis left, Dr. Kelley arrived. They barely had time to process Adam and Marianne's death before the doctor grasped Jake's hand.

"Congratulations. Sophia and the baby are perfect. Did Marianne get here?"

"She..." Everyone in the room was in shock. Too much had happened too quickly. "Marianne and her husband, Adam, were killed in a car accident tonight. On the way here."

Dr. Kelley's smile disappeared, and all the joy he'd brought with him melted away as if they had imagined it. "I'm so sorry. Sophia will be devastated."

Jake scrubbed his hand over his face and glanced at his watch—the first of June. He fucking hated the month of June. "I need to tell Sophia."

"Not tonight. She's had enough excitement for one day."

Emily reached out to stop Dr. Kelley when he headed toward the door.

"When can I see my mom?"

"She's resting right now. How about you let your dad see her first? And you can have her all day tomorrow." Turning to Jake, he added, "Just for a few minutes."

Chapter 39

The crucifix over the bed reminded Jake of the one that hung over Marianne's. He shivered and turned his gaze to Sophia, determined never to lose sight of her again.

Her body curled into itself, reflecting the stress she had endured these past months. It was up to him to tell her that her loss was even more than any of them could have imagined. This loss was forever. But she didn't need to know that tonight.

"Hey, can I come in?" He stood quietly, waiting for admittance.

Sophia's eyes said he was the last person she wanted to see, but she nodded, wrapping her arms protectively around her middle, her need for him in the delivery room a fading memory. He pulled a chair over to the bed, wanting to pick her up and hold her, protect her from all she would soon learn. But he couldn't protect her from anything.

"Did Marianne get here? Has she seen Mia?" Sophia's voice was no more than a whisper.

"No." That was the correct answer, but it didn't come close to the truth. His eyes shifted to the crucifix, and he backtracked. "I don't know."

Sophia struggled to a sitting position, releasing a small gasp of pain. "Haven't you seen her?"

"No." *There's been an accident.* Officer Ellis's words echoed in his head, growing louder with each beat of his heart. He forced himself to continue, raising his voice to block out the words of the man who had simply been doing his job. "I'm sure she'll be here soon." He looked everywhere but at Sophia.

She cocked her head as if she were weighing the truth of his statement. "What's going on? What are you keeping from me?"

"Nothing." *Everything. They're dead, Sophia.* His eyes skittered across the room, searching for a diversion. "Please. Can we not talk about Marianne for a minute? Can we talk about us?"

"Us?" The word held no warmth. No hope. She snatched the call button from the bedside railing.

"What are you doing?"

"I'm calling the nurse to find out if Marianne's been to the nursery."

He grabbed the button out of her hand. "You're supposed to be resting."

"Asking for a nurse is hardly going to wear me out." She held out her hand. He placed the call button on the bed between them—Switzerland lying benignly between Germany and France.

"I need to tell you something."

"I think you've told me enough for one day." She seemed to think about that, adding, "I'm not sure you ever need to tell me anything again."

Sophia grabbed the call button and held it tightly to her chest. If he wanted it, he would have to wrestle her for it.

"But..."

"But what? You're *sorry*? You ruin our lives and think that apologizing will make it all better. Make me forgive you? The baby is the only thing I can think about right now. I need to know if Marianne has seen her baby."

Jake rubbed his eyes, willing his exhaustion to disappear. "How can you be so concerned about Marianne... after everything?" He would never understand. *Why doesn't she hate her? Why isn't she the last person—other than me—she wants to see?*

"Because of the baby. The baby needs to see her mother."

Dr. Kelley might never understand, but Sophia would not rest until she knew the truth. He wrapped his hands around hers.

"The police were here." He stumbled over words that were still too raw. "There's been an accident."

"What do you mean?"

"A car accident. A... a drunk driver." His pulse raced, and his jaw throbbed. Once again, he glanced at the crucifix over Sophia's bed as if it would absolve him of his sins.

"What are you talking about? What car accident?"

Jake pulled his eyes from the wooden cross, knowing sorrow would replace Sophia's agitation.

"I'm sorry, Soph. They..." He could barely spit the words out. "They didn't make it."

Sophia's eyes shifted from him to the empty doorway to the windowsill, where a bouquet of gerbera daisies already brightened the room, their very presence making his announcement a travesty.

"*Who* didn't make it?"

Sucking in a mouthful of air and slowly letting it out, Jake struggled to answer. "Marianne. And Adam. They died tonight on the way to the hospital." *They died tonight while I prayed that Marianne would be late so that I could take her place in the delivery room. They died while I helped you deliver the baby. They died while I cut the umbilical cord. They died...*

He repeated Officer Ellis's message, hoping he hadn't caused more harm. "By some woman who drove into their car."

Sophia lowered herself back onto the bed as if she were made of glass and might shatter at any moment.

"Soph?" He rubbed her fingers, hoping she knew he was still there. Would always be there for her.

Long minutes later, she turned toward him. "*Dead?* They're *both* dead?"

He nodded. Releasing her hands, he swiped across his face as if he could wipe the strain of these last few hours away. But it wouldn't be that easy. Neither of them would forget Marianne.

"But the baby's here. She's in the nursery." Bewilderment filled Sophia's voice.

"I know."

"What's going to happen to Mia?"

His heart stuttered. He had never reconciled how easily Sophia and Marianne had gone from talking about "the baby" to calling her by her name as if she were real when there were still months before she would be born. He guessed the baby had been real to them the moment Dr. Kelley confirmed Sophia's pregnancy.

Shaking his head, Jake forced himself to answer Sophia's question. "I don't know. They're going to need time to review the will. To see who Marianne named as guardian."

Sophia swallowed. "Guardian?"

He leaned forward, gently urging a stray curl back behind her ear. "You know they had to name a guardian."

Sophia's fingers splayed against the white sheet. "But we never thought... why was Adam even with her?"

"What?"

"Adam. They're practically divorced. Why was Adam with her in the car?"

Jake had wondered the same thing. "I don't know. Maybe... maybe they were getting back together. Maybe he'd changed his mind about the baby." *I hope that's true. That after all this, they found each other again.* "I guess we'll never know."

As if Sophia hadn't strayed from the topic of guardianship, she plunged back in. "Her cousin Kerry from one of the Carolinas—I forget which one—is the guardian. Bring me my purse. It's in the closet."

It didn't surprise him that Sophia knew who Marianne had named as guardian and that he had no clue. The two women had shared everything about this pregnancy. What shocked him was that Marianne hadn't named Sophia guardian.

Sophia extracted a business card from her wallet and glanced at it. "She's from South Carolina."

"Why didn't Marianne name you guardian?"

Sophia's entire body froze. "That's not exactly encouraged in surrogacy situations. Besides... besides, I couldn't do that to you. You never wanted another baby." She closed her eyes briefly, and grief washed across her face as she extended the card to him.

"Give this to the police if they're still here. Or call them. I'm not sure they'll need it or if the hospital has provided any information from the surrogacy center, but it can't hurt."

He reached for the card, but Sophia held on as if even that small piece of cardstock was difficult to relinquish. When she finally released it, the card fluttered toward the floor before he scooped it up.

"And then stop at the nursery and tell them to bring Mia."

"Dr. Kelley says you need to rest."

"I'm sure I do, but I need to hold that baby first."

This was the moment Jake finally accepted that Marianne's baby was in the nursery, alive, and Marianne was dead.

Chapter 40

Nothing would console Emily until she had seen Sophia. And even that wasn't enough. She spent the night in Sophia's room while Jake paced the hallways, wanting to find a place to close his eyes yet never wanting to close them again.

The following day, he found his daughter asleep, snuggled up to Sophia, one arm draped across her chest. Emily must have made quite a fuss for the nurses to allow her to stay. He was almost sorry he'd missed it. Yawning, he canvassed the room and caught sight of a cot, most likely meant for Emily.

He gently nudged her, hoping to get her moving but not disturb Sophia. "Hey, time to wake up."

Emily stretched like she had the bed to herself, opened her eyes, and gave him the briefest of smiles, but the moment reality hit, her smile disappeared, and she looked away.

"Mom's okay." He kept his voice low and reassuring. "She needs to rest. How are you doing?"

Relief, followed by anger, flickered across Emily's face. Finally, she muttered, "Marianne and Adam are dead." Her words held everything he felt.

"I know." They both went silent. Swallowing the truth of the last twenty-four hours took all his strength. Emily likely felt the same.

"What's going to happen to Mia?"

That is the question. "I don't know, sweetheart." He didn't have it in him to explain that the baby would move away and they'd likely never see her again.

There was no time to say more. A nurse arrived with a screaming baby in her arms. Sophia awakened instantly. The look on her face reminded him of when Emily woke in the middle of the night so many years ago. This time, sorrow wedged itself in with all that expectation.

"This little girl is hungry." The nurse's voice grew louder as the baby's screams intensified, but even distracted, she caught sight of Emily and added, "And aren't you supposed to be in that cot?"

"Give her to me," Sophia interrupted, exposing her breast before the baby was even in her arms. Unwrapping the tightly bound swaddling, she lifted the baby to her breast and sank back into the pillow when the baby latched onto her nipple.

Jake had to look away rather than give in to the sense of loss that immediately overwhelmed him.

Sophia had readily agreed to nurse the baby for the first few weeks after her birth because it was good for both of them. He wasn't surprised that she hadn't changed her mind after discovering he'd spent the night with Marianne. Nothing about Sophia surprised him.

The sound of the baby nursing filled the room. These personal moments were meant to be shared between his wife and the woman he'd once agonized over. The woman who was now dead. Aware that he didn't belong here but refusing to leave, he focused on Emily. It was safer to keep his eyes on her while she ignored the chastising nurse and settled in, her eyes glued to her mother.

"How do babies know to do that?"

Sophia yawned. "Instinct, I guess."

The baby's eyes closed, and her mouth loosened its grip on Sophia's nipple. Only then could he look at the infant in Sophia's arms.

"Can I hold her?" Emily pulled herself into a sitting position, leaning forward with anticipation, and directed the question to her mother.

"Certainly not," the nurse responded. Lifting the baby from Sophia's chest, she glanced at Emily's crestfallen face and reversed her answer. "You can hold her when I bring her the next time. As long as you're out of this bed and your hands are washed."

Sophia was drifting toward sleep when Emily carefully lifted herself from the bed, but the slight movement was still enough to nudge her awake. She touched Emily's wrist. "Where are you going?"

"Dad wants to take me for breakfast." Emily's tone suggested she wasn't looking forward to spending time with him, but at least she'd agreed to leave the room.

"Hey, go easy on him, will you?"

Sophia's look told him unequivocally that she was doing this for their daughter's sake. Not his.

"Like he's been easy on us?" Emily moved toward the door without checking to see if he was following.

Sophia stopped her before she escaped. "Honey, I know you're upset. We're all upset, but this is between your father and me. You need to trust me to handle this."

Emily hesitated, looking like she wanted to object, but instead, she backtracked, kissed Sophia's cheek, and left the room. He hurried to catch up to her.

Expecting his daughter to be sullen at breakfast since Sophia wasn't there to intervene, Jake was pleased when she gushed about Sophia breastfeeding the baby as he followed her through the hot food line in the cafeteria. Not that breastfeeding was a topic he wanted to think about, let alone respond to, but she could pick any subject as long as it meant they were talking.

Balancing his tray that held coffee and food he had no taste for, he paid the cashier and headed to a table facing the wall at the back of the room, uninterested in conversing with strangers in various degrees of either grief or joy.

"I'm glad we're having breakfast together." Pushing aside his omelet, he wrapped both hands around his mug of coffee, his first sip reinforcing his belief that nothing good ever came out of a hospital cafeteria.

"Mom told me I had to be nice. Remember?"

Jake took another sip of the bitter brew, letting it roll around in his mouth. He considered spitting it out but swallowed instead. "Well, at least you're honest."

He reached across the table to gently cup her face, but she jerked away, and when his hand dropped to the table, he felt something sticky beneath his fingertips. Shuddering, he wiped his hand down the leg of his jeans when he discovered they'd neglected to grab napkins.

"Your mother and I will work this out. Everything's going to be all right."

She looked at him with eyes that had seen and heard too much in the last twenty-four hours. "Not so long ago, you told me that everything would be all right, and within hours, I discovered you had slept with Marianne. I hardly think you're in a position to make promises."

"What happened to being nice?"

"What happened to honesty?" she shot back.

Emily's response told him she was done being nice. At least to him. He wanted to say everyone deserved a second chance, but he'd had more than one chance.

"Finish your breakfast, then Matt and Christine will drive you home. I'm going to stay a little longer."

"I don't want to leave without Mom."

His patience was wearing thin. "Look. I get it. I don't want to leave without her either, but the hospital is not going to let us stay, and Mom needs rest more than anything. I need you to listen to me."

Emily's left eyebrow rose as if she were prepared to argue, but then, she looked away and kept whatever complaint she had to herself.

Wanting to make his demand more palatable, he added, "If you want, you can call Nonna and Grandma and tell them about the baby."

"And should I tell them that Marianne and Adam are dead?"

She was busting his balls. He got it. He raked his hand over his face, the stubble on his cheeks like a rough grade of sandpaper, and offered her a smile, pulling every bit of parenting advice he'd ever heard out of his ass so he didn't lose his temper.

"They don't know Adam and Marianne, so I hardly think that's necessary."

Visiting the nursery before Emily went home with Matt and Christine, she pressed her face to the window next to the *Do Not Lean On The Glass* sign. Sucking in her breath, she pointed out the Barclay name card attached to the bassinet.

"Barclay. There are no Barclays."

Wanting to take away her pain, he wrapped his arms around her, but she stood motionless and unyielding in his arms.

Chapter 41

The woman beside Sophia's bed looked vaguely familiar, but Jake was positive he didn't know her.

Sophia appeared exhausted. Her hair looked like she'd just run her hands through it, but she pulled herself together enough to make introductions. "This is Kerry Ackerson. Marianne's cousin. From South Carolina."

He saw it then—the resemblance. Tall and slim like Marianne, with a similar hair color, but hers was short and edgy, while Marianne's had been hair a man wanted to bury himself in. Kerry Ackerson exuded sophistication. Marianne's idea of well-groomed meant jeans without holes. Jake still couldn't believe she was dead.

Emily glanced from Kerry to Sophia. With suspicion in her eyes, she didn't beat around the bush.

"Why are you here?"

If the woman was startled, she didn't show it. "I'm Mia's guardian. I've come to take her home."

Emily blanched. "To South Carolina?"

Again, she turned to her mother, who looked like she was dealing with her own sorrow. Sophia had hoped to keep the baby in her life in some small way because of the friendship between the two women. But after he confessed his night with Marianne, she would want distance from her and the baby that would always remind her of his broken wedding vows.

But now that the baby had no one, what did Sophia want?

"It's what Marianne wanted," Kerry continued as if she owed Emily an explanation when she owed her nothing. "Marianne spoke of you frequently," she added. "She loved how good you were to your mom and how excited you were about Mia."

Emily hung her head. Whatever thoughts she had, she kept to herself.

"She spoke about you, too, Sophia. You gave her the one gift she wanted, and she loved you for it."

He would never know how Kerry missed the momentary bitterness that crossed Sophia's face, but rather than provide an explanation, Sophia redirected the conversation. "Have you seen the baby? Her name is Mia. It means 'mine.' Marianne chose it after Adam left."

"I have. She's beautiful. I knew she would be."

Emily had been so quiet that he almost forgot she was still in the room until she spoke, her voice direct, with no time for the niceties Kerry and Sophia danced around. "When will you be flying home?"

"The airline says the baby has to be two days old, but I'll need to be here at least a week because of the cremation."

"Cremation?"

Kerry glanced at Sophia as if asking permission. The woman obviously had no more experience talking to children than Marianne had.

"It's in their wills. They want to be cremated, with no memorial service or burial. I'm to scatter their ashes on one of the hiking trails on their property. I've already verified—well, my assistant verified—that it's legal. Getting the ashes from the crematorium takes about a week, so I'll—we'll—go home next week."

Kerry looked as if she expected applause for her organizational skills.

"Everything will be ready for the baby by then. I've hired a nanny. Decorators for the nursery. It's amazing what a couple of phone calls can do."

"A nanny? You're not planning on taking care of her yourself?" Emily asked.

Emily'd had no experience with nannies—even babysitters had been a rarity. Sophia hadn't taken a job until Emily had entered seventh grade.

But Kerry knew none of that. "Yes. She came highly recommended by young friends of mine." She twisted the rings on her fingers, most likely not expecting to be cross-examined by a teenager.

Sophia pulled the blanket up to her chin, chilled, maybe, even though the room temperature was set to keep the babies comfortable.

"It's been a shock, becoming a mother in a matter of hours. People make plans, agree to do the right thing, but never really expect to be called on to do it."

Jake took that to mean Kerry regretted her decision. He was beginning to doubt her ability to take on the responsibility of a newborn, and if he had to guess, he'd have said Sophia had the same concerns. He was no expert on guardianship or why someone would agree to become one if they didn't have their own children, but he would at least have assumed that Kerry *liked* children. It didn't seem that she even knew any children. She had no idea what she was getting herself into.

"I'm a forensic anthropologist, rarely home."

Kerry looked at Sophia as if she would find compassion for her situation, at the very least, understanding.

"I'm forty-five years old—I've never had children. Never been married."

"Why did Marianne ask you to be Mia's guardian?"

Whatever Sophia was feeling, he couldn't see it on her face or hear it in her voice.

Kerry shrugged. "There wasn't anyone else. I'm Marianne's only relative. Both her parents are dead, and she had no siblings. She never really developed lasting friendships." She seemed to think about that for a moment. "*Adam* was her best friend."

Sophia nodded—even though Jake knew she'd thought *she* was Marianne's best friend. But Kerry was right. That was how Adam and Marianne were. Together. Until they weren't. Illogically, Sophia zoned in on what seemed the least important information Kerry had shared.

"A forensic anthropologist?"

"Like that author, Kathy Reichs? She does what I do but also writes crime novels. I'm not nearly as glamorous, but I travel worldwide to different crime scenes and help solve them."

Again, Sophia seemed confused. "Why did you ever agree to be Mia's guardian when you have a full-time job, especially one that involves so much traveling?"

"I've been asking myself the same question." Kerry's laugh bordered on hysteria. "The best answer I can give is that, like all of us, I never expected this to happen."

She looked at her watch and then at the three of them. "You must all be exhausted, and I'm feeling a little weary myself—between the shock of all of this and my nonstop phone calls to get my home ready to accommodate a newborn—I could use a break too. Why don't I let you rest and return this evening?"

No sooner had the door closed behind Kerry than Emily erupted. "Mom, you can't let that woman take Mia. She knows nothing about babies."

Sophia looked heartbroken, but before she could answer, Matt and Christine arrived with a bouquet of wildflowers and a box of Godiva chocolates.

"We're not staying," Christine assured everyone as she set the flowers on the windowsill and opened the box of chocolates. After selecting the biggest truffle for herself, she handed the box to Sophia. "We just wanted to see that you're okay with our own eyes."

Sophia eyed her friend, struggling to catch up with the change in atmosphere from Kerry's departure to their arrival. They all were. But she recovered faster than Emily and Jake.

"And eat my chocolates. I'm fine. Just tired." She looked at the candy and passed the box to Emily as if the thought of putting something sweet into her mouth somehow offended her.

"I can't believe you guys are still here," Sophia said.

"We're going and taking Emily with us. I'll check in with you later." Hugging Sophia, she added, "Try to get some rest."

Matt and Christine trooped out of the room, taking Emily—who opted not to complain—and bypassed Jake without a word.

And then they were alone.

"It appears that I am dead to them."

Sophia didn't offer sympathy. "I need to sleep. If you could come back later?"

"Sure." He left the room with no more resolved than earlier, but at least she hadn't said she never wanted to see him again.

Chapter 42

Hospitals were not the place to spend time unless you were so damn sick you had passed praying to live and moved directly to the God-kill-me-now phase of your sorry life. Jake hadn't reached that stage yet, so he moved from waiting room to waiting room—picking up and discarding newspapers and magazines, trying not to think about the number of fingers that had touched them—until it was time to see Sophia again.

He knocked on the door and entered Sophia's room, keeping his expectations in check. All afternoon, Jake thought about what to say. He wanted desperately to save his marriage. The question was, did Sophia? And then he saw Kerry, and his thoughts scattered.

Kerry seemed just as flustered when she looked from him to Sophia to the baby attached to Sophia's breast and backed up toward the door.

"I can come back," Kerry said.

"You're fine. Stay," Sophia assured her. "I wanted to talk to you both anyway. This makes it easier."

Jake stood about two feet inside the door, frozen, while Kerry stepped slowly forward as if any sudden movement would startle the baby.

"Don't worry." Sophia laughed. "At this point, nothing will distract this little girl." Sophia gently removed her nipple from the baby's mouth and burped her then placed her at her other breast. "I've been thinking that since you plan on staying for a few days, you and Mia should stay with us. We would love to have you."

Jake's eyes locked on Sophia's, but she didn't even blink.

"Oh, I couldn't," Kerry responded before he looked away from Sophia. "I've arranged for a crib at the hotel. I only need to get... some things for the baby."

"Kerry. It's no imposition. You've already told me you have no experience with babies. I can help you. Admit it," Sophia added quietly, "You don't know what kind of *things* Mia even needs right now. Do you?"

"Well, no." Kerry glanced in his direction as if waiting for him to reassure her that she was welcome, and when he stayed silent, she looked down at her hands.

"Jake doesn't mind, do you, honey?"

Both women turned to him—Kerry with maybe a look of relief and Sophia with not a drop of doubt in her eyes.

"Not a problem." Jake supplied the correct answer, knowing he had no choice. "We'd love to have you." He stepped maybe a foot farther into the room, figuring he at least deserved that much after being railroaded.

"Really?" Kerry looked back to Sophia for confirmation. "It won't be too much of an imposition?"

Sophia repeated his words with more enthusiasm than he had offered. "We'd love to have you."

"But you need to rest when you go home, not take care of me and Mia."

"I won't be taking care of you. I'll be teaching you how to care for Mia."

As if to prove how good she was, the baby's mouth loosened from Sophia's nipple, and she fell asleep wearing a slight smile. Sophia snuggled her in closer to her body.

It will not be easy for her to give this baby up, even with... everything.

"The doctors are discharging us tomorrow afternoon." Sophia looked around the room until her eyes settled on the closet. "Get my purse, will you?"

Kerry handed it to her, and within a minute, Sophia held up a single key on a pewter chain.

"This is the key to Marianne and Adam's house. Marianne gave it to me when Adam left. In case..." She shook her head. "I'm not sure why." She held the key in her hand as if keeping it warm. As if she couldn't bear to hand it over. But finally, she did.

"Their cabin is about two hours away, so you'll want to wait until the morning. Bring diapers. Clothes. The dresser's filled with everything. Take enough for a few days—a week. Actually, it all belongs to you, so you might as well bring everything. If there's too much to take home on the plane, I'll ship it to you."

Sophia closed her eyes for just a moment. "Bring the bassinet. And don't forget the baby's car seat. It's sitting on the rocking chair in the nursery."

She looked at him as if expecting him to fill in the blanks of what else they might need, but then she paused. "Oh! Was the car seat in the car when..."

Sophia shouldn't have to voice that question. Jake jumped in. "I don't know. Kerry, if the car seat isn't at the house, call me, and I'll buy one, and when you get back, we can run it over to the police station."

Kerry stuffed the list she'd made of the needed baby items into her purse. "Whatever for?"

Sophia looked at him as if to say, "See? This woman needs help."

"To make sure the seat is installed correctly in your rental." If he had to guess, he would say Kerry was in way over her head. "And once you get home, take the seat to your local police station and let them install it correctly in your car."

"That's just one example of what I don't know about caring for a baby."

The agonized look on Kerry's face was honest, but Sophia was not letting her off the hook. "You can learn. No one knows everything. It's the one job in the world where you will mess up repeatedly and pray to get it right the next day. But you won't. All you can do is keep trying. That's all any of us do." She lowered her voice. "I'll help you. Try not to worry."

The color in Kerry's cheeks heightened—she was obviously aware of how ill-prepared she was for motherhood. Finally, she grabbed her purse and hustled out of the room.

Sophia sank back into the bed while the baby slept soundly in her arms. "I blindsided you."

He had to laugh. "You did." It was the closest Sophia had sounded to the woman he loved in what seemed like forever.

"Thanks for coming."

"Of course." *How did we become so formal with each other?*

"We need to talk."

"I know, Soph. But let's wait. At least until you get your strength back." All he had thought about was talking. But now that Kerry and the baby were staying with them, it was the last thing he wanted to do.

Chapter 43

Jake couldn't think past driving home with the baby strapped in her car seat. Thankfully, she would be facing backward, and he wouldn't catch sight of her in his rear-view mirror.

There'd been some question about which car the baby should ride in, but the look on Kerry's face when Sophia suggested she take her made it clear that the woman would rather transport a crazed tiger that had escaped from the zoo than an infant who might stop breathing at any second. At least to him, it was clear.

The car ride home would be their first opportunity for serious discussion—reconciliation, separation, divorce—since Emily was home, adding the last "welcome home" decorations to the house rather than in the back seat, listening to their conversation.

Sophia couldn't seem to get her message out fast enough. "You can sleep on the couch in your office until Kerry leaves. Then, you can move into the guest bedroom."

Not that he was surprised. To Sophia's credit, she left unsaid, "You sure as hell aren't sleeping with me."

He might have been offended by Sophia's need to make their sleeping arrangements clear so quickly if he hadn't been keeping an eye on Kerry, who was following in her rental car.

"Why do you keep looking in the rear-view mirror?"

Jake hadn't thought he'd been that obvious. "I keep waiting for Kerry to turn off somewhere and get the hell out of town. Without the baby."

Sophia laughed. "She's not going to leave without the baby. Don't be so pessimistic. Kerry will be fine."

He'd no sooner parked the car in the driveway, determined to keep his negativity to himself, than Emily rushed out the front door. She unlocked the infant seat carrier from the car seat, and she and the baby disappeared into the house.

"Aren't you afraid Emily will become so attached to this baby that she'll be crushed when Kerry leaves with her?" *So much for suppressing negative thoughts.*

"First, you're afraid Kerry will leave without the baby, and now, you're worried Emily will suffer when Kerry does take her. How do you sleep at night with all that worrying?"

Sophia opened her car door, adding, "Mia and Emily will be just fine. Emily understands what's happening. Yes, it'll be a little hard for her when they leave. It will be hard for me, too, but we'll be fine. And so will Kerry. Just stop."

Maybe she was right, but he didn't relax until Kerry pulled into the driveway.

He wasn't wrong. From the moment they entered the house, Marianne's cousin treated the baby like an antique porcelain doll that would shatter into a thousand pieces if she even tried to pick her up. When forced to hold her, she kept her arms outstretched, leaving the baby dangling in the air instead of having her close to her body. Even he could tell things were not going the way Sophia had hoped.

"Didn't you babysit when you were a teenager? Have younger brothers or sisters? Have you ever *seen* a newborn before?" To no avail, Sophia grilled Kerry, attempting to get to the root of the woman's fear.

Kerry shook her head at every question, eyes imploring Sophia to take the baby. But equally adamant, Sophia persisted.

"Bring her closer. Let her feel your warmth." In exasperation, Sophia finally took her from Kerry's quaking arms.

Sophia insisted she could reach Kerry's maternal instincts. Jake did not see that happening.

By Friday, Kerry had yet to bathe the baby, and they were days from leaving for South Carolina. Late that afternoon, Sophia jumped ship to visit Christine, leaving Emily in charge while the baby slept.

Sophia was only gone a couple of hours, but Emily watched over the baby like it was her life's work. No one would need to teach her how to be a mother. Watching Emily care for the infant was more difficult than when Sophia held her. Jake saw how Emily's eyes lit up when the child was in her arms. What he couldn't understand was why Sophia didn't see it.

When Sophia entered his study later that day with the baby in her arms, she looked more relaxed than he'd seen her in days.

"How was your escape?"

She grinned. "That's just what it felt like. I adore taking care of Mia. I do not adore forcing Kerry to care for her, so my escape was delicious, especially since it included a glass of wine."

"Wine?"

"Don't look so shocked. According to my doctor, a glass of wine won't hurt if I don't nurse for at least two hours. And I fed Mia not long before I ran over to Christine's. Plus there's pumped milk in the fridge. *Yes*, I can have wine."

"Good. I'm glad you had a break. I'm also glad to see you here." Sophia hadn't stepped foot into his study since he'd told her about his night with Marianne.

"I'm here because we need to talk."

He felt like she'd thrown down a gauntlet, but he refused to pick it up. "Didn't we talk enough in the car the other day? I thought we decided to wait until Kerry and the baby leave before we make any decisions."

"I think you decided that. We need to talk about Kerry, or I need to talk about Kerry, and I need you to listen."

Not at all sure where this conversation would take them, he nodded.

"How can she not be affected by this sweet baby? I've tried
everything I know to entice her with the incredible feeling of holding
a precious new life, and she looks at me like I'm offering her a piece
of raw liver to chew on."

Grimacing at the image, Jake leaned back in his chair and
watched as Sophia laid the baby beside her on the couch. Wrapped in
blankets, she looked incredibly small to have so much drama in her
short life.

"What's going to happen if things don't improve?" It had been
on his mind for days. He did not see Kerry and the baby flying off
into the sunset to live happily ever after.

"I don't know. I'm still hoping Kerry will turn around and surprise us all, but I've never seen a grown woman so terrified of a baby."

He didn't respond. In his opinion, there wasn't a chance in hell
that Kerry would give up her life to fulfill her promise to Marianne.

"What?"

"I didn't say anything."

"You don't have to. I can see it on your face. You don't think Kerry will take Mia."

He wasn't ready to talk about this, maybe because, like Sophia,
he hoped for a miracle in which the forensic anthropologist morphed into mother of the year right before their eyes. But Sophia was
forcing the issue.

"You are pushing a woman who has never had children to raise
one," Jake said.

"I'm not doing anything of the sort. Kerry signed guardianship
papers. What did she think was going to happen?"

"I'm pretty sure she didn't expect Marianne and Adam to die."
The pain started low in his belly and exploded into his jaw at his cal-
lous statement as the memory of Officer Ellis's message taunted him.

"There's been an accident...no one survived." Will I ever stop hearing those words?

"None of us expected them to die, but they did."

It surprised Jake that Sophia could say this out loud. He had always suspected she was stronger than him—a thought he preferred not to dwell on.

"Have you ever asked her *why* she hasn't had children?"

Sophia squared her shoulders. "No, I've never asked her. I know that not all women want babies, but when one is right in front of you and needs to be loved, wouldn't you think she would love her back?"

"Like you have?"

Sophia's cheeks turned pink. "I..."

"Don't. I've seen you with that baby. Not all women will uproot their entire lives for a baby."

"You mean like me?"

He didn't answer.

"I promised you. Mia will not become a member of our family."

He didn't believe her, but for one instant, he thought about watching the baby grow up as part of his family. He wouldn't be able to breathe with her in the house.

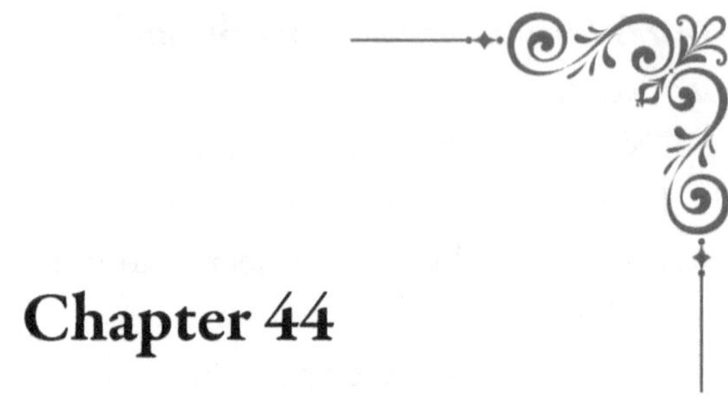

Chapter 44

The law books lining the shelves in Jake's study taunted him, reminding him of his last meeting with Stephen when he'd refused the LINE case. *Am I even a lawyer if I don't have a job?*

"It's not too late to back out of this case." He'd been sure he could convince Stephen that taking this lawsuit would be a mistake. But the mistake was that he'd tried to persuade Stephen of anything.

When the new business cards with his name and "Senior Partner" engraved on them didn't sway him, Stephen had shown his true colors. "I'd like to say I'm surprised, but I always knew you didn't have what it takes."

At one time, Stephen's words would have crushed him, but the statement wasn't unexpected.

"If what it takes to succeed is climbing into bed with people who aren't concerned with the public's welfare, then I disagree. I have what it takes." His words had been brave, but even as he'd uttered them, he still hoped Stephen would change his mind.

As Jake sat in his study, he pulled the business card out of his pocket—his memento from that day. He figured he'd hang onto it until he could blow the tiny fragments into the universe with one half-hearted breath. Considering how often he ran his fingers over its creamy surface, it shouldn't take long. Until then, it reminded him of everything he didn't want in his next job.

His future was at the top of his concerns, but so was his worry about Sophia's growing attachment to the baby. Emily showing up with Lilly trailing behind her was a welcome reprieve. The sight of his daughter put all thoughts of the law on hold.

Emily plopped onto the couch beside him while Lilly twirled around a few times and settled at her feet. It was the first time Emily had chosen to be in the same room with him since the night of his father's birthday dinner.

A weight lifted from his chest. Maybe they would get back to normal. "Where's Miss Molly?"

Emily rolled her eyes. "Where she always is. With Mom. Are you and Mom getting a divorce?"

He winced. "Why would you even ask that?"

"The nanny quit."

His head shot up from where it rested on the back of the couch. "What do you mean, she quit?" Jake was sure she was mistaken. "She hasn't even started yet."

"Kerry's housekeeper called. The nanny got a better offer—traveling to Italy for six months with the family who hired her then settling back in South Carolina. She said it was an opportunity of a lifetime, and she wasn't passing it up."

"She's going to hire another nanny, right?"

"Dunno. Mom told her that's what she needs to do. She told her to take off work until she locates a good nanny then make her sign a contract." Emily snorted. "You should have seen the look on Kerry's face. You would have thought Mom asked her to amputate her arm and feed it to Lilly."

"How do you know all this?"

A thin veil of guilt swept across Emily's face. "I might have been standing in the hallway."

"Eavesdropping."

Her shoulders hunched. "Well, sort of."

Bypassing the implications of listening to conversations that were none of her business, Emily gave her opinion on what she'd learned. "I don't understand how the woman doesn't see how much Mia needs to be loved. Kerry should be thrilled to have her. Thrilled that Marianne thought enough of her to ask her to be Mia's guardian. But she acts like this is nothing but a big imposition."

"You know this isn't your concern."

"No?" Emily sputtered as if he'd thrown cold water in her face. "This is Marianne's baby. Of course I'm concerned."

"I'll admit, this is complicated. But it's between Mom and Kerry."

"Well, the matter might be out of their hands because Mia won't take a bottle from Kerry even though Mom keeps pumping breast milk. She won't even take it if Mom gives her a bottle. Just screams until Mom opens her shirt."

Jake flinched at the image.

"Kerry doesn't want Mia. I think Mom wants to adopt her."

"Mom?" He drew in a sharp breath, unwilling to admit he was worried about the same thing. But would Sophia make that decision without talking to him? "You probably misunderstood."

"Pretty sure I didn't. They were arguing. I probably could have heard them from my room instead of the hallway. Mom said that Kerry signed the papers and that she couldn't desert Mia. And then Kerry started crying. She agreed. Apologized all over the place for being so emotional—I doubt the woman ever cries. She says she'll resent Mia if she takes her. And that Mom should adopt her because anyone could see how much she loves her."

Even if Emily had taken everything she heard out of context, which was doubtful, he knew Sophia loved that baby.

"Mom said she couldn't take Mia because she swore to you she wouldn't. That's when..."

"What?"

Emily blushed.

"What were you going to say?"

She struggled to explain. "Look, it's one thing if I bust on you—you're my dad. You'll always be my dad, no matter how much you piss me off. But Kerry's a stranger. Even more so now that she doesn't want Mia."

He was beginning to get the picture. "So what did Kerry say about me?"

Emily let out an exaggerated sigh. "Kerry knows about you and your... fling. Marianne confessed. Kerry asked Mom why she should worry about her promise when you broke the biggest one. Mom said—"

"Enough." *Did Marianne's confession to Kerry go any better than when I talked to Matt?* Something else he didn't want to think about.

"Mom wouldn't make a decision about the baby without talking to me first."

"Then why would Kerry sign over the Barclays' property to her? Even Mikie."

Jake tried to inhale, but the air caught somewhere along the way, and the pain was sharp, as if someone had plunged a knife into him. "Are you sure?"

Emily nodded then added, "I want Mom to adopt Mia, but what if she moves to the cabin?"

"Why would you even think that?" The look on Emily's face told him everything he needed to know. "You overheard Kerry and Mom talking."

"Well, yeah..."

"I suppose you'd want to move with her?" The thought made his heart hurt even more. He couldn't imagine coming home to an empty house. No matter how many doors she slammed or how loud she played her music, he would want Emily to be here.

"I want to live with Mom. But not in the cabin."

"No?" The disbelief in his voice was clear, but Emily didn't comment.

"My friends. School. Everything is here." Emily looked like she'd thrown Sophia under the bus.

Almost lightheaded with relief, he offered comfort. "Well, it's a good thing we are not getting a divorce and that no one is moving out of this house." *Who am I trying to soothe? Emily? Or myself?*

"I don't think deciding who lives where is up to you. Or whether you and Mom get divorced. You know? Once you decided to screw Marianne?"

Jesus. She really is like me. "That's kind of harsh, don't you think? And maybe you shouldn't say things like that."

"Maybe I wouldn't say things like that if you didn't do them." Lifting her chin, she spat out concerns he would have known if he hadn't been so self-absorbed in his own worries.

"Do you expect me to *choose* between you and Mom? How can I do that? How can I let her live in that cabin alone with Mia? Don't you see what you've done?"

He lost the staring match that ensued. "You have no idea how sorry I am about all of this."

"It's not me you need to be telling that to."

He couldn't argue that point. "I've apologized to your mother."

"Did she forgive you?"

"Not yet." Everything good in him came from Sophia. *But what if she doesn't forgive me? What if she can't?*

Emily squirmed in her seat until she faced him. "Do you think she will?"

He closed his eyes, wishing he could have a drink, but he was trying to keep his promise to Sophia. One he'd made long before he met Marianne, long before he'd screwed up his life with Sophia. "I don't know. I hope so."

She searched his eyes. He hoped she found whatever it was she was looking for.

"Do you think God punished Marianne, and that's why she died? And Adam died because he was with her? Is God going to punish you too?"

Emily's questions came out in a rush, and he wanted nothing more than to hold her in his arms and tell her everything would work out, like he'd done a million times when she was a little girl and had scraped her knee or flubbed a line in the school play. But she wasn't a little girl anymore, and he wasn't willing to bet on God's compassion. He had wondered the same thing himself.

But he couldn't admit that to Emily, so he said nothing.

"How could you do it?"

How do I explain that I'm not perfect and I made a mistake? How do I explain my nightmares or my father or my brother's death in a way that she can understand without giving her nightmares of her own? How do I explain that I was afraid and confused?

Of all the things he had done in his life that he was sorry for, sleeping with Marianne was the one he regretted most. He scrubbed his hand over his face. "I don't know, Emily. I have no excuse. What I did was wrong, and I will live the rest of my life trying to make it up to you and your mother."

She shifted away from him as if she needed to separate herself from the passion of his words. "I don't know if I believe you."

"Fair enough. I guess I'll have to prove it to you."

"Does Mom believe you?"

He had no idea if Sophia believed him.

Chapter 45

Sophia paced from one end of the kitchen to the other with the baby in her arms. She had pulled her hair into a messy ponytail with little curls framing her face. Shadows lay under her eyes from lack of sleep, and her shirttail hung out from the waistband of her jeans.

He'd rarely seen her this unkempt. Or this beautiful.

"We need to talk," Jake said.

Even after Emily shared what she'd overheard, he didn't think Sophia would sacrifice the life they had built together. It was true that this past year had been hell—a hell of his own making that he regretted with every fiber of his being—but before that, they had loved each other. They still loved each other. They belonged together.

"Shh. I'm trying to get her to fall asleep."

Jake waited until he couldn't wait any longer. "Soph?" Her silence made him wish he'd never promised to cut back on his drinking, but he held fast to his oath. He would never have another drink if it meant they'd be together.

She finally faced him after placing the sleeping baby in the cradle. "I don't want our marriage to end because of Mia."

His knees buckled with relief. Reaching out to pull her into his arms, Sophia held her hand up as if to ward him off, and he froze. Had he misunderstood?

"What?"

Sophia closed her eyes for a second. Exhaustion? Pain? He had no idea.

"No one could have predicted this." It was as if she had pulled each word up from the depths of her soul and laid it on the floor for him to see.

"Kerry doesn't want this baby. She's no good with children. She doesn't *want* to be good with them."

"Soph..."

"She won't even hold her. There is no warmth in that woman's body for Mia."

He knew where this was going. He couldn't stop it, but he had to try. "Please..."

Without even acknowledging his plea, she kept going. "She says she can't learn to love Mia. That she's not made that way."

"No..."

They stood inches apart, yet the distance between them was insurmountable. Jake knew it was over, but he couldn't walk away.

"What happens now?" Her answer would define the rest of their lives.

"I can't abandon her." She looked everywhere but at him.

"You promised." He sounded like a child reprimanding his parents for breaking an agreement to visit the zoo.

She finally raised her eyes to him, and he saw they would both lose.

"Don't you think I *know* that?"

The anguish in her voice cut through him like he'd been cleaved in two. Tears slid down Sophia's cheeks.

"Kerry wants me to adopt Mia."

His heart was nearly exploding. "I made a mistake. You have to believe me. Can't we go back to the way things used to be?"

He wanted that more than anything—just him, Sophia, and Emily.

"This isn't about you and Marianne. This is about Mia."

The baby. Marianne's baby. Marianne would hate his next words—she would hate him—but he was willing to accept that. He had to save his marriage. He had to get rid of the baby.

"Let someone else adopt her if Kerry refuses to take her."

They stared at each other for long moments. Jake's response was harsh, but he couldn't take it back, even though he feared that he'd just ended his marriage.

Sophia recoiled as if he had slapped her. "Do you realize that this baby exists because of me?"

"That's not true." His voice thick with emotion, his movements shaky, he took a chance and drew her to him. Holding her was like wrapping his arms around a mannequin. She did not hold him back.

Releasing her, he whispered, "Anyone could have been the surrogate."

"But anyone *wasn't*. I was." Putting more distance between them, she added, "I cannot abandon this baby."

"But you won't be abandoning her. We'll find a good family to adopt her. There are lots of people who can't have their own babies. You've said so yourself. Some people are unable to do IVF. They pray to adopt a baby. We can help them."

"No."

"You'd rather abandon our marriage?"

A shadow passed over her face, and when it disappeared, it seemed she was someone he'd never seen before. "I think it was you who did that."

Sophia chose Mia. He wanted to tell her the baby could stay, but the words remained deep inside him.

Chapter 46

Emily freaked when Sophia chose to move into the cabin with the baby. Jake knew this was what she'd feared most. She couldn't desert Maddie. Couldn't leave their place close to Church Street, where she met up with her friends, grabbed a bite, and checked out the sales. The cabin was obviously way too isolated for Emily's comfort.

But Emily's nightmare was the one bright spot out of the whole godforsaken mess Jake had made of their lives, and it gave him the ammunition to approach Sophia with a counteroffer. He found her going through the linen closet, removing sheets and towels, placing them in boxes, and then rearranging the shelves so they didn't look like someone had pilfered their stuff.

He stopped her when she knelt to seal the box.

"The baby can stay. We can work things out." He searched for words that would make a difference. "We can go to counseling. Maybe we can both adopt the baby." He silently begged her to agree. "And Emily is beside herself. She doesn't want to leave school and her friends but wants to live with you."

Sophia's hand hovered over the packing box, tape in one hand. "Emily and I have already worked this out. I know the cabin is too remote for her liking, so she'll live here and stay with me as often as she wants. On weekends and holidays. We'll figure it out."

"But what about—"

"You don't have a say in this. I've never seen you pick up Mia or tend to her in the middle of the night. It's as if she doesn't exist to you. So it's not nearly as simple as you might think. Babies need to know they are loved. There is no love within you for this child."

"But I love you."

She put down the tape to seal the box and lowered her head as if she were praying. *He* was praying, and he never prayed.

"I understand that," she said. "Don't you see that that's not enough?"

"But it is. I can learn to love her. It's the perfect answer, and Emily will be thrilled that we'll still be a family. You want that, too, don't you? We can make a nursery out of the spare room that is currently no more than a room-sized junk drawer. I'll clean it out and repaint it. Whatever color you want. We can move all the baby things here from the cabin. It'll be perfect." He grinned. "Even Mikie won't be a problem. He's one of the most well-behaved dogs I know."

As if she wasn't listening to how simple it would be to get their lives back, Sophia taped up the filled box, labeled it, and grabbed another. She threw a bottle of Oribe Gold Lust shampoo into the new box, dug it back out, and handed it to him. "Here, I won't be needing this at the cabin."

"Will you stop packing and listen to me?" His words echoed in the hallway. Lowering his voice, he tried again. "I'm trying to tell you we can get our lives back."

"Jake, you never even call her by her name. Why would you want her to live here permanently? Why would you even think about adopting her?"

Confused, sure that she was wrong, he thought back through these last few months and any time he had mentioned the baby. "I call her by her name."

"No. You call her 'the baby.' Her name is Mia."

I know that. "Don't you think you're splitting hairs?"

She glared at him. "Don't you think you're sounding desperate?"

That was the thing. Jake was desperate. He'd never been more desperate in his life. And he wasn't ready to give up. Kneeling next to her, he closed his hand over the bottle of mouthwash she held.

"What about Emily? If you move into the cabin, you are two hours away from her. Your *real* daughter. Can't you move somewhere closer? Or stay here? I'll move out if that's what you want. Then at least nothing changes for Emily."

"You don't get it, do you? If you move out, Emily will end up moving with you. I love Emily, and she loves me, but no matter how much you've screwed up this past year, you are her dad. Where you go, she goes."

She finally said something that stopped him. "She said that?"

"She didn't have to. You have always been her person."

Chapter 47

Several weeks later, Christine and Matt did their best to look invisible while waiting for Sophia to grab the rest of her things so they could head to the cabin in St. Johnsbury. Wanting to look anywhere but at them, Jake glanced out the window when Emily took Lilly over to Susan Johnston's house, where the dog would stay until Emily picked her up later that night. He saw the moving truck in the driveway and swore the damn thing leered at him.

Even though his former friends witnessed his humiliation, he continued pleading with Sophia. "This is crazy. I don't understand why you want to move there."

"Why not? Because you spent the night with Marianne in that cabin? Everything I've imagined a million times about that night is in my head—I doubt it matters where I live—I'll still see you in bed with her. But don't worry, *that* furniture will be the first to go."

He deserved that.

It wasn't like Sophia to be so snide. She must have thought the same thing.

"To be honest, I'm not sure how I can do this either, but I'm going to try. The cabin meant a lot to Adam and Marianne. It's Mia's home, and everything in it is Mia's history. The child deserves to know where she came from. What her parents left her. How much Marianne loved and wanted her."

She leaned against the wall, balancing the last boxes meant for the truck. "Maybe I am making a mistake and won't be able to spend one night in that house. I don't know—but it's my choice, and either way, whether I stay there or not, I won't be coming back here. This house holds too many memories." Eyes glassy with pain, she added, "Besides, you've always loved this place more than me."

Jake was beyond desperate. "But what about your job? You'll be two hours away at the cabin. And even if you're crazy enough to make the commute, who will watch the baby?"

"I already talked to David—I'm extending my leave for another twelve months. After that, I plan on buying a small house closer to work. But I'm keeping the cabin for Mia. Then, she can decide what she wants to do with it."

"If we live together, you won't need to work. I can support you like I did when Emily was a baby. Wouldn't you rather do that?"

"Stop, Jake. I'm leaving."

"If you are determined to move there, I'm coming along to make sure you have everything you need."

Based on the look she gave him, Sophia didn't seem to think that was a good idea. He wasn't sure what he could accomplish, but she didn't say no.

Emily, the baby, and Miss Molly rode with Sophia. Jake followed, watching Emily and Sophia's heads bob back and forth, talking and laughing as if they were out for a Sunday drive, while Jake agonized over everything he'd said these past few weeks to convince Sophia she was making a mistake.

Not in leaving him. He'd given up trying to convince her he didn't deserve to be left. He deserved it. She knew it. Hell, the entire neighborhood knew it. But he wasn't sure he would ever reconcile himself to Sophia living in Marianne's house.

When they pulled into the driveway, Matt and Christine jumped out of the truck while Emily followed Sophia onto the porch. He couldn't take his eyes off the front door. The door where Marianne had initially welcomed him and then barred his entry once she discovered he was married to Sophia. Her friend. The woman who carried her baby. He shook his head. So many things had happened so quickly. And now, Adam and Marianne were dead.

He had too many memories here. Climbing out of his car, Jake walked through the big double doors, maybe for the last time.

It didn't take long to empty the truck. Besides Sophia's personal things, the only furniture she'd brought was from the guest room, planning to buy what she needed once she bought a house closer to Shelburne. Until then, she'd make do with what was here. Except for the furniture she couldn't bear keeping.

He found Sophia in Marianne's bedroom. Never in his wildest dreams had he imagined Sophia and him together in this room. The sun peeked in through the windows and danced across a straw gardening hat perched on a hook, creating patterns of light and shadow before skittering across the room. Marianne had liked those windows bare since the closest neighbor was a mile away, but Sophia probably planned to cover them as soon as she had time.

They avoided the bed, although he couldn't miss the crucifix that leered down at him. The same one, he swore, that hung over Sophia's hospital bed when she delivered the baby.

Sophia quickly organized the men from Goodwill when they arrived, advising them to strip the room bare. They had no sooner picked up the first dresser than they put it back down again.

"Excuse me, ma'am? This here dresser's got stuff in it. We'll wait while you empty it."

Sophia paled, shooting him a look of desperation. *Damn.* He wasn't surprised that Kerry didn't think to empty the dressers before she hightailed it back to South Carolina without the baby, but he imagined there wasn't a chance in hell Sophia wanted to go through Marianne's things.

This was why he had come. To reduce the burden of this god-awful day. "Take it all. Whatever's in the dressers, everything. I'm sure someone can use this stuff."

"Wait. I'll keep this quilt. I can give it to Mia when she's older." Sophia grabbed it off the bed, brought it close to her body, appeared to think better of it, and laid it on a chair.

He imagined it would go through the wash before she touched it again.

Leaving the Goodwill people to finish emptying the bedroom, he followed Sophia into the kitchen, where Emily had released Mikie from his leash. Mikie ran to Jake when he caught his scent, and Jake knelt, scratching behind the dog's ears and whispering nonsense, taking a break from the stress that clutched his soul.

Emily hung Mikie's leash on the peg by the door. "Mrs. Stellar said Mikie was an excellent guest, and you should call anytime you need a place for him to stay."

Sophia's hand grazed Mikie's head. "You had a nice long visit, didn't you, boy? And you were a good dog?"

As soon as Miss Molly caught Sophia's words, she hustled herself—as much as she could—to get some of that same attention. There had never been a question of where Miss Molly would go. Even though Emily had wanted her, and he had bought her, Sophia had claimed ownership the moment she'd laid eyes on her.

The question was what to do with Mikie, who, along with everything else, had been willed first to Kerry and then transferred to Sophia. The obvious choice had been for him to take the dog because Mikie had attached himself to him first, but he couldn't do it. The dog was used to having land to roam, and living in Burlington would have stunted his lifestyle. Besides, Mikie would protect Sophia.

The dogs sniffed at each other, tails wagging, while Sophia gave them equal attention.

"Look," Emily said as she held out treats, "they like each other!"

"It appears they do." Sophia scanned the kitchen as if she wasn't sure what to tackle next when Christine carried a box into the house that he recognized. Their wedding album was in that box. They might have stood before a JP, but they had memorialized the occasion with tacky pictures and then bought the most expensive album to keep them safe for posterity.

Emily grabbed the box he had his eyes on.

"This one's not marked. Do you want me to go through it to see where it belongs?"

"Leave it!" Sophia said quickly.

Mikie barked at Sophia's sharp tone.

She lowered her voice and added, "Put the box in Mari—the big bedroom."

Sophia averted her eyes when she caught him staring at her. And that gave him hope. He was the only other person in the room who knew what was in that box, and he wondered what it meant that she had brought the album with her.

The end of moving day came too quickly for him, but Sophia could barely stay awake. The baby was sleeping and the dogs were down for the night when Christine and Matt hugged Sophia goodbye.

"You sure you don't want one of us to stay?"

"Don't be silly. I'll be fine. I may not be able to see the neighbors, but I know they're out there, and I have their phone numbers."

The goodbye was harder for Sophia and Emily.

"Maybe this is a bad idea." Emily slapped a smile on her face and grabbed Sophia's hands. "I can move here. I always wanted to live in a log cabin."

Sophia reached out and pulled Emily to her. "Don't be silly. You can live here every weekend if you want. Maddie wouldn't know what to do without you." She looked at him. "Neither would your dad."

Even he could see the relief in Emily's eyes.

"You're sure?"

"I'm sure. Now, go. Try to stay out of trouble. I'll see you next weekend. And bring Lilly with you."

He tossed Emily the keys to his car.

"I'll be right out."

He stood before Sophia, finally alone, determined to have his say.

"I know that you needed to leave. I destroyed our marriage and our lives. I hope someday, you can forgive me. But why move here? I'll never understand how you can live in this house."

He wasn't expecting an answer, but while he waited, he looked around the great room: the sofa, the fireplace, the side table where he'd first noticed Adam's pipe, and he wished with all his heart that he'd done things differently. Or not done them at all.

Chapter 48

It wasn't like Jake had an office where he could bury himself in work when Emily spent her first weekend with Sophia, but he hoped the solitary days would get better once he'd survived the first.

By the time Emily came home, he was torn between wanting to know what Sophia looked like, what she said, how she laughed—if she laughed—but most importantly, if she mentioned him. At all. Even the tiniest reference. She didn't.

"Mom added her crocks and quilts to make the place feel more like home. She even unpacked her collection of school bells. I bet she packs them right up again when Mia is old enough to ring them—like she did when I wouldn't leave them alone."

She stopped talking long enough to pour a big glass of milk and toss a treat to Lilly. "You should have seen this girl. She was so excited to see Mikie and Miss Molly."

As if Lilly knew Emily was talking about her, she ran between them, smiling and whining for attention. "Lilly and Mikie spent hours outside. Miss Molly was excited to see Lilly, too, but she doesn't play outside anymore. I can't believe how gray her fur is."

The excitement in Emily's voice dwindled, and her eagerness to share the events of her weekend came to a shuddering halt.

"And?"

"She barely leaves her bed except when she needs to go out. And treats don't excite her like they used to."

Miss Molly never passed up food or treats. Jake assumed they'd all be together to help each other through this phase and the one that followed. He never thought he'd be hearing about the dog's decline secondhand.

"Remember when Miss Molly came to live with us? Adam said she wasn't healthy. Wouldn't live a long time."

"I *know*, Dad. All I'm saying is that knowing she's reaching the end of her life makes me sad. It's okay for me to feel sad."

Emily had always been more mature than her years, and she rarely failed to remind him of it.

"It is. It makes me sad too. But we gave Miss Molly a good life—that's important to remember. Your mom must be feeling pretty bad."

"She won't even talk about it. Acts like Miss Molly's going through a phase, and she'll perk up again."

He suspected that Sophia had reached a saturation point with grief, but she'd do what was right when the time came.

When he asked about the baby, Emily was halfway up the stairs with her overnight bag. She whipped around and gave him a withering look.

"Mom's right. You never call her by her name."

"That's not true. I just asked you how she's doing."

"You asked how the *baby* is. Her name is Mia. Why don't you ever say her name?"

"I do..." He didn't understand why they were making such a big deal out of this, and he was too tired to argue. "So, how is she?"

"*Mia's* sleeping through the night, which means Mom's sleeping through the night. Mom says they reached an agreement—she feeds Mia on demand during the day, and in return, Mia sleeps at night."

He didn't know what "on demand" meant, but at least Emily had answered his question. He had news also, but for the moment, he kept it to himself until he could share it with Sophia first.

He'd felt adrift without a job but had wanted to take his time before deciding what to do next. He didn't want sixteen-hour days, clients he wouldn't dream of sharing a meal with, facts and figures conveniently lost or contrived so that the client appeared innocent. He didn't want his livelihood determined by his acceptance of shady deals. He was no longer willing to put himself in a position where he felt threatened. He did not want to go to his father for advice.

Jake hadn't been sure who was surprised most when he finally figured out his starting point—himself or Becky Boden. He remembered everything about the first time he'd been in her office, and nothing had changed when he'd visited her several weeks ago. She still had a great view from her office window and insisted he call her Becky.

He got right to the point. "The last time Sophia and I were here, which seems like years ago, you talked about how important surrogacy is to your staff. I'm wondering if it's the same for your in-house counsel. Do they also have a history with surrogacy?"

He had been impressed with the team of lawyers associated with the surrogacy center both before and after Marianne and Adam died. Once he decided he didn't have the stomach for corporate law and started looking into other avenues to put his degree and experience to work, the surrogacy center seemed like a natural starting place.

"Some of our lawyers do have a history with surrogacy. Either they were surrogates, or their wives were." Her expression altered. "I know you're a lawyer. Tell me, what are you thinking?"

He laid it out for her. "I quit working for my former firm." Playing those words over in his head, he went for full disclosure. "To be more accurate, my boss fired me because I refused to take a specific case."

"The LINE case? I remember reading about that. As I recall, that didn't go well for either your previous law firm or the defendants."

"No." He didn't want to talk about the case. He'd answered questions in court only because he'd been subpoenaed.

"I've taken a few months off for several reasons—the Barclays. Their baby." Sheepishly, he looked at her, adding, "My marriage."

Burlington was a big city, but somehow, when a couple died the same night their child was born, word spread as if he lived in a small village with a few hundred residents. So there was no point in pretending that Becky didn't know more than what was socially acceptable.

"Becoming a surrogate was important to Sophia. I'm proud of what she did and why she did it."

Becky watched him with an intensity that made him think before he uttered his next words.

"I'd like to know more about the legal side of what you do here before I contact headhunters who are more concerned with their commission than with a satisfying placement. I'd like to know if there's a place for me here." Jake felt like he'd been talking for an hour. "Is this something you can help me with?"

If Becky was surprised by his request, she had the grace to withhold her reaction. "How about I introduce you to the head of our human resources department?"

He was joining the legal team for We Make Families in one month. That was what he wanted to tell Sophia.

Chapter 49

The news Jake shared with Sophia wasn't about his new position, and he delivered it in the middle of the night, when no one ever wanted to answer the phone.

When his mother called, asking him to come to the hospital, he reached across to Sophia's side of the bed in search of the woman who had been at his side for every life-altering event of his adulthood, only to find it empty. In his grogginess, he had forgotten she hadn't lived with him for months.

Miss Molly was snoring when Sophia answered the phone. He heard the rustle of covers and pictured her pulling herself up, then he noticed the quiver in her voice as she struggled to wake.

"Jake? What happened? What time is it?"

He looked at his watch. "It's late. I'm sorry. I... I shouldn't have called. I needed to talk to you."

"Where are you?"

"I'm at the hospital. My father had another stroke." His voice was raspy, his words swollen. "This one was bad," he added, emitting a slight laugh that ended in a hiccup. "He didn't make it."

Not that long ago, they had celebrated his birthday. Robert had looked in perfect health, but that was the thing—he only let you see what he wanted you to see.

"Oh, Jake. I'm so sorry. How's your mother? How are you?"

"I don't know what I feel. Or if I even feel anything. But Mom's doing pretty well, surprisingly. I always thought she'd lie down and die with him when he took his last breath. But I've seen a change in her recently. Who knows? Maybe I'm imagining it. She asked me to call. To let you know. But I wanted to talk to you anyway. You're the one person who can understand how confused I am."

"Just give yourself some time. How's Emily?"

Emily had jumped out of bed when he woke her, insisted on going with him, said all the right things to his mother, kissed her grandfather goodbye, and yet when he'd mentioned organizing the funeral on the drive back to the house and suggesting she look in her closet for something appropriate to wear—preferably black—she'd looked at him like he'd lost his marbles.

"I have no intention of honoring a man who thought more of himself than his family."

He'd been exhausted. Nothing she'd said made sense to him. "What are you talking about?"

"Did you think I never noticed how he treated you? And Grandma? And he treated Mom like she should be seen and not heard. I'm not going."

He'd left it alone. But when Sophia asked how Emily was, he hesitated, then he responded that she was coping.

"I'll call her in the morning."

"Thanks. I have no right to ask, but will you come to the service? It's on Thursday, at Christ Presbyterian."

"Don't be silly. Of course I'll come."

Jake poured himself a cup of coffee the following morning and joined Emily at the table. Breakfast for both was hot and liquid, not nearly what they would need to get them through the day.

"Mom called. She's coming over to help me find something appropriate to wear for the funeral."

"You're going?"

"Just don't. I know you talked her into convincing me I should respect my elders no matter how I might feel about them."

Sophia had read between the lines, but Emily didn't need to know that.

The service was a spectacle worthy of Robert's position in the community. The church filled with almost everyone who had attended his birthday celebration, along with the mayor of Burlington and the governor of Vermont.

A wave of relief washed over him when he caught sight of Sophia in a pew at the back of the church, squeezed between one of the clerks from Price Chopper and Chuck Coleson, their mailman. He would have loved for her to sit next to him, Emily, and his mother, but that was too much to ask.

The service was long and filled with the drama of a life cut short too soon, the minister obviously forgetting that his father would no longer be available to write large checks in the name of the Lord. Sooner than he'd hoped, it was time for him to give the eulogy. But when he pulled his notes out of his jacket pocket, Emily put her hand over his, withdrew the notes, kissed him on the cheek, and headed toward the dais. His breath caught in his throat.

Back ramrod straight, Emily looked out over the people who had come to pay their respects to his father and smiled. She looked at his notes, still crumpled in her hand, and shoved them into her pocket. He had no idea what was going to come out of her mouth.

"Thank you for coming. My grandfather would be honored to know that you took time out of your busy day to see him off on his final journey. And, knowing my grandfather, he would tell you all it was time to get back to work." She beamed at everyone, raised one eyebrow at Jake as if to taunt him, and then returned to his side.

He leaned toward her, but she cut him off before he could say a word and whispered, "Mom told me to keep it short and sweet."

Of course she did.

If some mourners felt short-changed by the brevity of the eulogy, others were trying desperately to hide their smirks. His father had not been as beloved as he thought.

At the end of the service, Sophia surprised him by throwing her arms around him in the receiving line as if she'd never let him go.

"Thank you for coming." It felt good to wrap his arms around her. It was what he missed most.

"Of course," she whispered.

He felt the loss of her the moment she stepped away.

Chapter 50

It was Jake's favorite time of year. Crimson and gold leaves announced the beginning of apple-cider season, carved pumpkins, hay bales, and scarecrows dressed in worn-out denim bib overalls. The scent of woodsmoke filled the air and tantalized his senses.

But he barely noticed the weather, the decorations, or the cider donuts highlighted at every farm stand he passed. His need to see Sophia gnawed at him until his chest was tight, and he could think of little else. Maybe a drive in the country would abate his hunger for her.

Instead, it brought him to her front door.

The last time he'd stood there was when Sophia moved in. But this time was different. He knew who he was and what he wanted. Filled with hope and terror, he knocked on her door.

Mikie's barking brought him back from his reverie. He swallowed hard when Sophia opened the door, his words melting away faster than an ice cream cone on a hot summer's day, while the dog's barking transformed into a whimper of joy when he caught Jake's scent. Before Sophia could object, Mikie scooted between her legs and through the partially opened door to greet him.

"Jake. What are you doing here?"

Surprised by the directness of Sophia's question, he faltered, feeling more than a little foolish. "May I come in?"

When she didn't respond, he added, "I just want to talk."

"What do we have to talk about?"

Her voice was not unkind or cruel. But it was different. She was no longer the woman he had married. She wasn't even the woman who had paid her respects at his father's funeral and flung her arms around him.

I want you back. I want my family back. He shook his head. This was no longer just about what he wanted. Offering a small smile, determined that what he had to say was vital, he asked again. "May I please come in?"

She looked at him as if judging the weight of his words. Finally, she nodded.

Lightheaded, he followed her into the family room. Mikie trailed closely at his heels as he made his way into the house and sat on the same couch he'd shared once with Marianne. This house held too much history, even though he'd only been there a few times.

Emily was right—Sophia had made the room her own. It no longer reminded him of Marianne, but there was no trace of him either. They had both been wiped out. Minutes passed while Sophia sat in the chair opposite him, waiting. Every time he opened his mouth, he shut it again. No matter what he said, it wouldn't be enough.

"Where's the baby?" *Jesus. At least I didn't comment on the weather.*

"She's napping."

He needed to say why he was here, but what if, no matter what he said, it didn't matter?

He remained silent until Sophia came to his rescue. "How's your mom?"

Jake relaxed just enough to answer the question. "She's an amazing woman. Without my dad holding her back, she's making a life for herself." *Like you.* A thought that he would rather cut his tongue out than vocalize.

He looked forward to telling Sophia the first part of his news. "My father left his law firm to me. According to his lawyer, he'd made that decision years ago." The wonder of it still amazed him. "Apparently, he'd always meant for me to have it."

Emotions flickered across Sophia's face—anger, sadness, joy—much like what he'd felt when his father's lawyer read the will. He also saw relief. Maybe pride.

"Oh, Jake, that's won—"

"I sold it."

This time, he saw confusion.

"But why? I thought that's what you wanted."

"I thought so too. But all I ever wanted was for him to love me. The firm means nothing without him."

Sophia reached out and touched his hand. "I'm so sorry."

His fingers twitched when she touched him, but he didn't want sympathy.

"It's okay. I don't want to be that kind of lawyer anymore. I don't want to be that kind of man. I joined the legal team for We Make Families. I could have gone to another surrogacy center—and would have—if they hadn't had a spot for me. I accepted the offer before my father's death.

Remembering Emily's comment when he'd finally told her, he laughed. "I wanted to tell you first, but I start next week and figured I should tell Emily before she caught me wearing a suit and tie at the breakfast table. I thought maybe she told you?"

He felt foolish when she shook her head.

"I made her swear not to say anything until I talked to you first, but Emily can never keep secrets from you, so I wasn't sure."

"Sadly, those days could be over. Now that Emily's dating, she seems to be mum on many subjects. What does she think?"

"Emily? To quote her, 'As long as you're not working yourself to death, I don't care what you do.'" He grinned. "She told me she was happy if I was happy."

Did Sophia resent that he made this decision after she'd moved out? Did she understand how difficult it had been to accept that he would never have been happy living his father's life?

"I love it." Her smile was genuine. "It's a wonderful decision, a big adjustment."

"You could say that. No more teak conference-room tables, that's for sure. And no more dreaming of becoming a senior partner." He exhaled, embracing the joy of his new position. "A fair trade when it means my livelihood doesn't depend on defending clients who see no harm in deceiving the public."

Comfortable that what he saw in Sophia's eyes was joy and not pity, he willed himself to tell her what was in his heart, but the momentum that had compelled him to knock on her door deserted him. He wasn't even surprised when Sophia calmly took control of the conversation—the past few months had been better for her than for him.

"Was there anything else you wanted to talk about?" There it was again—her confidence-filled voice.

Jake's hands lay flat on his knees as if to keep him tethered, but he was still unable to get to why he was there. "I was sorry to hear you lost Miss Molly."

A shadow crossed Sophia's face, and he regretted mentioning the beloved dog, but then, she lifted her head and smiled.

"She's not lost; she's in our hearts."

Again, he was amazed at her strength.

Forcing himself to address the history of their surroundings because if he didn't, he feared there would be no future for them, he asked, "What's it like? Living here?"

Her eyes glistened with sorrow as they darted from the bookcases filled with her favorites to the cross-stitch samplers on the walls and back to him. But then, she blinked, and he thought he'd imagined it.

"The last time I'd been in this house, before it became mine, before... everything, I thought my life was over. And when I walked through the rooms the day I moved in, I had no idea how I'd be able to stay. Remember? I even told you I wasn't sure I'd make it through the night."

The memory haunted him. He'd thought about that day ever since he left her here to conquer her fears on her own. He'd seen her strength, though, and he knew she'd survive. He'd never been prouder.

"It got easier once I—once we—dealt with the bedroom. Thank you for that. I moved from room to room, making decisions without spending too much time deciding what was right or wrong. A neighbor does all the outside work, but I might plant a garden and care for that myself."

And you kept our wedding album. The thought slipped into his head unbidden. It had been a great source of hope these past few months.

"Anyway, you all helped me move, and Emily seemed so happy running around with Mikie. I needed to give it a try. It's a house. The house had done me no harm."

Jake bent his head, remembering all the harm he had done. "The place looks good."

"Everything's finally unpacked. However, sheets still cover the bedroom windows. I never decided what to do about them, and now that Mia's crawling, I have much less time to think about anything."

When Emily had first started crawling, two of them kept track of her, at least on the weekends. Jake had wanted to hire a nanny during the week to help her—even though they could hardly afford one then—but Sophia wouldn't hear of it. So he did what he could and installed baby gates throughout the house.

It was painful to hear Sophia relay a life that had nothing to do with him, yet he was happy that she had created more than just an existence for herself. Maybe "happy" wasn't the right word, but he didn't want her to suffer.

"I know you don't understand how I can live here—neither do Matt and Christine. And to be honest, I had considered taking Emily and moving out of state, but once I remembered how much I had loved Marianne... I thought I was strong enough to try. Besides, I couldn't take Emily away from you."

He hadn't realized how close he'd come to losing Emily. He would never have contested the move, not after everything he'd done to set all of this in motion.

"Of course, on moving day, the hardest thing was saying goodbye to our girl. That nearly destroyed me." She laughed. "Emily handled it better than I did."

"I miss you." He blurted the words out, knowing he shouldn't have reverted the conversation so quickly to himself and what he wanted, but he couldn't help himself. "I'm sorry. I shouldn't have said that. I wanted this to be perfect, but I'm like a kid asking a girl out on a first date. Christ, my hands are even clammy."

Unable to sit a minute longer, he stood. The action forced unwanted memories—Marianne lighting a fire and rubbing her hands over her arms to ward off the sudden chill in the room.

To still his thudding heart, he would have loved to pile wood and kindling in the hearth and strike a match, even though sweat ran down his back and he wished like hell he could pull off his sweater.

"The house is empty without you." *What is wrong with me?* "I am empty without you." He caught her eye, praying that what he saw was hope. "Emily misses you."

"I see Emily almost every weekend. She's fine."

He hadn't swayed her. Exhaustion gave way, and once again, he sat on the couch, no closer to telling her how much he loved her than before.

"I know. Weekends are the days I hate the most."

It occurred to him that Sophia could say no. That she was happy with the way her life had turned out. And yet he had to ask.

"I want to try to put our family back together." He released a deep breath, glad to have the words out.

She didn't look surprised, but he couldn't begin to know what she was thinking.

"Because you're lonely?"

"I... no. Because I love you." His admission was a reminder that once, they'd meant everything to each other.

"Did you love her?"

She had asked this once before, the night the baby was born. But he'd never really answered. And when it seemed he wouldn't respond this time, she asked again.

"It's a simple question, Jake. Did you love her?"

Things would be different. He saw that now. "I don't know." *This is no more than I deserve, whether I expected Sophia to be capable of being so explicit or not.*

"I... I thought I did." Her slight intake of breath gutted him, but he refused to look at her. He couldn't.

Even if she didn't believe him, even if she couldn't forgive him, he wanted to be honest with her.

"I thought I could be different with Marianne, but then, I realized I didn't want to be different. I want to be better. You make me better."

He had some crazy notion of grasping her hands, of pulling her to him, but one look told him she was not his wife to touch. "Everything that happened was wrong. Was my fault. And I'm sorry. It was one night that I will regret for the rest of my life."

The events and his responsibility for them were clear in his mind. "I should have told you, but I was afraid I would lose you. I thought I could ask you to give up Mia and you would do that for me. Because I loved you." He lowered his head in shame. "I was wrong."

Sophia looked at her hands, possibly to shy away from his confession. He had no idea if anything he had said mattered, but then, she raised her head, her eyes glistening with unshed tears.

He never meant to make her cry. "What?"

"Mia. You called her by her name."

Emily had said the same thing. *"You never call her by her name."* He saw it now. When he said her name, he made her real. No different than Emily. "Yes."

"I'm going to adopt her." Sophia's entire face lit up.

This was his chance. "I want us to be a family—you, me, Emily, *and* Mia. I want to adopt her with you. I thought I wanted everything to return to how it was before you became a surrogate. I thought we were happy. But we can't go back. I know that now."

"You make it sound so simple."

"It's not simple. Not at all. I made one huge mistake and then kept compounding it by not telling you. Before I knew it, I'd made a million mistakes." He pulled her to him. "I never stopped loving you."

He willed her to say she loved him too, but she stepped away, already separating herself from him.

"Why should I believe you?"

He'd thought about it himself—why *should* she believe him? He had to get this right. His entire future with Sophia depended on it.

"The choices we make define who we are, and yes, I made poor choices, but I'm not that man." He had never felt so sure of anything in his life. "I am *not* that man. I can't force you to believe me. But I'm hoping you will."

Sophia's silence was unbearable. Minutes went by, and she wouldn't even look at him.

He'd done everything he could to convince her that they belonged together. He was different. He would love her for the rest of his life, but he didn't blame her for not wanting to take the risk. And that was what he was—a risk.

It was over. He would grieve later. "I should go."

All too soon, he was at the front door. He closed his mind to everything. *Just leave. Go home and learn to live with this sorrow of your own making.*

Surprisingly, Sophia reached up to kiss his cheek. "Tell Emily I'll see her next weekend."

"I will."

The door closed behind him. It was almost twilight. The sky reflected the fall hues of the season, and he would have found it beautiful at any other time, but tonight, the scene was just one more thing to break his heart.

When the door opened again, Jake expected Sophia to shoo him off her porch. Instead, she reached for his hand and pulled him back inside.

Acknowledgments

Thank you to my publisher, Lynn McNamee, owner of Red Adept Publishing, and my agent, Liza Royce, of Liza Royce Associates, for their continued faith in me.

Thank you to Red Adept's editors, proofreaders, cover designers, and fellow authors for your knowledge and support—a special call-out to editor Meghan Portillo for making this book shine.

The following people offered invaluable feedback and encouragement:

My critique partners, Lee Bukowski and Sarahlyn Bruck: fabulous friends and the best two people to have your back in the writing trenches. I love your attention to detail and your ability to listen to me whine yet still manage a smile.

My beta readers, Densie Webb, Diane Barnes, Samantha Verant, and Grace Sammon: Thanks for reading and sharing your thoughts on improving this book. I appreciate you all!

C. D'Angelo: Christine was also a beta reader and weighed in heavily on the psychological aspects of this novel. And yes, Sophia's friend and neighbor Christine is named after this fabulous Christine.

Nancy Fagan and Sarah Branson provided medical advice. Any errors are my own.

Ginny Henning is not only an excellent lawyer but also a dear friend. She offered advice on the workings of private law firms and directed me to Vermont Law and Graduate School for surrogacy issues in Vermont. Willow and George are Ginny's beloved Great Danes.

Thank you to Jessica Thomas and her husband, Jeff (who was more than willing to share a male point of view on surrogacy), Whitney Newquist, and Steph (Anderson) Thompson for sharing their surrogacy stories. Without them, I could never have written this book. Please note—their stories were the exact opposite of Sophia's in this book. Their husbands and families could not have been more supportive when they embraced surrogacy.

A special note to the surrogacy centers in Pennsylvania and Vermont: Thank you for your time and dedication to all the families you assist.

A huge thanks to the Women's Fiction Writers Association, a community that comes together to share diverse experiences, deepen connections, and hone the craft of writing. Don't let the name fool you—this organization is open to all genders.

If I've forgotten anyone, I apologize. I started research for this book in 2021, and although I tried to keep my notes and emails organized, some wonderful people may have slipped through the cracks. If that's you, I thank you!

Beagles and the Beagle Freedom Project have played a part in all my books. Anyone who knows me knows how much I loved my rescue beagle, Miss Molly—who has a supporting role in this book and now runs pain-free in Doggy Heaven.

The Beagle Freedom Project can be found here if you have it in your heart to donate or adopt a rescued beagle: https://bfp.org/.

Special thanks to Renee Anderson, webmaster, graphics creator, and technical assistant—she makes all things possible.

A heartfelt thank you to my family for their support and encouragement—I love you all.

A BIG thank you to every reader who picks up this book and reads it. Without readers, there would be no need for writers.

Author's Note:

I named my imaginary dog rescue organization Homeward Bound, unaware of the real Homeward Bound animal shelter in Middlebury, Vermont—simply a coincidence.

Addresses in Vermont were primarily created in my imagination. I also took some liberties with pregnancy superstitions just for fun.

The last time I spoke to my brother, we were arguing on the phone, and I hung up on him. Life is fragile. Family even more so. If you or someone you love is considering suicide, please dial 988.

About the Author

Barbara Conrey worked in the health care industry for many years before opting for an early retirement, which lasted all of three months. She then accepted a position in finance, for which she had absolutely no background, with a national company, and four years later, she decided to write a book. But not about finance.

In the early morning hours, people can find Barbara walking her neighborhood streets, head down and deep in thought.

Travel is her passion, along with reading, writing, hiking, and exploring antique shops. Her greatest love is Miss Molly, her rescue beagle. There are stories to be told about beagles, and Barbara hopes to incorporate some of them into her books.

Barbara lives in Pennsylvania, close to family and friends.

Read more at https://www.barbaraconreyauthor.com/blog.

About the Publisher

Dear Reader,

We hope you enjoyed this book. Please consider leaving a review on your favorite book site.

Visit our site to find more quality books!

Read more at https://RedAdeptPublishing.com.